THE CAT STAR CHRONICLES

SLAVE

CHERYL BROOKS

sourcebooks
casablanca

Published by Sourcebooks Casablanca, an imprint of Sourcebooks, Inc.
P.O. Box 4410, Naperville, Illinois 60567-4410
(630) 961-3900
FAX: (630) 961-2168
www.sourcebooks.com

Library of Congress Cataloging-in-Publication Data

Brooks, Cheryl
  Slave / Cheryl Brooks.
     p. cm.
  I. Title.

PS3602.R64425S57 2008
813'.6--dc22

                          2007049212

Printed and bound in Canada
WC   10   9   8   7   6   5   4   3

Dedicated to anyone who enjoys the occasional escape from reality.

Acknowledgments

My heartfelt thanks to:
My husband and sons for their love and support;
My buddies at the hospital for their enthusiasm and encouragement;
My editor, Deb Werksman, for giving me a chance;
My horses for forgiving me for spending more time at my computer and less time at the barn;
And all the cool aliens and sword-wielding men on horses who have ever inspired me.

Chapter One

I FOUND HIM IN THE SLAVE MARKET ON ORPHESEUS Prime, and even on such a godforsaken planet as that one, their treatment of him seemed extreme. But then again, perhaps he was an extreme subject, and the fact that there was a slave market at all was evidence of a rather backward society. Slave markets were becoming extremely rare throughout the galaxy—the legal ones, anyway.

I hitched my pack higher on my shoulder and adjusted my respirator, though even with the benefit of ultrafiltration, the place still stank to high heaven. How a planet as eternally hot and dry as this one could have *ever* had anything on it that could possibly rot and get into the air to cause such a stench was beyond me. Most dry climates don't support a lot of decay or fermentation, but Orpheseus was different from any desert planet I'd ever had the misfortune to visit. It smelled as though at some point all of the vegetation and animal life forms had died at once and the odor of their decay had become permanently embedded in the atmosphere.

Shuddering as a wave of nausea hit me, I walked casually closer to the line of wretched creatures lined up for pre-auction inspection, but even my unobtrusive move wasn't lost on the slave owners who were bent on selling their wares.

"Come closer!" a ragged beast urged me in a rasping, unpleasant voice as he gestured with a bony arm.

I eyed him with distaste, thinking that this thing was just ugly enough to have caused the entire planet to smell bad, though I doubted he'd been there long enough to do it. On the other hand, he didn't seem to be terribly young. Okay, so older than the hills might have been a little closer to the mark. Damn, maybe he *was* responsible, after all!

"I have here just what you have been seeking!" he said. "Help to relieve you of your burden! This one is strong and loyal and will serve you well."

I glanced dubiously at the small-statured critter there before me, and its even smaller slave. "I don't think so," I replied, thinking that the weight of my pack alone would probably have crushed the poor little thing's tiny bones to powder. I know that looks can often be deceiving, but this thing looked to me like nothing more than an oversized grasshopper. Its bulbous red eyes regarded me with an unblinking and slightly unnerving stare. "Its eyes give me the creeps, anyway," I added. "I need something that looks more…humanoid."

Dismissing them with a wave, I glanced around at the others, noting that, of the group, there were only two slaves being offered that were even bipedal: one reminded me of a cross between a cow and a chimpanzee, and the other, well, the other was the one who had first caught my eye—possibly because out of all the slaves there, he was the one seeming to require the most restraint, and also because he was completely naked.

I studied him out of the corner of my eye, noting that the other prospective buyers seemed to be giving him a wide berth. His owner, an ugly Cylopean—and Cylopeans are *all* ugly, but this one would have stood out in a crowd of them—was exhorting the masses to purchase his slave.

"Come!" he shouted in heavily accented Standard Tongue, "my slave is strong and will serve you well. I part with him only out of extreme financial need, for he is as a brother to me, and it pains me greatly to lose him."

His pain wasn't as great as the slave's, obviously. I eyed the Cylopean skeptically. Surely he couldn't imagine that anyone would have suspected that his "brother" would require a genital restraint in order to drag him to the market to part him from his current master!

Rolling my eyes with disdain, I muttered, "Go ahead and admit it. You're selling him because you can't control him."

"Oh, no, my good sir!" the Cylopean exclaimed, seemingly aghast at my suggestion. "He is strong! He is willing! He is even intelligent!"

I stifled a snicker. The slave was obviously smart enough to have this one buffaloed, I thought, chuckling to myself as it occurred to me that no one around here would even know what a buffalo was, let alone the euphemism associated with the animal.

I blew out a breath hard enough to fog the eye screen on my respirator. Damn, but I was a long way from home! Earth was at least five hundred long light-years away. How the hell had I managed to end up here, searching for a lost sister whom I sometimes suspected of not wanting to be found? I'd followed her trail from planet to planet for six years now, and had always been just a few steps behind her. I was beginning to consider giving up the search, but the memory of the terror in her wild blue eyes as she was torn from my arms on Dexia Four kept me going.

And now, she had been—or so I'd been informed— taken to Statzeel, a planet where all women were slaves and upon which I didn't dare set foot, knowing that I, too, would become enslaved. The denizens of Statzeel would undoubtedly not make the same mistake that the slave trader had, for I was most definitely female, and, as such, vulnerable to the same fate that had befallen my lovely little sister. That I wasn't the delicate, winsome creature Ranata was wouldn't matter, for a female on Statzeel was a slave by definition. Free women simply did not exist there.

Which was why I needed a male slave of my own. One to pose as my owner—one that I could trust to a certain extent, though I was beginning to believe that such a creature couldn't possibly exist, and certainly not on Orpheseus Prime! I was undoubtedly wasting my time, I thought as I looked back at the slave. He was tall, dirty, and probably stank every bit as much as his owner did. I was going to have to check the filter in that damn respirator—either that or go back and beat the shit out of the scheming little scoundrel who'd taken me for ten qidnits when he sold it to me. I should have simply stolen it, but getting myself in trouble with what law there was on that nasty little planet wouldn't have done either my sister, or myself, a lick of good.

As I glanced at the man standing there before me, he raised his head ever so slightly to regard me out of the corner of one glittering, obsidian eye. Something passed between us at that moment—something almost palpable and real—making me wonder if the people of his race might have had psychic powers of some kind. That he was most definitely not human was quite evident, though at first glance he might have appeared to be, and could possibly have passed for one to the uneducated. There weren't many humans this far out for comparison, which was undoubtedly why I'd been able to get wind of Ranata's whereabouts from time to time. She seemed to have left a lasting impression wherever she was taken.

Just as this slave would do, even with the upswept eyebrows that marked him as belonging to some other alien world. His black, waving hair hung to his waist, though matted and dirty and probably crawling with vermin. I had no doubt that his owner hadn't lied when he had said that the slave was strong, for he was collared and shackled—hand, foot, and genitals. I'd been through many slave markets in my search, but I'd rarely seen any slave who was bound the way this one was, which spoke not only of strength, but also of a belligerent, and probably untrainable, nature. The muscles were all right there to see, and while they were not overly bulky—appearing, instead, to be more tough and sinewy—their level of strength was unquestionable.

This man had seen some rough work and even rougher treatment, for jagged scars laced his back and a long, straight scar sliced across his left cheekbone as though it had been made with a sword. He had a piercing in his penis, which appeared to have been done recently, for the ring through it was crusted over with dried blood.

A chain ran from the metallic collar around his neck, through the ring in his cock, to another metal band that encircled his penis and testicles at the base. The pain that such a device could inflict on a man was horrifying, even to me, and I'd had to inflict a lot of pain in the course of my travels—though never to someone so defenseless and completely within my power as a slave. My never-ending search for Ranata had left me nearly as tough and battle-scarred as the slave was, and I'd often had to fight to the death in order to stay alive. So far, however, I'd never stooped to torturing a slave, and sincerely hoped I never would. This slave owner obviously had no such qualms, and it made me want to take a shot at him, just on general principles.

Call me an old softy if you will, but I must admit that I considered buying this slave, if for no other reason than to set him free of his restraints. I might feed him first, though—and perhaps buy him some clothes.... I cocked my head to one side as I considered him again. You're a fool if you think feeding this thing will tame it, I told myself. A bona-fide fool...

And fools didn't last very long around these parts. This was the dirtiest, toughest, most lawless region of space I'd ever been to, and I was ready to get back in my ship and get gone—if for no other reason than to be able to breathe fresher air again. But I'd been on Orpheseus for over three weeks now, haunting the slave markets, and this was the first humanoid possibility that I'd run across. Even though he didn't look very promising, I felt that I at least had to ask a few questions—he might turn out to be my last, best chance at getting what I needed.

"How much?" I asked.

"He will be in the auction!" the Cylopean protested. "He will bring a high price! To sell him now would be…"

"A wise move," I said firmly. "Just look at what you had to do to get him here! Oh, no, he will not sell at auction, my friend! At least, not for as much as I will pay for him now. In fact, I'd be willing to bet that in the auction, I'll be the only one bidding when he's up there on the block. I'll probably get him for less than it cost you to bring him here."

He knew I was right, of course, but I'll swear he had the soul of a Bedouin horse trader! "I will not sell him outright!" the man insisted, flapping his arms and kicking up dust with his feet as he stomped them in a gesture of outrage. "I will auction him!"

It occurred to me, eyeing him with disfavor, that while Cylopeans never look very agreeable, this one looked even less so than most. Sort of made me want to turn around and leave right then, just so I wouldn't have to look at him anymore.

I shook my head sadly. Stupid, stubborn man! My God, they were everywhere, on every planet, and in every system! I could take this one for the price of a slave he couldn't control—though he might consider it a good bargain in the end. On the other hand, the one I was thinking of buying was obviously pretty stupid, and stubborn, too, or he wouldn't have been in such a state in the first place. I revised my earlier opinion of his intelligence, for a smarter man would have been more docile and wouldn't have required such a horrendous level of restraint. Of course, I had no idea what had been asked of him. For all I knew, he might have been forced to commit some heinous crime, or maybe he just wouldn't do windows. It was also possible that the Cylopean was just a sadistic little bastard who enjoyed such things. Glancing at the slave again, I wondered how many men it had taken to hold him down while that genital restraint had been applied.

I tried another approach. "Where did he come from?"

This question seemed to surprise him, for he appeared to be rather puzzled for a moment. "Originally? I have no idea, though I believe he was a prisoner of war at one time. He is a fine fighter and has fought by my side in many battles."

A soldier, then, I decided. One whose loyalty could possibly be bought with the promise of his eventual freedom. I could use a good mercenary; one who would fight and see that I stayed alive long enough to reward him. I was still a bit skeptical, however, and asked what I felt to be a rather pertinent question, given the circumstances.

"So, tell me, how did you manage to keep him from killing *you* instead of the enemy?"

The man shrugged. "If I die, he dies," he said simply. "It was in his best interest to see to my continued welfare."

Which spoke of other means of control, like one of those poisons that don't work until you *stop* taking them. I wondered if, in, say, three day's time, my new acquisition would suddenly begin writhing in agony and then die a rather nasty, painful death.

Deciding to leave that question for later on, I asked, "And now? Have you no further concern for your own, um, welfare?"

I thought he hesitated for a moment before answering me, but I believe he was telling me the truth when he said, "I have no need of a fighter any longer." He left it at that and I didn't press him any further, for just looking at the man told the story pretty plainly. That he was every bit as seedy-looking as anyone there on the auction block was easily observed, and if he'd ever been blessed with any degree of wealth, it certainly wasn't apparent at this point. Quite plainly, he needed the money, and if he was desperate enough, I still might be able to pull off a deal with him.

"Mind if I make a closer inspection?" I asked cautiously. "Is it safe to approach him?"

"Oh, yes! He will not harm you. Not while I have this," the Cylopean replied, holding up a remote control of some kind. I didn't ask what would happen if he turned the dial on it since I was already too creeped out by the outrageous forms of control I could see with my own eyes.

I nodded and walked around the slave. *Yes, he will do very nicely!* I thought. There weren't very many open wounds on him, though I had no doubt that there were probably sores beneath those restraints. He seemed healthy enough, too: no wheezing when he breathed, no cough, and his color—what I could discern of it from beneath the layer of dust and filth caked on his skin— seemed normal enough, though it might not have been for one of his kind.

"May I touch him?" I asked.

"Certainly! Touch him, if you will!" the Cylopean urged. "Feel the firmness of his muscles, the strength of his bones!"

Actually, all I really wanted to do was to knock some of the crud off of the sores on his back to see if there was anything festering under there. I didn't have to feel him to know that he was strong. Stepping up behind him, I flicked the crusts off with my glove. No pus, I noted, but the cuts appeared to be recent—perhaps they simply hadn't had the time to become infected as yet.

"Any sickness?" I asked.

"Oh, no, he is quite healthy, I assure you!"

"What about his teeth?" I inquired. "Are they rotten?"

Where I was going, a man with bad teeth would stick out like a sore thumb (not that this man would blend in anywhere, mind you). It was just that I didn't want him to appear as though he had been the one to have been a slave, rather than myself. On Statzeel, with the women enslaved, all the men had personal groomers who kept them in tip-top condition—even to the point of brushing their teeth for them.

"Not at all!" came the reply. "Wait, I will show you." The Cylopean stepped forward and gestured to the slave, who promptly opened his mouth. "You see? All present and in good condition."

And sharp enough to cut through most conventional tethers, with canines a full quarter-inch longer than his other teeth! Damn, he looked dangerous! What the hell was I thinking? I should move on. Then it occurred to me that the command to open his mouth had been unspoken.

"Can he hear and speak?" I asked quickly. "Does he understand Stantongue?"

This was important since he'd have to be doing the talking for me on Statzeel, and possibly on other worlds, as well. A mute would be of no use whatsoever, and I didn't want to have to take the time to teach him a new language, either.

I was looking at the slave when I asked that question, and noted the faint flicker of a dark, feline eyebrow. Oh, yes, he understood me, all right.

"Yes, of course he can!" I was assured. "He is quite fluent!"

"Let me hear him, then."

"You may speak, slave," the Cylopean said in an offhand manner and with a callous wave of his hand which made me long to punch his beady little eyes out.

My own eyes were drawn once more to those shining, black orbs which flashed as the slave raised his head, an act which drew the chain between his collar and the genital cuff taut and lifted his penis by the ring running through the top of it. If I'd previously assumed that his posture was one of submission, I'd have been wrong, for obviously it was merely the position of the greatest comfort for him. Well, the position of the least *dis*comfort, anyway.

"What would you have me say, Master?" the slave asked. The words were respectful, though his tone was carefully neutral.

"Tell me where you come from," I asked.

His dark eyes narrowed and the tips of his eyebrows became more vertical.

"You may speak," the Cylopean said with a depre-cating wave. "Answer the questions as you wish."

My, that was brave of him, I thought! I might ask him what a rat his master was—of course, "Master" still held the remote and would probably zap him if he said anything out of line. Then again, I might not like his answers, either, and I decided that if he gave me too much lip, I wouldn't mess with him. I wondered if he realized that his freedom was hanging in the balance with his reply.

"I come from the planet Zetith," he replied.

There was a slight accent in his speech, one that I couldn't quite place. Of course, I'd never heard of Zetith, but then, I'd never run across another specimen that was anything like him, either—and I'd seen a lot of strange beings in my search.

"How did you come to leave your planet?"

"We were at war with other worlds," he replied. "I was taken prisoner along with others in my unit. We were to be executed, but were sold as slaves, instead."

Well, so far that coincided with his master's story; however, hearing him talk was a bit like listening to a computer spitting out information. His inflections and syntax seemed acceptable, but his replies were clipped and short, and he didn't seem to relish the idea of giving me any information about himself. I tried again.

"Would you like to return to your home world?"

"I cannot."

"And why is that?"

"It is gone."

Which might explain why there were so few of his sort scattered throughout the galaxy—and also why I'd never heard of the place. It was safe to assume that if he had any relatives, they were as dead as his planet. Of course, I'd heard of planets that had been largely destroyed by war, but never one that had been completely obliterated.

"Do you mean that all life is gone, or that the planet itself is gone?"

"The planet itself," he replied. "An asteroid struck it, and it was destroyed."

"And how would you know that?" I inquired curiously.

Those dark eyes regarded me unblinkingly. "I watched it happen," he said shortly.

"And how did you do that?" I asked, rather intrigued. "Were you watching from another world, or from a ship, or what?"

"In my mind," he replied. "I saw it in my mind."

Well, that certainly sounded interesting! I wondered if he had seen it happen prior to the actual event and was therefore able to escape—although, if that were the case, with space travel being extremely common on most worlds, the rest of the people on the planet should have been alerted in plenty of time to evacuate, as well. Unless, of course, no one else believed him and they all perished as a result. There was obviously more to that story.

"What else can you see in your mind?"

His glittering black eyes narrowed again, and the satyr-like expression returned.

"The ones responsible," he replied.

Even more interesting! "So it wasn't an accident, then?"

"It was an act of war."

I glanced at the Cylopean just then, and judging from his rapt attention to the conversation, it was safe to assume that he'd never bothered to ask any of these same questions, himself. I wondered if anyone had, but left it at that for the time being. By now, I'd heard enough to know that he was articulate enough for my needs, and with a bit of care and feeding, he would probably clean up very nicely. I did note at this point that other than his eyebrows and lashes and the long mane of hair on his head, he had no other facial hair whatsoever, and if his overall unkempt appearance was anything to go by, I would have to assume that this was his natural state. Body hair, he did have, however, which was as dark and curly as the hair on his head.

I moved closer to him, wishing that I dared to remove my respirator long enough to get a whiff of him. Some species had extremely unpleasant smells associated with them, whether they were clean or not, and it was possible that he might have fallen into that category. Unfortunately, the best I could have said was that I didn't notice that the smell working its way through the lousy filters on my respirator seemed to change appreciably. One thing was certain, however— though my close proximity didn't do anything to further my own enlightenment, apparently it did something to him.

I hadn't been standing in front of him for long, but as I studied his face, I observed a slight quiver to his nostrils and a flicker of some recognition or reaction in his eyes. He was a tall man, though I was nearly as tall myself— my two-meter height not being at all uncommon among

Earth women anymore—and though my eyes weren't quite on the same level as his and were shielded from the glare of the sun by the brim of my cap, I could see his own quite clearly. There was a message there, of some kind. I just wasn't able to read it.

The Cylopean made an odd little sound, interrupting my thoughts. If he'd been human, I'd have said he was saying, "Ahem!" but this was an altogether different noise—sort of an atonal hum.

"Must be a receptive female in the area," he commented.

Turning quickly, I cast a questioning glance in his direction. Noting that, unlike his utterance, his gesture, as well as his expression of embarrassed chagrin, were so remarkably human, I almost laughed aloud. Then I followed his gaze to the slave's genital region and jumped backwards a full meter.

The slave's cock seemed to have bloomed while I was standing before him, and for a moment, all I could do was stare at it. It was long and thick, and while it might have been overly engorged due to the restraint which surrounded it at the base, it still had a fairly showy head, sporting a corona complete with a serrated edge that looked as though it had been crimped like a piecrust. Though I'll admit to never having made a study of such things, I knew for a fact that I had never seen anything to compare with it on any biped before. On the occasional quadruped, perhaps, but never on a primate. In fact, the only time I had ever seen a penis that came even close to it had been on a stallion back home on Earth. This one was similar, though scaled down to human size—large enough to tantalize and catch the eye, but not so huge that it would scare anyone off.

My eyes flew back to meet his glittering stare. He knew I was female, though just how he had discerned it was beyond me to guess. I might have done or said something to suggest it, but I knew that in my flight coveralls and cap and with the respirator covering most of my face and altering the tone of my voice, he should have had no obvious clue. Scent was the other possibility, but in the stench of that hellhole of a planet, I doubted that even a bloodhound would have been able to pick a skunk out of the crowd. Then again, I reminded myself, I *had* been standing right under the man's nose! I wondered if he always did that around females. If so, it might pose a problem—especially at a time like this when my ability to appear to be male, rather than female, was a definite advantage to the preservation of my own personal safety and general welfare.

Unfortunately for my little charade, my reaction to his erection had been a decidedly female one, and I knew I had to change my attitude if the Cylopean were to remain convinced that his assumption of my gender had been correct.

"You should have castrated him," I said with a chuckle, which sounded rather forced, even through the respirator.

"It has never been a problem in battle," the slave trader commented. "I suppose I might have done it if he had been a house slave."

I nodded. "Well, it doesn't concern me overly," I said, in an attempt to seem nonchalant about it—though, I'll admit, it was difficult. "It was a bit of a surprise, though. Perhaps you should clothe him."

The Cylopean shook his head. "Not for the auction," he said firmly. "Slaves sell better unclothed."

While I might have agreed that female slaves probably did, this wasn't that sort of auction. Still, I had to admit, he was impressive—which is a slight understatement of the facts. I had no doubts that many a noblewoman would have considered buying him to add to her stable of male attendants, if for no other reason than to enjoy the distinct pleasure of looking at him.

"Aren't you concerned that he might be burned by the sun and bring less in the sale?"

The slave had skin which was slightly darker than mine, but he was, overall, a little on the pale side when compared with most natives of hot planets such as the one upon which we found ourselves. I hoped that his covering of dirt offered some protection.

The trader shrugged. I smiled as I thought how I'd always found it odd that such a human gesture seemed truly universal. It was like saying "okay," which was a word understood throughout the galaxy as far as I could tell. There might not have been very many humans this far out from Earth, but we'd still managed to put our stamp on the general lexicon. For example, the word "shit" was universally understood, and so, of course, was the word "fuck," which was to my knowledge the only word referring to the act of procreation that could be used as a noun, a verb, and an expletive, all in the same sentence—unless you were to include "screw" or "nail," which somehow just didn't pack the same punch as the

F-word. Generally speaking, I tended to use that one as an expletive, myself, but I must admit that after looking at this man's equipment, I was thinking more along the lines of the verb.

Not for myself, of course. I'd never had much use for such a meaningless waste of time. I'd been far too busy working my ass off my whole life, and now that I was tracking my lost sister across the galaxy, I really didn't have time for it! Before I'd started searching for Ranata, I'd been too busy bartering my way to a fortune—though at this point, my fortune had diminished somewhat. I still had more than enough to keep going, and along the way I'd managed to accumulate a few extra dollars, credits, markers, or whatever the currency of the area I was passing through might be called. For some reason I was pretty good at it, and had always instinctively known what was going to be the hot item wherever I traveled. I'd thought that perhaps my wealth had been the reason for Ranata's kidnapping, but when no ransom demands ever came, I realized that whoever had taken her had other motives in mind, or they might have taken me, instead.

The Cylopean obviously didn't consider a case of sunburn to be a problem, but I'd been buying and selling things long enough to know when it was best to leave the diamond in the rough and when it was best to give it a bit of a polish. He could have sold this particular slave for much more if he'd cleaned him up and dressed him nicely, but some people just never learn.

Feigning a lack of further interest, I wandered away after that and waited in the shade of an awning over the outdoor café across the plaza from the slave market. I took a seat at a small, rickety table and ordered a talansk—a local beverage which was the only thing I'd tried so far on this planet that didn't taste like shit. My dusty, tired little waiter brought it to me with a respirator-compatible straw, and I sipped it while I waited for the auction to begin. As I suspected, my slave from Zetith drew a few stares, but most of the potential buyers avoided him like the Scorillian plague.

I put my feet up on the empty chair at my table and leaned back to watch the show. The little grasshopper slave was demonstrating his jumping ability and the one that looked like a cow-chimp was showing off his strength—which, for its size, was considerable. The Cylopean was still extolling the virtues of his slave, but few appeared to be listening to him, for the Zetithian slave simply looked to be more trouble than he was worth.

I was just starting to get comfortable—well, as comfortable as one could be in a place like that—when a Drell shuffled over and tried to relieve me of my foot-stool without so much as a by-your-leave.

"Fuck off, you fuckin' Drell!" I growled.

Drells are notoriously rude, but, for some reason, can't abide being sworn at. The hairy little lump drew back with a squeal and scuttled off to stand quivering in the shadows near the bar. Damn thing should have known I'd be grumpy. I was about to starve to death, but didn't dare take off my respirator for so much as a bite. My pack had food in it, of course, but I'd have had to breathe the foul air in along with it, which would undoubtedly have rendered even the most succulent meal completely inedible. I would eat when I got back to my ship.

Gods above, but I was getting tired, and I was nearly at my wit's end! I'd come up with this plan to get to Statzeel to find my sister, but so far, it wasn't progressing very rapidly. It seemed that all I did these days was wait, and this was simply one more place to wait out the time in, just like a thousand other places I'd patronized during my search. Ranata had been moved from planet to planet so many times, I'd lost track of the number—but I *did* know how long I'd been searching. I'd been on the move for six long, dirty, dusty, uncomfortable, and stress-filled years! If I hadn't sworn to my father that I would find her, I'd probably have given up long ago. I'd been sort of hard-bitten, as women go, even before this started, but I was a true cynic now. I trusted less and didn't hesitate to take the advantage whenever it offered itself. I'd gotten in and out of a lot of tight spots and had even had to kill a time or two, and while those things weighed upon my soul, they affected me less than the terror in Ranata's eyes when she was taken. I still had trouble sleeping, sometimes waking in a sweat as though I had been desperately running after the pack of Nedwuts who had snatched her right out of my hands.

"Stay close," I had urged her. "This is no place for a woman like you!"

The poor kid had followed me into a meeting with some other traders, and I knew from the moment she set foot in that dive that every eye was upon her, for Ranata, as a woman, is everything that I am not. Taller than I, and with our mother's willowy build, she is blonde and fair like our father, while I, on the other hand, am dark like my mother and, unfortunately, built more along the lines of our father. "Amazon," had been a frequent epithet applied to me, and though the origin of the true meaning of the word had been lost with the passage of time, it still meant a tall and rather tough-looking woman. It was no wonder that with my face covered the Cylopean had assumed I was male. No one seeing the vision that was Ranata would have ever mistaken us for siblings, either, for Ranata was ethereally beautiful, and I was anything but. I should have considered myself fortunate to have been blessed with plain features, for, as a result, I had never been a target for male attentions, and didn't want to be. It was a curse to be beautiful, I decided. If you doubt me, just pause for a moment to consider what had happened to my lovely sister Ranata.

Her trail hadn't been too hard to follow, for no matter where she went, the inhabitants always seemed to remember her and how beautiful she was. Once I had gotten a line on her on Dracus Five; the trail might have been a bit chilly, but not impossible to follow. The trouble was, whoever had her always seemed to know that I was on their tail; just when I was about to pounce, she would be spirited away once more, and then I had to pick up her scent all over again, which isn't an easy thing to do in space! I'd had to do more lying, conniving, and wheeling and dealing than I would have thought a person could do in a lifetime, let alone in six years.

And now, rumor had it that she was on Statzeel, a planet which women avoided like death itself, for on that planet, the women were all slaves. It could be argued that the same could be said of many worlds, but Statzeel had a reputation like no other. I had once observed a discussion between two men, one from Statzeel and the other who, from his style of dress, I took to be a Davordian prince. The Statzeelian male had a woman with him, held to his wrist by a chain connected to a collar around her neck. I'd been in a café similar to the one in which I now sat, and had watched from a dark corner as the heated discussion progressed to a dangerous argument, whereupon the woman—a scantily clad beauty, I might add—was thrust to her knees by the male and ordered to suck his cock while their talk continued. She complied, getting on her hands and knees to lick and suck him until he ejaculated right in her face. When the prince objected at such scandalous treatment of a female, the man had said of his slave, "Be thankful that she was here to allay my anger, or you, my good prince, would no longer be living." From other reports I'd heard, this type of behavior was typical of the men of Statzeel, so, essentially, my sister had been enslaved on a planet populated with belligerent, pompous, controlling assholes. I think "asshole" is another of those Earth words that has become universal over the thousand or so years since we Terrans first began to explore the galaxy. I hadn't found anyone yet who didn't know what it meant.

The Standard Tongue had gradually developed over that period of time, and it incorporated words and phrases from many worlds, including a good chunk of words from my own planet. There were regional dialects and colloquialisms, just as there were in any country on any world, and there were local accents, as well, but it was easily understandable throughout the known galaxy. Some planets had adopted Stantongue, as it was often referred to, as their primary language, which made things much easier when other species came to visit. There was also a universal sign language for those intelligent beings incapable of articulated speech, though I'd seldom had cause to use it.

The galaxy had come a long way, but there was still war, still crime, still poverty, and still the occasional abduction of a beautiful woman. There was no united governing body to regulate space trade or travel, and, for those like myself who roamed through space, there was a greater freedom, but a little law and order might have improved things a bit. Most star systems had a central government which regulated their own territory, but, for the most part, space travelers were pretty much on their own. It was a bit like Earth's Wild West in that respect, with distances so vast that patrolling an area of space was even more difficult than what the cattle barons had faced on the open range, and it was rare that anyone even bothered to attempt it.

The slave trade was something I would have preferred to see abolished entirely, but, there again, every planet had its own culture, and the rules that worked quite well for one didn't always work for another. Take Orpheseus Prime, for example. This particular slave market was typical of many of the more backward planets, though on Earth, such a thing was considered abhorrent, and hadn't been an accepted practice for nearly two thousand years—ancient history, as they say, and we Terrans had learned a few things in that time. Slavery was a bad thing, of course, but human nature being what it is, our society wasn't perfect by any means, and there were still a few bad apples in every basket.

Like the one I was about to bid on. My only hope was that I could deal with him, find out what it would take to motivate him, or I was simply going to have to take a loss on him and let him go. I wouldn't dream of selling him again unless I was desperate for funds, which, at the moment, I was not. No, I would give him a few credits and some decent clothes, and then set him free. Ordinarily, I wouldn't have considered buying a slave at all, but at that point, I simply didn't see any alternative. Hiring someone to pose as my "master" was dangerous, though buying a slave wasn't much better, for either way, I might very well end up as a slave myself.

Damn! Of all the places she had to wind up! If the bastard that took her was looking for a place where he knew I wouldn't follow, he'd probably chosen the right planet. My only other option was to pretend to be male myself, which I had considered since the males of Statzeel and I were of similar height and build; however, they had a tendency to dress in a fashion which left little to the imagination when it came to their gender. The female I'd seen suck off her master hadn't had to look far to find his penis, for it had been hanging right out in plain sight. Cocky bastards! I thought with a chuckle. Some women might like it, though. Of course, my future slave—I was that confident I'd get him—had a much more interesting phallus than any I'd ever seen before.

Not that I'd seen every species, mind you, but I had seen quite a few—enough to know that it would either hurt like hell to be fucked with it, or it would be the best ever. I was fortunate that there weren't any women there to buy slaves, or I would have undoubtedly had more competition for him.

The auction began and the little grasshopper went first, followed by two others that were unremarkable except that they appeared to be denizens of Orpheseus—a squat, toad-like species that didn't seem to mind the smell. I wondered how they had managed to become slaves. Had they gambled their way into debt and been subsequently taken in payment, or had they been born into slavery? The Zetithian slave had been a soldier, which was unusual among slaves, and I hoped no one was in the market for a promising gladiator, or I was going to have to shell out far more credits to get him than I'd hoped.

I crossed the plaza as the cow-chimp went on the block, knowing that the Zetithian would be next. The Cylopean looked nervous, twisting his ugly, gnarled hands in a gesture which was also universal: sweaty palms. They occurred on nearly every world in every system in one form or another—you just had to know where to look.

The cow-chimp went cheaply and the owner looked downright pissed. He should have kept it because the cow-chimp didn't look very happy when he saw who had bought him—a big, furry creature who had a lot of baggage in tow, which, no doubt, the slave would now have to carry. Perhaps he shouldn't have been quite so anxious to display his strength.

When my Zetithian male was led to the block at last, I noticed that, for the moment at least, his penis had quieted down considerably. He walked with his head lowered to avoid yanking on it, and I hoped he didn't see me or get a whiff of me or whatever else it might have been that had triggered that amazing display of his manly attributes, or I just might lose him to another woman. I chuckled to myself thinking how odd that sounded— almost as though I considered him a lover whom I feared might be taken from me by a more beautiful competitor.

The auctioneer looked a little afraid to be standing so close to what was obviously a very dangerous specimen, but managed to contain his fear long enough to ask for the first bid.

The silence that followed was nothing short of deafening. It appeared that I had been right about no one else wanting him, and the Cylopean *really* started wringing his hands, then!

"He is strong and willing to work!" the man exhorted desperately. "He is the best the market has to offer!"

The silence went on, broken only by scuffling sounds as beings of all kinds took a few steps backward. The Cylopean, in a sudden fit of rage jerked hard on the chain and his slave roared out in pain and anger. It reminded me of the sound that a Euclidian lion makes when its tail gets twisted. Really loud and really pissed! I'd obviously waited too long.

"Five credits!" I shouted, though I believe I could have whispered it and still have been heard quite clearly.

The Cylopean forgot his anger and began to sputter in protest. "Five credits? He is worth more than fifty!"

Which was about what I would have paid for him if the arrogant bastard had been willing to sell him before the auction. I wished I'd had the opportunity to smile evilly at him, but with the respirator on, my facial expressions were wasted. So I settled for a gesture which is also universal: I flipped him off.

"Sold!" the auctioneer shouted, obviously quite anxious to put as much distance between himself and the Zetithian slave as possible.

I stepped forward and laid the credits on the table. "I'll take that," I said to the slave trader, indicating his remote as he and my slave stepped down from the block. The money lay there taunting him, a mere fraction of what he might have made if he'd only been just a little less greedy. The auctioneer's assistant took two of the credits and pushed the other three toward the Cylopean.

With a snarl, the bastard slammed the remote on the table and snatched up the credits, which disappeared instantly into his robes, but not before I heard another roar from the Zetithian slave. The remote obviously controlled the genital restraint which had tightened painfully in response to the inadvertent triggering of the device. Although, judging from the smirk on the Cylopean's face, he'd probably done it purposefully, as a parting shot, if you will.

Fortunately, it only pulsed for a moment and didn't remain engaged until it was released, for my slave relaxed after a second or two, though I could see the anger boiling within him. He wanted to kill that man so badly he could taste it. Deciding that I would test my control over my new slave right now, I took the chain from the guard who had taken it from the Cylopean, lest he attempt to damage my purchase any further before handing him over.

I stared up into those dark eyes, now sparkling with hatred, and noted that they seemed to be the reverse of those of the average house cat, having a bright golden pupil and a black iris. His pupils seemed very cat-like, however, being glowing, vertical slits rather than the dark, round pupils of a human.

"Kill him, if you wish," I said quietly. "No one will stop you."

He was sorely tempted, I could tell, but, instead, gave a nearly imperceptible shake of his head. "Not worth killing," he muttered.

"Good answer," I said tersely, and I led my new slave out of the plaza.

Chapter Two

IT OCCURRED TO ME, AFTER WE'D MADE OUR WAY A FEW paces down the dusty, sun-baked street, that I was now parading a filthy, chained, and also very naked man through the town. Deciding that he'd probably appreciate some clothing at the very least, I stopped and glanced around for a shop. He might have been able to wear some of my tunics, of course, but I hadn't brought one with me, never dreaming that any slave I bought might come without clothing of his own. Of course, the chains presented a problem, for his wrists were chained to his ankles and would have made it impossible to get a tunic and trousers onto him without first removing them. I still held the remote in my hand and looked down to study it. The buttons on it were labeled, but in a language that I couldn't decipher.

"Any idea how this thing works?" I asked him. "I suppose I should have asked that little scumbag for the owner's manual, but at the time, I didn't think of it."

The Zetithian's reply was simple and to the point. "Do not press the star-shaped button."

"Oh? And what does that one do?" I inquired.

"It tightens all of the cuffs."

"Even the one around your neck?"

He nodded in reply.

"Gotcha!" I said with a quick nod. "Don't touch the star button." I took a deep breath and went on, "Seems simple enough! What else?"

"The knobs on the top increase the tightness of the restraints and the length of time that they remain tight."

"Which way do you turn it?" I asked. "To release them, I mean."

He shrugged. "I do not know."

"Well, then how the hell am I ever gonna get all this stuff off of you?" I demanded. "I'm afraid I'll kill you if I just start experimenting with it!"

Tilting his head to one side, he regarded me curiously. "You plan to remove them?"

I stared at him with a blank expression. "Do you mean to tell me that he kept these restraints on you all the time?" No way could I go to Statzeel with a man wearing a restraint on his dick! The locals would *never* understand....

He shook his head. "Not all at once," he replied. "But always one. Usually the one on the neck."

"A remote choke collar!" I said in a horrified whisper. The sort of thing you'd use on a dog—a really nasty dog, too. I shuddered and looked up at him questioningly. "You're not gonna be that much trouble...are you?"

"I am a slave and a prisoner," he informed me. "I will attempt to escape."

"Well, isn't that just ducky!" I grumbled. "I might as well just give you this thing and let you go right now!" Noting his astonished expression, I went on. "I require the help of someone I can trust, Kittycat! I didn't pay enough for you to go to a lot of trouble just to make you

stay with me, and I can't afford to waste any time
hunting you down, or trying to keep you in line. I've got
enough trouble trying to find my sister as it is."

I studied his enigmatic face for a long moment before
letting out a pent-up breath. This just wasn't going to
work....

"Well, it was just a thought, anyway. I'll have to figure
out something else. Here," I said, handing him the
remote. "Hold this." I fished into my pocket and put the
other forty credits that I would have paid the Cylopean in
his hand. "Good luck to you, my friend," I said, looping
the end of the chain over his arm. "I wish you well."

I turned away, hitching my pack up on my shoulder,
and set off down the street, leaving him behind. I would
simply have to come up with a different plan. I could try
to pretend to be a man myself. Perhaps not every man on
Statzeel walked around with his dick hanging out, and if
they did, I could always wear a strap-on.

Of course, if I pretended to be a man, then I'd probably need my own slave woman. Crap! I heaved a sigh
of utter weariness, thinking that maybe I could buy a
woman and then let her go, too. The idea had merit, and
it would undoubtedly end up being much easier than
dealing with a man I wasn't sure I could trust. It had
been pretty damned stupid of me to think that my slave
would behave any better for me than he had for his
previous owner—even if I *had* made his dick hard. I'd
have thought that perhaps a former soldier would have
had more of a sense of honor. Oh, well....

I stopped at the crossroad to let a cart pass, which was
being pulled by a tired-looking smedreck. They were

sort of like horses, but not nearly as pretty, being more reptilian than anything. I missed horses, for I'd never found any animal like them on any other planet. They were unique to Earth, it seemed, and rightly so. I thought it fitting that we should hold claim to at least one thing that was beautiful and not to be found anywhere else. It made Earth seem that much more special and made me long to return home that much more.

As I tramped on down the street, I realized that I was getting hungrier by the second and decided to head back to my ship to get out of this damned respirator so I could eat something. It had been a very long and fruitless day—not to mention the fact that I had paid forty-five credits for a slave that I didn't keep for more than ten minutes. I just hoped Ranata would stay put on Statzeel long enough for me to come up with a different plan. I figured I'd eat something and then sleep on it and see what else might come to mind, because at the time, I was fresh out of ideas.

I'd left my ship parked unceremoniously on the flat plain outside the town, and even though there were no amenities whatsoever, had been charged fifteen credits to keep it there. Wondering how far away I'd have had to land to park it for free, I keyed open the hatch with my thumb and went inside, closing it quickly in a futile attempt to keep the stench out of my ship. I knew I'd have to turn the filtration system on high to clear it out before I even thought about taking off the respirator, for, hungry and slightly nauseated as I was, even a whiff of that stink would probably have been the death of me. Of course, the respirator hadn't helped a hundred percent:

that little snit on Dadred had taken me to the cleaners on that one! I figured I ought to go back and punch the sonofabitch's beady little yellow eyes out since it seemed I had plenty of time now—unless an inspired plan to rescue Ranata suddenly came to me like a bolt from the blue.

I gave it a few minutes before I pulled off the respirator and plopped down in my big, comfy chair with a bowl of leftover stew. My ship was a good one, with all the amenities, which was fortunate because, on most planets, I hadn't cared to stay in the local lodgings, some of which catered to very different creature comforts than those to which I was accustomed. I wasn't terribly adventurous when it came to soaking in steaming mud baths, or lounging on a bed that was largely made of sharp stones, for example.

I wondered if my slave had managed to free himself yet and I hoped he wouldn't waste the money I'd given him on something stupid like getting drunk or getting laid. It was possibly enough to buy passage off this horrid planet if he was frugal, but who knew what a recently freed Zetithian would choose to do? I'll admit, I was feeling a bit guilty about having left him so abruptly, thinking that I should have at least stayed long enough to find food and clothing for him and to get him loose from those god-awful restraints!

I hadn't admitted to myself yet that I'd left him like that because he hadn't been able to see that I was a decent sort who would take care of him rather than abuse him. Perhaps it was the crack about having him castrated, which was something that I would never have done even if I *had* kept him as a slave, but, of course, he couldn't have known that. I hadn't given him much of a chance, had I? And I certainly hadn't factored the length of time it might take to convert him into the equation when I'd considered buying a slave for this purpose. I'd been on this planet too damned long, I decided, and I needed to get the heck out of Dodge. I was desperate to the point of actually considering just blundering onto Statzeel alone and taking my chances—which wouldn't have done at all. I mean it really would've sucked to have come so far and taken so long, only to end up screwing the pooch at the last minute.

I finished my stew and sat there for perhaps fifteen minutes before getting to my feet, deciding that I would go back and look for the stupid sonofabitch and try to give him all the help I could. Of course, with a pissed-off Cylopean around, I'd probably end up getting myself killed in the process, but I felt that at least I had to give it a try. I had a fairly good chance of locating my little slave, since he was fairly conspicuous. He shouldn't be too hard to find....

Unfortunately, neither was I. The Cylopean was waiting outside the hatch when I opened it, and while he still looked rather pissed, I suppose it might have been the pulse pistol he was pointing at me that gave me my first clue.

"You have something of mine," he snarled. "I want him back, or I want the full fifty credits he is worth."

I was armed, of course—I never went anywhere without Tex, my trusty pulse pistol!—but at the time, my weapon was holstered and I knew I'd probably have to talk my way out of this one.

"Listen, you little shit!" I snarled back at him. "That slave was worthless! He was wild and uncontrollable and I couldn't trust him, so I gave him forty credits and the remote and left him in the street! Go find him yourself if you're so damn worried about him." When in doubt, tell the truth.

"That's a lie!" the Cylopean hissed. "He's here on your ship! He was seen in this area."

I sighed and shook my head. "Why is it that no one ever listens to me? I'm an honest person and I tell the truth on a fairly regular basis, so I shouldn't seem all that untrustworthy! It's a curse, I tell you! A curse!" I sighed again. "Look, if he was seen in this area, then he must have come here on his own. I left him not thirty meters from the plaza. You can search my ship if you like. He's not here."

"Why would you give him money when you wouldn't even pay me what he was worth?" he demanded.

Again, when in doubt, tell the truth. "Because I felt sorry for him and I didn't feel the least bit sorry for you—asshole! Besides, he had a nice cock." *Oops, I think I might have let the cat out of the bag with that one.* "I would have paid you more before the auction began," I went on, "but, no! You wouldn't listen to me, would you? Just had to be greedy, didn't you?" You know, it's really difficult to face someone down and sneer at them when you're wearing a mask that covers most of your face. I found it to be a decided disadvantage. "Are you really wanting to get him back or are you just here to kill me or rob me because I pissed you off by being right about how the auction would go?"

I hoped I wasn't giving him any ideas, but, somehow, I doubted it. He'd had enough time to come up with plenty on his own, and considering what he'd done to his slave, I knew he'd have no qualms about doing some pretty nasty things to me. You know, I just hate people like that! I've never understood why some people are so damned mean! I suppose it might have been their upbringing, but some people are so awful that they had to have been born that way. I think Cylopeans were, because I'd never yet met one that was very friendly. Their reflexes aren't very good, either, because we both saw the Zetithian at the same time, and the dumb-ass Cylopean was still pointing his pistol at me when his former slave lowered his head and launched himself at him—chains and all—with a deep-throated roar.

My reflexes, on the other hand, were pretty good and I had my own weapon in the palm of my hand in less time than it takes to tell it. I knew I'd better do something pretty damn quick, because if that creep got hold of the wrong chain…well, let's just say it could get messy! I got closer and kicked the pulse pistol out of the Cylopean's hand as they wrestled in the dirt, noting that the Zetithian was attempting to wrap the chain that ran between his right hand and foot around the Cylopean's neck, while the former slave master tried to grab the chain to the genital cuff. Muttering, "Oh, what the hell…," I set my own pistol on a wide stun and shot them both.

"Whoa! Good shootin', Tex!" I said as I holstered my weapon. As split-second decisions go, it was probably one of my better ones, for not only did it stop the fight without killing anyone, but it also meant that I didn't have to take any lip off of either of them. I struggled with the impulse to simply get back on my ship, close the damned hatch, and take off, but once again my softer side got the better of me. I dragged the Cylopean clear of the blast zone for my take-off, rolled my slave onto a blanket, retrieved the remote from where he'd dropped it—along with the credits I'd given him—and pulled him aboard. Then I closed the hatch, fired up the engines, and took off. I just hoped that my second decision was as good as the first, because if not, I was going to have an extremely unhappy little slave boy on my hands.

After getting clear of the solar system, I set the autopilot to fly while I consulted the star charts. Statzeel was only about five light-years away, but going there first was probably not the best idea, unless I just wanted to turn the Zetithian loose there. I needed somewhere to take him to if I didn't decide he was worth the trouble, or at least find someone to get his restraints off if we couldn't figure it out between the two of us. I hoped he would be a bit more cooperative and not too pissed to listen to reason when he woke up. On the other hand, the Cylopean had said that he'd been seen in the area around my ship. Could it be that he had been looking for me, and *not* his former master? But, why? Did he realize he needed my help, or what? Had he attacked the Cylopean because he was threatening me, or just on general principles? I hoped he'd at least be honest with me, but I also knew I couldn't count on it.

I glanced up from my charts to see him lying there, still inert upon the floor. In my haste to depart, I had simply left him there, just inside the hatch, sprawled out on the blanket and fully exposed. He was certainly an interesting looking creature, with definite feline characteristics, for, in addition to the vertical pupils and rather pronounced and sharp canine teeth, I also noted that he had slightly pointed ears which I hadn't been able to see before due to the mass of filthy, matted hair that covered them. His penis, of course, I had gotten a really good look at, and it was still quite impressive even in its flaccid state. I was pleased to note that he hadn't ripped the ring out of it when he'd attacked his former master, either. He was still extremely dirty, however, and as such, didn't exactly smell like a rose. Fortunately, he didn't smell anything like the atmosphere of the planet we'd just left, for if he had, I'd have been sorely tempted to space him.

I picked up the remote and studied it, wishing that whoever had made it had seen fit to use pictographs instead of the local symbols to describe the function of each control. I toyed with the knobs on the top, thinking, *righty tighty, lefty loosey.* I wondered if that was as universal wherever this device had been manufactured as it was on Earth. I thought that perhaps the ship's computer could decipher the symbols and I was scanning them into it when my new shipmate began to stir.

"Take it easy there, big guy," I said as reassuringly as possible. "I'm trying to figure out how this thing works, and hopefully I'll be able to get it off for you. Just curl up there and get some sleep if you like, this may take a while." Then it occurred to me that he might be hungry or need to pee or something. "Bathroom is around the corner, and the galley is over there," I said with a wave of my hand. "I don't know what you like to eat, but laying in supplies for you wasn't exactly what I had in mind when we left." I heard a low growl emanating from his direction. "Hey, I'm not gonna have to use this on you, am I?" I inquired with a wave of the remote.

Honestly, one more display of ingratitude on his part and I was going to seriously consider spacing him! However, the fact that it was impossible to do such a thing on this particular ship without getting sucked out into space myself would have made it an idle threat. Still, it might be worth mentioning at some point if he ever got completely out of control…. "And if you're thinking about killing me, too, then let me remind you that I *am* piloting this ship, and unless you were once a pilot yourself, you might want to consider keeping me safe until I land you on solid ground somewhere."

He growled again. "I was not going to kill you."

"Well, I can't even begin to tell you how pleased I am to hear that!" I said in a voice heavily laced with sarcasm. Of course, I had no idea whether or not sarcasm was a concept he was familiar with, but at the time, I simply didn't give a damn. "So, if you weren't plotting my demise, would you mind telling me just what the devil you were doing hiding underneath my ship?" I glanced over at his filthy, naked body and gave him a nasty little smile. "I mean aside from the fact that you aren't exactly dressed for a tea party and it might be a trifle embarrassing for you to be seen out in public."

My adorable little slave kitten rolled onto his hands and knees and pushed himself up off the floor. Head down, he advanced in my direction, glaring at me from beneath those flying black brows, his cat-like pupils glowing almost brightly enough to cast a shadow. Even not knowing him well, I would have to assume that he was a bit out of sorts, himself.

"You released me and gave me credits," he said as though it were the nastiest thing anyone could have ever done to him. "You have placed me in your debt." He bit out the words as though they tasted bad, and I think that perhaps in another circumstance he might have followed that statement up with a hiss. I was still holding the remote, however, so perhaps he felt it best to leave that part unsaid, though it seemed to be understood.

I sighed and shook my head. I had bought him, released him, and had given him enough money to keep himself in cat food for a good, long while, and he had the audacity to be hateful about it!

"Story of my whole fuckin' life!" I said irritably. "You do something nice for a guy, and he hates you for it! I should have pressed the fuckin' star button and left you writhing in the street!" I felt an odd little pain in my chest when I said that. Must have been from eating that stew so fast, I decided. Yes, that was it. I was just having a bit of indigestion. I ate too fast, and I was mad. Okay, that explained it. "Go on, Cat," I said, turning my back on him to stare into the computer screen once more, "go take a bath, or stuff your face, or take a piss—or, better yet, go fuck yourself. I don't give a shit what you do. Just go away."

Unbelievably, I felt that same twinge in my heart again and my eyes grew damp with tears. I hadn't shed a tear in so long the sensation was as alien to me as the feel of cool grass between my toes. What made it so unusual was that not only was I angry, but I was hurt, though it pained me even more to admit it, and I hadn't thought I had enough feeling left in me to ever experience that again. It wasn't the first time I'd felt that way, of course, but it had been many years, indeed, since I'd experienced that kind of pain. It reminded me of the way I'd felt the first time a man had singled me out for his attentions just so he could get closer to my beautiful, and otherwise unattainable, sister. Oh, yeah, just exactly like that....

I heard him take a step closer, his chains clinking together as he moved.

"I *said*, go away!" I warned through my tightly clenched teeth. I raised the remote and put my thumb on the star button. "Back off!"

I never looked up, but I heard him move away and when he was gone, I dropped my forehead into my hand as hot, unaccustomed tears coursed down my cheeks. Damn, I thought miserably. I'm so unlikable, I can't even get a stray cat to want to stay with me! I didn't think it was asking too much of him to say thank you, either. You know, just a little, "Hey, by the way, Jack, thanks for buying me and letting me go." Then again, perhaps it was. I mean, what did I know about him, really? Maybe his kind didn't appreciate it when someone took pity on them. He'd been a soldier at one point, apparently—maybe it was a duty and honor sort of thing. They all had their own little codes of behavior, and I suppose I could have unknowingly violated one of them when I set him free. It was also just possible that I hadn't made my intentions entirely clear to him.

"Hey, Cat!" I called out as I wiped away my tears. "Come back here!"

I heard the rattle of his restraints as he returned to the pilot's console. He stopped about two meters away.

I didn't look up. "My sister was kidnapped and I've been trying to find her for six years," I said in a low voice. "Where she was taken, I cannot go alone, and I need your help. I will pay you for your services and when she is safe, I will pay you a substantial bonus and then our ways will part. You will be freed, for I have no use for a slave and consider slavery of any kind to be an affront to the dignity of all beings on all worlds. I will carve that in stone, if you like."

"My last master promised me freedom after the battles were won," he said flatly. "You see what comes of trusting someone who would purchase a slave."

I spun my chair around to face him. "Well, isn't that just ducky!" I spat out. "I'm sitting here trying to be sincere, and you're comparing me to that asshole of a Cylopean! You are not—and I repeat, not!—scoring any brownie points here, Kittycat! I'm not the one who put your balls in a vice! I'm just the one sitting here trying to figure out how to get you loose from all that crap while you stand there and insult me!" I glared up at him with as much ire as he was directing back at me. "Don't you get it, you stupid feline? I'm one of the good guys!"

"You gave me no chance to agree to help you," he said accusingly. "You left me behind."

"What?" I demanded. "Is that why you're acting so damned testy? You couldn't have hollered after me? You had plenty of time to say something—I wasn't walking that fast! You could have followed me, caught up with me, and offered to help. Really, you quiet, stoic types just get my goat! 'You gave me no chance to agree to help you,'" I said, mimicking his tone. "You could have at least given me a fuckin' thank you! I could have left you there without the remote and without any money, you know. Did you ever consider that? Huh? Answer me! Well, did you?"

To my surprise, he smiled. "You are like the women of my home world," he said. "Fiery and very, very stubborn."

"Ha! Look who's talking about being stubborn! The pot's calling the kettle black, if you ask me." In response to his puzzled expression, I added, "Old Earth expression. You know, like, 'it takes one to know one.'"

His nod was tentative. "You are very odd," he observed.

"Is that a problem for you?"

"I believe I like odd."

"Don't you try to sweet-talk me, you big ol' tomcat!" I warned. "All I want from you is a simple thank you and a promise that you won't try to kill me while I'm sleeping!"

He smiled again. "Thank you and I promise not to kill you—whether you are awake or asleep."

"Well now, that's more like it!" I said, somewhat placated. "So, are you going to help me or not?"

"What would I be required to do?"

This is where things might get a little sticky. "Are you familiar with the customs of the planet Statzeel?"

He nodded. "Women are enslaved there."

"Yeah, well, that's where my sister is," I declared, "so that's where I have to go. I need you to pose as my, um, master."

He stared at me in frank disbelief. "You bought a slave so that you could pretend to be *his* slave?" he asked incredulously.

"That just about sums it up," I replied. "Are you game?"

He hesitated a moment before asking: "Explain what you just said."

"Yes, I bought a slave so that I could pretend to be his slave," I said patiently. "Do you want to help me or not?" I hesitated a moment before adding, "Have I made myself perfectly clear?" I rolled my eyes as it became quite obvious that he was still in the dark about something. "Do you understand?" I enunciated each word deliberately and very distinctly, and then laughed to myself thinking of all the old movies I'd seen where the people who spoke only English thought that they could be understood by the native tribesmen if only they spoke very, very slo-o-ow-ly.

"Yes," he replied. "I understand, and I will help you— but for my freedom only. You do not have to pay me any more than you already have. I will keep the forty credits you gave to me as payment for my…services."

I nodded. "Fair enough," I said. "And I'll cover the cost of your food and clothing and whatever else you might need in the meantime."

His lips curled into a sly grin. "And will you carve that in stone?" he inquired.

Well, at least he was learning! "If you like," I replied, heaving a sigh of relief, and thinking that perhaps this would work, after all—but not unless we got his restraints off. I'd seen enough to know that often such things were booby-trapped to kill if you tampered with them. Slave owners, as a rule, did not want their property running off, and the promise of death if they ever made the attempt was a pretty effective deterrent. We would have to be very, very careful. "Okay, now, tell me again," I said. "Whenever any of your restraints were removed, did he have something else he used, like a key or other device?"

My cat shook his head. I decided that I would have to figure out something else to call him. I couldn't just keep on calling him "Cat." I hoped he didn't have any strange, cultural beliefs about sharing his real name with me. You just never knew about such things. I'd met a man on some planet somewhere who said he wanted to have sex with me, but wouldn't remove his visor because he couldn't let me see what color his eyes were. Pretty weird, huh?

Anyway, my feline friend didn't seem to mind being nude all the time, although I wondered if he might be getting just a bit chilly since my ship's environmental settings were considerably lower than those we had been experiencing on the surface of Orpheseus Prime. If he'd been like other cats and had a nice covering of fur, it wouldn't have been a problem, but since he didn't, he obviously needed some clothing. Of course, this presented the same problem as before, because in order to dress him, I still had to get the damned restraints off. I thought for a moment and decided that perhaps he could wear a sheet wrapped around him like a toga. It might have looked a little silly, but it would cover up that penis of his, which, I don't mind admitting, I found to be just a tad on the distracting side. And besides, I didn't want him getting any funny ideas because I couldn't keep from staring at it.

"And speaking of food and clothing," I said, as casually as possible. "I don't suppose you'd like something to wear in the meantime? You know, while I try to figure out how this remote works?" Then I came up with another idea. "I could cut a hole in a blanket and then you could at least have a poncho of sorts to put on. Aren't you cold?"

"No."

Since I had asked two questions, I wasn't completely sure which one he'd answered. "No, you aren't cold, or no, you don't want something to wear?"

"No, I am not cold, and no, I do not want something to wear."

"We're gonna have to teach you to speak with contractions," I muttered. "The way you talk drives me nuts." Judging from his expression, I'd lost him again. "Never mind," I said quickly. "Getting back to the original subject, are you absolutely sure you don't know how any of this works? Never watched while he fiddled with the dial?"

He shook his head. "He never let me see what he was doing with the controls. He would threaten me by turning the dials on the top and also with the star key. I know nothing else."

By this time, my computer had finished searching through the known character database and with a cheery little beep reported that it had, as I might have guessed, come up with absolutely nothing. So much for technology. It was becoming apparent that good ol' trial and error was going to be the only way to solve this little dilemma.

"Well, okay, then, since you don't know anything, and the computer doesn't either, I'm afraid you're going to have to go through a little pain here, Kittycat. I promise I'll try not to hurt you too much."

He didn't say anything, or even nod, but if his stoic expression was anything to go by, I had to assume I could take that as a yes.

At first glance, the controls seemed simple enough: three rows of two buttons each—no doubt corresponding to each of the cuffs—the star key, and the two dials on the top. The central button in the top row was somewhat worn and had obviously been used the most, so I figured that it must correspond to the collar restraint. Deciding it was best to leave that one alone for now, I pressed the one next to it experimentally, and he responded with a jerk of his left arm.

"Well, if that's the arm, this must be the foot, and so on," I muttered to myself. I turned the dial on the top right counterclockwise and pressed the left arm button again. "Feel anything?"

He shook his head. "Almost nothing."

"Okay, then, we at least know how to turn down the intensity." Apparently the righty tighty, lefty loosey thing was universal after all. I dialed down the other one, which I assumed was the duration control and examined it again. It had to have some sort of power source, obviously, and though there were no screws holding it together, I had an idea that if I could get it apart somehow and take out the batteries, all the restraints would just pop off. If we were lucky, that is. Of course, that sounded much too easy, and I had to assume that the remote was probably booby-trapped and might explode and kill us both if I tried prying the casing apart. I toyed with the idea of just cutting the chains and leaving the cuffs on him for the time being, but that cock ring had to hurt and the cuff around his genitals couldn't have been good for his balls. Besides, it went without saying that I couldn't take him to Statzeel like that, which would make him pretty much useless in my search for Ranata.

"Tell me again, when he took cuffs off, he did it using the remote, right?" I asked. "Never took them off manually using a key?"

He nodded. "Yes."

"Well, then it must be a sequence thing." I paused for a moment as another thought occurred to me. "Tell me, did he ever actually press the star key, or did he just threaten you with it?"

He shook his head. "No, he only told me what it would do."

I chuckled slightly. "And if you ever got hold of the remote, that was absolutely the *last* button you would ever dream of pushing to attempt to escape, right?"

"Yes."

"Well, hold on, Cat. Here goes nothing!" I said, as I pushed the star key, followed by the left arm control.

My slave started to lunge forward to stop me and began to roar, but stopped short as the left arm cuff sprang open. If he'd been from Earth, his response would undoubtedly have been, "Well, I'll be a son-ofabitch!" but since he was from somewhere else, he just blinked and stared at his free hand in complete and total disbelief.

"Should have known a big, fat liar like that wouldn't have told you the truth about it, now, shouldn't you?" I chided him.

"I must be very stupid," he remarked, still marveling at his left hand.

"Nope, just a little too trusting of a known liar," I said with a chuckle. "Like my old Grandpa used to say, 'A thief can only take what you've got, but a liar can get you killed!'"

I popped off the rest of his limb restraints and noticed that we had an additional problem: the ring through his penis didn't appear to be removable. "Better hold onto that chain," I suggested, "or your ying-yang might get yanked."

Cat did as I told him and I popped off the remaining cuffs. "Don't worry about that ring," I said. "I've got some tools and we can at least cut through the chain, even if we can't remove the ring—although I doubt it's made of something so hard that I can't get it out with my bolt cutters."

In a classic male response, I noticed him wincing when I mentioned the bolt cutters. "Don't worry, I'll be very careful!" I assured him. "I won't have to cut through your penis to get it out." He went slightly pale when I said that. "Oh, don't be silly! It'll be just like taking out a pierced earring!"

"No," he said firmly. "It will not. A penis is *nothing* like an ear lobe."

"True," I conceded, "but like I said, I'll be very careful. You won't feel a thing."

He still appeared skeptical. "Now, where have I heard that before?"

"Ha!" I exclaimed. "So you *do* have a sense of humor! I was beginning to have my doubts." I went off to the storage area and, after a bit of rummaging around managed to find my tool box. It's amazing just how much a person can accumulate during six years aboard the same ship— like a house that you've lived in so long that you either need to get rid of some stuff or just give up and move.

Returning triumphantly from my search, I brandished the bolt cutters with a few quick chops in the air to demonstrate how they worked. "Here," I said, handing him the cutters, "you ought to be able to handle this yourself." I certainly hoped so because I wasn't about to touch his dick or even get that close to him, not after the reaction he'd had to me in the plaza!

He took the tool from me, but then just stood there, holding the chain and the cutters like he had no idea what to do with them.

"Is there a problem?" I asked, thinking that perhaps he hadn't been paying attention to my little demonstration.

"I will not be able to hold the chain and cut the ring at the same time," he replied.

"Well, just sit down and lay the chain across your legs and then cut the ring, dummy!" I said. "It shouldn't be that hard to do!" He'd already claimed to be stupid; now he seemed to be proving it. Well, he only cost me five credits, I thought, and, after all, you get what you pay for.... Of course, I'd assumed that he would only be belligerent, not dumb as a box of rocks! Then it occurred to me that he might have been remembering the ring being put in—which couldn't have been fun, and I seriously doubted that whoever did that to him had bothered to use a local anesthetic. "Are you okay?" I asked.

He swallowed hard and sat down heavily in the nearest chair. "No," he replied.

So, of course, I just *had* to ask, "If you don't mind my asking, how on Earth did they get you to hold still for that?"

His glittering eyes avoided mine for once and he stared down at the floor as he spoke. "My master choked me with the collar until I passed out after I lunged at him when he informed me that he was not going to set me free as he had promised, but intended to sell me at auction. When I regained consciousness, I was strapped to a table with the other restraints already in place and they were getting ready to put in the ring. It was sharp and red hot to cauterize the wound. Then they melted it together with a torch. It was…" He paused, wincing and blinking rapidly at the memory of the pain. "…the worst thing that had ever been done to me."

I looked at all the scars that covered what should have been a truly superb body and started crying all over again. Up until that day, I thought my tear ducts didn't work anymore, but now I was pretty sure that they worked just fine.

His hands started shaking then and he dropped the bolt cutters. Obviously, he was not going to be able to do it himself. I dashed the tears from my eyes and picked up the tool. Then I remembered that great stuff I'd found on Derivia.

"Hold on a minute," I told him. "I'll be right back."

I went into the bathroom and found the tube of oint-ment without too much trouble—my bathroom was a little neater than the storeroom, though not by much—and returned quickly.

"This is the best stuff ever! It prevents infection and relieves the pain just like that!" I said with a snap of my fingers. "It makes cuts and scrapes heal up almost overnight, too. Somebody gave me a tube of it when I got a little banged up on Derivia, and I liked it so well I bought several cases of it. It sells very well on other worlds, too." Noticing his questioning look, I went on to explain, "I'm a trader, Kittycat. It's what I do for a living—aside from chasing after my sister."

He nodded dumbly and just sat there. Obviously, I was going to have to do most of the dirty work here. I leaned over and applied a good-sized dollop of it to his penis. "We'll just let that set for a minute, and then you should be able to get the ring out without any problem."

I waited for about five minutes and hoped he'd be able to relax enough to do it himself, but there were scars on this man that weren't visible to the eye. He simply couldn't do it. So I did. It wasn't that hard to cut through the ring, but it did seem to be sort of stuck—though whether from dried blood or cauterized tissue, I couldn't be sure. I bent the ring open and slipped it out after lubricating it a bit with the ointment.

"Thank you." The words were clear, but his head was still lowered.

"Hey," I said gently, taking his chin in my hand and raising his face to look into his eyes. "You will never be abused like that again—at least not while you're with me, Kittycat. I can promise you that." I felt an overwhelming desire to kiss him just then, but I stifled it, just as I stifled most of my desires. They'd been on hold for so long already, a little longer wouldn't make much difference. Besides, anytime I'd ever let my emotions rule me, my business dealings had suffered, and I couldn't afford to let myself slip up now, not when I was so close to finding Ranata.

So, instead of kissing him, I decided it might be best if I introduced myself. "My name is Jacinth Rutland," I said, holding out my hand. "Welcome aboard the *Jolly Roger.*"

Not being native to Earth, he probably hadn't gotten the joke, but he probably didn't feel much like laughing just then, anyway. I suppose it could have been said that I was sort of like a pirate. Some of my customers might be inclined to refer to me as such, though I made it a rule never to be dishonest with anyone unless they tried to swindle me first. After that, I figured they were fair game. However, since I usually paid for things rather than stole them, I was more of a good pirate than a bad one—if there truly was such a thing as a good pirate. I wasn't sure about that, but the ship had already had the skull and crossbones painted on it when I bought it, hence the name. Mom had thought it was pretty funny, anyway. My, how she would laugh when I came home with Ranata! Of course, she'd probably cry her eyes out first—*then* she would laugh.

"I am Carkdacund Tshevnoe," he replied, taking my hand in a firm, warm grasp. He was recovering quickly, it seemed. "But you may continue to call me Cat."

"Thanks," I said, grateful for not having to wrap my tongue around a handle like that every time I spoke to him! "What the hell do your friends call you for short?"

"I have no friends," he stated simply. His voice held no expression of regret. It was merely a statement of the truth.

"Sorry," I muttered ruefully. "Should have thought about that before I opened my damned mouth." I heaved a sigh and added: "My friends call me Jack, but you can call me anything you like."

"Jacinth is a very beautiful name," he observed, and, you know, it really *did* sound beautiful the way he said it—almost like it had more letters in it or something.

"Yeah, I know," I grumbled. "Too bad it doesn't suit me. I think I look more like a Jack, myself."

"I disagree," he said. "To me, you look like a Jacinth. I will call you that."

Which was about the nicest thing anyone had said to me for quite some time—perhaps ever. I did my best not to let it show, though. "Sure," I said with a nonchalant wave of my hand. "Whatever."

Standing as close to him as I was now, and without the benefit of a respirator, my nose told me that a bit of washing up might be in order. I just hoped I didn't have to do that for him, too, but was surprised when just the idea of bathing him gave me a little twinge of…well, I don't know exactly what you'd call it, but suffice it to say that it revised my opinion of whether or not I would refuse to do it should it ever become necessary.

Clearing my throat and backing out of range of whatever it was about him that was making me *not* want to move away, I said briskly, "Okay, then, Cat, why don't you go get cleaned up a little and I'll fix you something to eat. What would you like?"

He looked up at me as though I'd completely taken leave of my senses. "I was a slave up until a short time ago," he reminded me, "and I have not eaten in two days. I will eat anything you give me."

"Silly me!" I commented dryly. "Well, it looks like you'll be an easy keeper, at least. And you don't seem to like wearing clothes much, so I won't be having to buy you a very extensive wardrobe, either." I was thinking of something along the lines of maybe, say, a loincloth and a vest at the very least, but, actually, I think it would have taken an awful lot more than that to camouflage his appeal.

"I have been in armor or restraints for most of my life," he said. "I think I would like to feel free to wear nothing for a while, if you do not object."

"No," I lied. "It won't bother me a bit. Just let me know if you get too cold."

He nodded and went to take a shower. I would have to remember to put some of the Derivian ointment on the sores on his back when he was clean and dry. And while he was gone, I thought perhaps I should turn down the temperature on the environmental controls. Maybe if he got a bit chilly, he'd at least put on a tunic—a really *long* tunic.

Chapter Three

CAT STAYED IN THE SHOWER FOR A LONG TIME. AT SOME point I'd have to tell him that, though the water supply was recycled, it took a little while and he might run out at some point if he stayed in there forever. But since it was possibly the first bath he'd had in years, I figured I'd let him enjoy it, at least this once. Apparently he didn't have the aversion to water that some Earth cats did, and it made me wonder just how many feline characteristics he had in common with them—did he purr, for example, and what would it take to make him do it?

I took him some shampoo while he was in there—it was the stuff I used myself whenever I happened to spend a little too much time around someone that I suspected had lice of some form. This was another commodity that I'd bought several cases of, and it sells well, too, especially on these dirty little back worlds like Orpheseus. I didn't have anything on hand to take out his tangles since my own short hair didn't require it, and I hoped we wouldn't have to end up chopping off those long tresses because I thought they would be quite attractive when they were clean. Maybe I'd have to comb it out for him—I could do it while he ate. After all, once you've pulled a ring out of a man's cock, combing his hair should be no big deal. Besides, I didn't have anything better to do while we flew to Statzeel, since apparently I didn't need to find another planet to drop him off on after all.

I heated up some more of the stew I'd had for dinner and set it out for him, wondering if he would use a spoon or eat it right out of the bowl. I'd seen some strange eating rituals during my sojourn in space; maybe I'd have to teach him how to use a knife and fork, too. After all, he'd said he would eat anything; he just didn't say *how*....

I'd seen the man naked, restrained, unconscious, sexually aroused, angry, terrified, and in pain, but I was wholly unprepared for just how incredibly good he would look right after coming out of the shower. The mere sight of him took my jaded, cynical, and completely unromantic breath away, and it was all I could do to point out the food that was waiting for him on the table. Cat didn't seem to notice my sudden afflic-tion, but merely smiled and pulled his hair back over his shoulders as he sat down to eat. I did have enough wits left to notice that he seemed to know how to use a spoon, but the rest of what I saw was pure animal attraction.

I drifted back over to the pilot's console and sat back, toying with my flight controls, but not really doing anything in particular while I watched him eat. Hungry as he must have been, I noted that he didn't wolf down his food, but sat there quietly savoring every mouthful. The stew was decent, but it wasn't *that* good and it made me wonder just what kind of garbage he'd been living on.

After studying him carefully, I came to the conclusion that if he were a typical specimen, then his people must have all been downright beautiful. As a general rule, I'd found most aliens to be unattractive, if not repulsive on the whole, but this one was decidedly the opposite, for, in addition to the other attributes which I have already described, his hair was the shiniest, blackest mass of spiral curls I'd ever seen on any native of any planet in any system. It was thick and luxuriant and made my fingers itch to delve into it, but I was denied that treat because he'd managed to get the tangles out all by himself and had even dried it using my handy-dandy Insta-Dry shower attachment that pulls the evaporated water back in to be recycled. He wasn't too stupid if he could figure out how *that* thing worked; I'd had to try twice before figuring it out myself.

Unfortunately, being clean and dry made his wounds and scars that much more prominent. He was nearly finished eating when I finally gave in to temptation and picked up the tube of Derivian ointment from where I'd laid it and went over to put some of it on the open sores on his back, firmly telling myself that I was *not* doing it just because I wanted to touch him. I had to move his hair out of the way to get to some of the sores and discovered that those curls truly felt every bit as good as they looked. I stood behind him, breathing in his essence, noting that whatever had smelled bad on him before was now completely gone. The funny thing was that I couldn't actually smell anything, but it did something to me anyway; and after the stench of Orpheseus Prime, he was a welcome change.

I had applied the ointment to all of his wounds and was recapping the tube when he got slowly to his feet and turned around to face me. "You forgot a place," he said.

Seemingly of their own accord, my eyes swept downward to follow the treasure trail of dark curls down to his groin. The spot to which he was referring was patently obvious, for his penis was fully erect and a droplet of blood had oozed from the site where his piercing had been. Surely he wouldn't insist that I do that as well!

He gazed down at me with those dark, but glowing, eyes and blinked slowly. He was so much more attractive now that he was relaxed and comfortable, and his nostrils flared ever so slightly, just as they had done when I'd been standing close to him in the plaza. Whatever it was that he had smelled then to arouse him in such a fashion, he must be catching whiffs of right now. What was it the Cylopean had said? A receptive female in the area? Oh, surely not! I chided myself. No one's sense of smell could be *that* good!—could it? And I certainly wasn't receptive—was I?

Then another of my questions about him was answered, for—honest to God!—he began to purr. He gestured toward his cock, and I pulled the cap off of the tube of ointment and held it out to him.

"No," he said, still purring softly, "do it for me, if you will."

I felt as though I were in some sort of trance and he was controlling me by the power of suggestion alone—I mean, I can't explain why I would have done what I did otherwise. Reaching down, I applied a small amount to the affected area and my eyes widened as his cock pulsed beneath my fingers.

"It has been too long since I have felt the gentle touch of a female hand," he murmured. "Too long."

Oh, how on Earth could I have been so stupid? Of *course*, any slave I bought would have been deprived of any pleasant experiences! He probably hadn't been with a woman in years, and now, here I was, alone on my ship with him! He was clean and well-fed and comfortable for the first time in who knew how long; the only thing missing was the sex. This was a factor I hadn't considered when making my plans for Ranata's rescue.

I couldn't afford to let it happen, though, because sex *always* clouded my judgment, making me botch the simplest of tasks and blow every deal I was involved in. This was definitely *not* the time to be making mistakes, for too much hung in the balance. I cleared my throat quietly.

"Perhaps we can find you a mate on Statzeel," I suggested, hoping my tone was more casual than my nerves were. "If the one I saw myself was any indication, their women are all very beautiful." I felt another twinge of pain in my heart when I uttered those words. It shouldn't have hurt me to say that, but, for some reason, it did.

"I would not want a mate who was my slave," he said quietly. "I would want someone like you, who was free and who wanted me." He studied me carefully with those gleaming eyes and inhaled again, as though rechecking my scent to assure himself that he had gotten it correctly. His purr grew louder as he breathed more deeply. "You do want me, do you not?"

My mouth went completely dry and my voice came out with a croak. "You can't possibly know that," I protested weakly. "I—I'm human. Have you ever met a human before?"

He shook his head. "Not before this," he said. "But the scent of desire is thick around you. So thick I can almost feel it."

I shook my head. Ranata, I reminded myself. Ranata must be saved! I can't lose sight of that now. Not when I'm so close…. "You're wrong," I said, shaking my head. "I don't desire any man. I…can't. And especially not now."

His purr intensified and he stepped closer, the flared head of his cock nearly brushing against my hand. "Touch me again, Jacinth," he purred. "I want to feel your hands on me. We saved each other today: you bought me and freed me, and I kept my old master from killing you. We should come together and rejoice in the knowledge that we are both still alive."

And suddenly, there it was again: that cloud, that fog in my brain that disturbed my normally well-ordered senses. I simply could not let myself fall victim to it! It could only cause me pain, for I knew he wouldn't want me again—not once he saw my sister, anyway. No man ever did, and he was no different from all the rest. I could not let myself be destroyed that way, not again, and especially not now.

"Yes, we're still alive," I conceded, "and I thank you for what you did for me, but my sister is still a slave and a prisoner. I can't let myself forget that, not even for a moment."

And with that, I turned away from him and retreated to the pilot's chair once more. I was Jack Rutland, I reminded myself. Captain of the *Jolly Roger*. I had deals to make and a sister to rescue. I didn't need a big pussy-cat to curl up with—no matter how attractive he was, or how good he smelled, or how fabulous he felt beneath my fingers. He would mess up my brain and fill it full of mush. I'd end up blowing everything and probably end up in slavery myself. Not that anyone on Statzeel would want me—though I'd probably be the type of slave that a man would leave at home to scrub the floors while he went out and paraded around town with one of his more beautiful possessions.

Of course, that way, at least I wouldn't have to fight it anymore. I'd just do as I was told and not have to worry about where I was going, or who I could find to give me information about my sister, or try to find another planet to search. I could simply work my tired fingers to the bone for the rest of my life and then die. I sighed deeply, thinking that it would almost be a relief, even a blessing in disguise. I wondered if Ranata felt the same way, or if she despaired of ever being found, much less of being rescued. Closing my eyes, I could see her quite clearly in my mind. Once more the terror in her eyes haunted me. No, I couldn't stop now, couldn't ever stop. Not until I found her and she was safe once more. Cat would simply have to get over it. I tried to blot out all that I was feeling, resting my forehead on the heel of my hand as though the pressure of it would force all the unwanted thoughts from my mind.

It was then that I discovered another thing about my shipmate that was very cat-like, for without all of those restraints dangling from his body, he could move without a sound. I had no warning that he was close until I felt his hands on my back.

"We will find your sister, Jacinth," he said firmly, as he began to massage my shoulders. I know I should have insisted that he stop touching me, but it felt so damn good I had to bite my lip to keep from letting out a groan. "Have you any personal belonging of hers?" he asked. "Something she wore or touched frequently? Something I could get her scent from? I am not the best tracker that I know of, but it may help us to find her."

I shook my head. "No, not a thing," I replied. "Just her photograph, though she probably looks quite different now. She was only nineteen when she was taken and she would have matured some by now. I wonder if she even remembers me."

"You remember her, do you not?" he inquired. "I am certain that she would not forget you."

I nodded. "You're right, of course. Though it's possible her memory might have been erased. I've seen stranger things done to people." Like putting rings through their genitals to control them, for example. I shuddered slightly at the thought of just how much that must have hurt my poor Cat!

It was odd that I still thought of him that way: *my* Cat. Like *my* dog, or *my* goldfish. I shouldn't think of him as a pet, I told myself. He was free; I didn't own him—and didn't really want to, even though it was a given fact that I would treat him better than anyone else ever had. I hoped whoever had Ranata was at least a benevolent master—though if the Statzeelian male I had seen was anything to go by, I couldn't have too many realistic expectations along those lines.

"I am certain that you will find her unharmed," he said, possibly assuming that my shudder had been because of my sister and not my Cat. There it was again: *my* Cat. I was thinking of him as my pet, which made me wonder if he would prove to be as hard to leave behind as my dog had been when I'd left home for a life in space. I also wondered what he would do once we found Ranata and his obligation to me was fulfilled. Would he take his forty credits and disappear, or would he follow me home like a stray dog? It was probably better for everyone if our ways parted— although if he truly wanted to stay with me and would keep on rubbing my neck like that…I might just decide to keep him.

It was the next logical question, so, what the hell, I went ahead and asked it. "What will you do once we find her?"

"I do not know," he replied slowly. "I would like to avenge the deaths of my people, but I am only one man. I cannot fight an entire civilization alone."

I shrugged. "I don't know, Cat. They say the pen is mightier than the sword, you know. You could just spread the word. Does anyone else know who was responsible for the destruction of your planet?"

Cat shook his head. "I do not believe so," he replied. "If it were known that I knew, I do not believe I would still be alive. I would have been hunted down and killed by now."

"Okay, now you've got my attention!" I said dryly, twisting around to look up at him. "Come on, out with it."

"Out with what?"

Either I was gonna have to stop speaking in Earth idioms, or he was gonna have to learn some of them. These constant explanations could get old. "Tell me what you know about who it was that destroyed your planet," I said carefully.

"I do not know what they are called," he said. "But they are an ugly, evil race, with fur-covered bodies and long, pointed snouts and vicious fangs."

"And really, really nasty, huh?"

"Yes."

At least he understood the word "nasty." I wasn't sure I could explain that one, unless I referred to his Cylopean master as an example. Of course, that guy was way beyond nasty, and anyone who would destroy a planet would be, as well. Sounded familiar, though, sort of like— "Nedwuts!" I exclaimed. "They were fuckin' Nedwuts!"

"What are Nedwuts?" he asked.

"The gang of slimeballs that kidnapped my sister were Nedwuts!" I explained. "I've always felt that the lot of them should be rounded up and interned on their own damn planet!" I said hotly. "They cause trouble wherever they go—although I must admit that completely destroying a planet would seem a bit ambitious for them. Mostly they're just petty thieves and sadistic little bastards, but sometimes they'll do much worse things— for a price." I looked up at him and went on earnestly, "Listen, Cat, if you want me to help you kill a few of them, I might actually consider it. I know I'd like to kill the ones who took Ranata!" I shook my head in disgust and spat out the word again. "Nedwuts!"

Cat seemed to focus on the most peculiar things. "What is a slimeball?" he asked.

I rolled my eyes, having to laugh just a bit. "Sorry, Cat. That's another old Earth expression," I replied. "I've made sort of a study of them. That one refers to…well, a ball of slime. You know what a ball is, don't you?" He nodded, and I went on, "Well, slime is goopy, slippery, sticky stuff that really grosses you out."

I was losing him, I could tell. My explanation was making it about as clear as mud. Then I realized I shouldn't be giving him the literal meaning, but the figurative one, instead.

"A slimeball is a real creep, Cat. You know, someone you can't stand to be around? Dishonest, greasy, sleazy—that sort of thing."

The light came on in his eyes as he caught my meaning. "So it is a bad thing to be a slimeball?"

"Well, yeah!" I said. "I mean, I certainly wouldn't want anyone to be calling me a slimeball! It's just about as bad as being called a blob of Redjbeck snot or a pile of Felderf dung—although I personally consider them to be much worse, and Nedwuts probably fall into that category, but it's just quicker to say slimeball."

I had collected quite a few other expressions in my travels—some of them quite colorful once you understood the reference. I still preferred the old Earth expressions, though. I knew some that dated back well over a thousand years, but, hey, when something works, why drop its usage just because it's old? I'd dug up lots of interesting idioms, some of which I'd attempted to revive, though they lost a bit of their punch when the person you were speaking to had no idea what you were talking about. Of course, you could insult someone and smile while you did it, and they'd never even know they'd been slammed. An odd hobby, I realize, but out in space, sometimes there's not much better to do than go through the literary database and read old texts. Occasionally the translator on my computer balked, but it was a way to pass the time.

Cat merely nodded, seeming to catalog this information away for future use. I wondered if he knew just how many euphemisms there were for that erection of his, which was still there, by the way. I also wondered what it would take to make that boner disappear—well, short of being stunned with a pulse pistol, that is. It hadn't looked like that when he'd been unconscious. If he could manage to keep it up, he would be very popular on Statzeel when he wore the crotchless trousers that the males of that planet seemed to favor. I would probably have to beat the women off of him, or at least spray a wide stun-beam with my trusty Tex.

Well, at least I felt a little better! A bit of laughter always helps, though I'd had to look real hard to find humor in some of the situations I'd been in. Of course, Cat could probably relate to that, too. I couldn't see him laughing about being bought and sold, for example— unless the slaves all got together later and made fun of the imbeciles out there bidding on them, which might prove to be amusing, though certainly one of the darker forms of humor.

I looked over my shoulder again. Yep, he was still there and still had that raging hard-on, which wasn't appreciably smaller than the one he'd gotten out in the plaza. I guess the genital restraint hadn't been as restrictive as it looked, after all. "Cat, what on Earth am I gonna do with you? You won't wear clothes and you stand around looking like something out of a holographic porn shop! Don't you have anything better to do?"

"No," he replied, with a shake of his mane.

"Well, surely there's something else you haven't done for a long time that you might like to do now."

"I have already done all of those things." He resumed his deep, soothing massage of my back, neck, and shoulders and began purring again.

"I suppose I could stun you," I suggested. "It seemed to help the last time."

"But I would not like that."

"I didn't think so, but at least your dick wasn't so hard while you were out."

"You do not like it when my 'dick' is hard?"

"Picked that one right up, didn't you?" I said approvingly. "No, I don't like—well, it does look very nice, but I really can't…"

"Tell my why you cannot," he persisted. "Do you have another mate?"

"No, it's just that being with men messes up my thinking," I explained. "I screw things up when I deal with men on anything other than a strictly businesslike basis. I just don't handle it very well. It's like someone who can't hold his liquor, you know?"

He understood that last reference, at least. "It intoxicates you?"

"Yes, something like that."

"Jacinth," he chided softly. "It is *supposed* to intoxicate you."

"Well then, I guess I just don't like being intoxicated," I grumbled. "I don't drink much liquor as a rule, either. I…lose control, and I don't like not being in control."

His purr took on a musical, laughing note. "But you *are* in control. You control me," he said. "I am your slave."

"Not anymore!" I insisted. "I let you go, remember? You are not my slave!"

"But I think I would like to be," he purred. "I believe I would like for you to tell me what to do for you. Things that would please you."

If he didn't stop that incessant purring and quit massaging my back in that deeply sensuous fashion, I really *was* gonna have to stun him again! He moved closer and leaned over me, sliding his hands down my arms and across my upper chest.

"If you're my slave," I countered, "I should be able to tell you to stop then, right?"

His mouth was right next to my ear and the purring was driving me insane. "You could tell me, but since I am not really your slave, I do not have to listen." His lips found my earlobe and he nipped it gently, pulling it through those sharp teeth of his. He sniffed my neck. "You smell of desire," he murmured. "I have not smelled it in many years, but I have not forgotten it. You smell like a female of my race, Jacinth. Just exactly the same."

I felt his tongue sweep across my skin: hot and wet and so very, very delightful.

"You taste the same, as well," he said against my neck. "Come and mate with me, my beautiful master, and I will give you joy unlike any you have ever known."

A likely story! Of course, I only *thought* that, though, because I seemed to have lost the power of speech all of a sudden. *Oh, God, he's doing it to me! I'm losing control….* He rubbed his cheek against mine, the way a cat will do when seeking a caress, and he followed with more of his body, stropping himself against me, making me wish he was doing it against my bare skin. Encircling my head with his hands, he brought my lips closer to his own and licked me firmly across the mouth until my lips parted in a sigh.

Kissing must have been an established Zetithian custom, for he certainly seemed to know how to do it— teasing me with his full, sensuous lips before delving deeply into the recesses of my mouth with his tongue as though he would find sustenance there. The sweep of his tongue across my own sent a warm gush of fluid from between my thighs which he must have smelled, for his purr grew even louder, becoming mingled with a deep, throaty groan—a groan which came from *me*.

I felt him take my hand and bring it up to wrap my fingers around his stiff shaft. I could feel the blood pulsing through it and thought about how he'd been abused. Poor Cat, he'd been hurt so much! Could I really refuse him this one, simple thing? All thoughts of my sister or my business or anything but Cat left my head completely. He had me now: it was going to happen, no matter what, and this was what I feared the most. This loss of will, of choice, of control. I felt my will slipping away as instinct took over and I grasped him firmly in my hand, caressing his strong cock as he pushed against me, fucking my hand with that fabulous cockhead. I was just about to surrender completely when the proximity alarm went off like a siren.

Not my own personal proximity alarm, mind you, but the ship's.

"We're coming up on Statzeel!" I gasped, releasing my hold on his cock and spinning around to reach the controls. "I've got to cut in the orbital engines or we'll crash right into it!"

Cat backed away and I shook my head in an attempt to clear the cobwebs out of it. You see! I chastised myself. This is what comes of getting too close to a big, horny tomcat! I should have insisted that he put on some clothes and then locked him in the hold. Or better yet, thrown him in the stasis chamber!

My fingers hesitated a moment as they switched from the hot, pulsating hardness of his penis to the cold, smooth surface of the control panel. It took a moment to adjust, and then my fingers began to fly over the console. There were too many distractions with him on board! What if I'd been underneath him at the moment of orgasm when that alarm went off, I chided myself. I can't do this right now! I need to focus! Fun and games must be put off until later, when I'd found Ranata and had somehow managed to set her free. Of course, if I made him wait that long, Cat would undoubtedly decide that he preferred Ranata, just like everyone else, and this whole thing would be a moot point.

Because, after all, I only smelled and tasted like a Zetithian female; Ranata probably looked, smelled, tasted, and felt like one. Hell, she probably even *sounded* like one! I let out a long sigh, thinking that there was a lot to be said for spontaneity, and also that timing truly *was* everything. I probably could have come up with at least ten other clichés to apply to this particular situation, but I was too pissed off at the time to think of them. What was I thinking to let him get so close? Was I feeling sorry for him, sorry for myself, or just plain willing to let him fuck me senseless and make me forget everything and everybody for a little while?

Maybe a little of all three, I decided as I heard the engines switch over. Statzeel loomed before us on the viewscreen, less than a million kilometers away, and I noted that it was a very attractive planet when viewed from space. The way my informant had described it to me, it sounded a lot like the whole world was one big planet-sized version of Hawaii, and it looked a lot like Earth from up there, all greens and blues and swirling clouds. I guess if you had to be a slave, it was as nice a place as any in which to live out your servitude.

"Where will we land?" Cat asked.

"Right about there," I said, pointing to a small area of land jutting out into the sea from another larger landmass. "I've been studying the maps for months. With any luck, we won't get lost."

Or encounter any of the other disasters that I had considered as possibilities for landing on a world like Statzeel. Actually, getting lost was among the more minor ones that had occurred to me. Being forced into lifelong servitude was the one that usually got most of my attention. What I mean is, being lost was a problem that could be remedied by finding a map, but being chained to some pompous Statzeelian asshole for the rest of my life was something else altogether. The thought of it got me to wondering just how often the women killed their husbands....

"My information was obtained from a smuggler who deals in black market goods. He sold me some clothing that should pass for the local garb and told me which areas to land my ship in to avoid detection, though we're not going to be sneaking in—at least not at first. I plan to go through the accepted channels as an honest trader and we should be able to find out plenty of information in the spaceport and the marketplace. This isn't a planet that people visit a lot, though, so I don't expect to be welcomed with open arms or put up in style at a Holiday Inn! He did tell me that traders aren't discouraged too much, so we can pull some stuff out of the hold and sell it while we're in the process of locating Ranata. She shouldn't be terribly hard to trace, given that she's from Earth, but the people might not be very talkative."

I hoped they were blind, too, for the outfit I had bought to wear while on my search was far too revealing for my own personal tastes, and had undoubtedly been designed for a woman much more well-endowed than I was—in the boob department, you understand. I suppose you might have figured out by now that I was as flat-chested as a boy, since I had considered it possible to masquerade as a man. The trouble was, I just didn't have the dick to complete that particular ensemble, so Cat would have to wear it. He'd probably look quite nice in it, actually, though it was difficult to picture him wearing anything at all since I'd only seen him in the nude—unless, of course, you were to count his shackles as garments, and I didn't think they qualified.

My smuggler friend had been the one to suggest that I get someone to go with me to pose as my master. He'd offered to do it himself, of course, but I wouldn't have trusted him not to sell me and leave me there to rot. He was a nice enough fellow, but since nearly all smugglers are seduced more by money than by any noble cause like freeing the slaves, I doubted that he would have been much help. He wouldn't have been allowed back on the surface of the planet if he'd made off with one of the women, either, which would have been bad for his business. Besides, finding Ranata was *my* job, and I doubted that she would have gone willingly with that particular smuggler anyway, for he was a bit creepy-looking—though certainly an improvement over any Nedwut I'd ever seen or heard tell of.

However, the information I received from him seemed to agree with what I'd already learned, so it seemed reasonable enough to believe him. I'd paid for the information, of course, and had put him onto a good bargain on another planet I'd visited; so he was pleased enough with the outcome of our deal to add another little tidbit of info for free, which was that if I was going to Statzeel, I'd better take along someone that I could trust. I just hoped Cat would fit the bill.

Chapter Four

I PUT THE *JOLLY ROGER* INTO ORBIT, SENT OUT A HAIL TO the surface, and sat back to wait. Some places take hours to respond to hails, so I knew better than to seem overly anxious by making the mistake of hailing them again. Some of those landing authority guys are real impressed with themselves and like to throw their weight around by making you wait for days just because they can. Besides, I had come a long way in six years and a few more hours of waiting wouldn't kill me, and hopefully it wouldn't kill Ranata either.

To pass the time, I went and got the clothes for Cat and told him to get dressed. He was still reluctant to put on anything, but I insisted. "Look, when they respond to our hail, they're gonna want to talk to the man in charge, and they're gonna want to see you, not me." I took a quick gander at what I was beginning to believe to be a permanent erection and added: "And don't worry about that, either. These clothes will accommodate it very nicely."

My smuggler friend had informed me that even visitors to the planet were required to dress like the natives, a practice which I found to be a bit odd—particularly since nearly every other world I'd ever visited didn't give a damn what the aliens had on, as long as they were wearing something decent. This was the first I'd ever heard of where the visitors to the surface were required to take things off, as it were. I could understand the women having to be properly clothed and chained, but I wondered why the men had to display their genitals. I never got a straight answer to that question, but the smuggler did tell me that a man could not legally even land on Statzeel without a female, which I assumed was to ensure that offworld men wouldn't run off with any of the local women.

The female dress was sheer and revealing, but stopped short of actual nakedness, which also seemed a bit odd to me. I mean, there were plenty of other places where the women wore virtually nothing, while you hardly saw any skin at all on a male. Then again, I reminded myself, I had seen plenty of other bizarre customs on my trek across the galaxy, and this was just one more to add to the list. I sometimes wondered if contact with other worlds was what had made them become even weirder—you know, just made them try harder to be different?—but I had no way of proving that hypothesis.

As I had thought, Cat looked spectacular dressed as a native of Statzeel. The white shirt had a high collar, billowing sleeves, and was open to the waist—it truly had no buttons on it whatsoever—and there was a black leather vest to wear over it. The black breeches were skin-tight and stretchy, but where on other worlds there would have been a fly or a cod-piece, on Statzeel there was a big hole surrounded with decorative embroidery, through which his cock and balls protruded. A red sash at the waist and black leather boots with Spanish tops to the knee completed the ensemble. He looked for all the world like a feline version of a swashbuckling pirate of the Caribbean with an exhibition complex. The only thing missing was the cutlass thrust through his sash.

"Well, if it isn't Puss in Boots!" I exclaimed. "Damn!" I swore softly. "You look good enough to—"

"Fuck?" he suggested with a hopeful lift of those exotic eyebrows.

"Well, yes, actually," I admitted. Of course, if I was being honest with myself, I would have to admit that he always *had*, even on Orpheseus Prime when he was filthy dirty and in restraints. Though I couldn't count myself among their number, I'm sure there were plenty of women who would have had an orgasm just from the mere sight of him standing up there on the auction block—though I must admit that seeing him dressed like this almost did it to me. Well, it made me think about it, anyway! I can't recall ever having had what you'd call a spontaneous orgasm in my life. Come to think of it, I hadn't had very many of the other kind either....

"If I had known that you would prefer me in such clothing I would have gotten dressed before this," he said ruefully. "I will have to remember that."

"Yeah, well, don't get too cocky, Kittycat!" I advised him. "Just remember we have a job to do and a sister to rescue." I was about to suggest that he keep his shirt on, too, when I realized that, at least in his current situation, the use of that particular expression to encourage patience would have been a bit ridiculous since, dressed as he was, he could service as many females as he chose without ever having to undo so much as a button. In fact, the more I considered the matter, the more I became convinced that it was quite possibly the most practical male attire I'd ever seen, and if you wanted to compare equipment size, it was unsurpassed. Of course, if your dick happened to be minuscule, there was no hiding that sad fact, and any woman would certainly know what she was getting into well in advance of any introduction, let alone an exchange of vows. I wondered why it hadn't caught on in other places throughout the galaxy, but decided that there were some people who preferred the element of surprise that came from unzipping their fly—and plenty of other guys who just didn't like the idea of their most prized appendage hanging out where someone might whack it off, whether accidentally or on purpose.

The hail came through just then and Cat took a seat at the communications console. "I am Carkdacund Tshevnoe of the trade ship—"

"*Jolly Roger*," I whispered.

"*Jolly Roger*," he went on smoothly, "requesting permission to land." He seemed very impressive, with his military bearing showing, and a firm, determined expression on his feline features. He could probably cow a few Nedwuts into submission just by looking at them like that, I decided. I was mentally patting myself on the back for my choice of slaves when the man on the planet asked if there were any females aboard.

"Yes," Cat replied. "I have one."

"Good. She must be properly clothed and chained to you before you will be allowed to leave the docking area, as is our custom. Your style of dress must meet with our regulations as well."

"I understand," Cat replied. "We will comply."

The man nodded and gave the landing coordinates and welcomed us to Statzeel. "The docking authority will give you further instructions on our trade regulations. I remind you that only legal commodities are allowed through the docking authority—no contraband."

What he was saying, of course, was that if we were smuggling anything illegal, we had to land somewhere unofficial. Not that we *couldn't* land somewhere else on the planet, mind you, just not in the main port. It was pretty much the same on any world in these parts: certain things were illegal only if you went through proper channels; if you didn't tell them about it, they would casually look the other way. I suppose even the most straitlaced Statzeelian might like a little Xedonian ale now and then, but you had to be really careful with the stuff because it had a tendency to explode—which is undoubtedly why it's illegal on most worlds. I'd carried it once and ended up losing a pretty nice cargo droid for my trouble, so I never bothered with it again.

Fortunately, I had been able to amass a fair fortune dealing only in legal goods, and it made me wonder sometimes why the smugglers went to so much trouble. Not only were their commodities dangerous at times, but I'd seen some of their covert landing areas, and even though I was a pretty decent pilot, I wouldn't have wanted to attempt it myself. Granted, drugs were easier to carry than, say, offworld furniture, for example, but I had a decent-sized hold in my ship and a good load-lifter. I guess the main difference between me and the smugglers was that I wasn't quite so greedy. Besides, to succeed as an honest trader, the trick is in knowing what to buy and when to buy it, and I was pretty good at that. Drug smugglers, on the other hand, didn't have to be particularly smart, just ballsy.

I fed the coordinates into the navigation computer but decided to take the ship in manually. Sometimes my reflexes were a little better than the *Jolly Roger*'s, especially if some idiot came flying in too fast from the wrong direction.

"We are landing now?" Cat asked as he noted that our heading had changed. From his tone he seemed to think such haste was unnecessary for some reason.

"Yes, of course, we're landing now," I informed him. "Why shouldn't we?"

"But you said that I looked good enough to fuck," he reminded me, his disappointment quite evident. "Why can we not do that while we are in orbit and *then* land?"

"Well, you certainly have a one-track mind, don't you?" I grumbled. "I thought you'd forgotten about that."

He swiveled his seat around to face me. "I do not forget things easily."

"Well, you're just gonna have to get over it, Cat, because I can't be screwing around and wasting time right now! God knows I wasted enough time looking for you, so let's just forget about it, okay?"

Cat didn't say whether he agreed or not, but it was fairly obvious that his dick hadn't forgotten yet since it was still pointing right at me. I pulled Tex out of his holster, checked the setting and aimed it in Cat's direction.

"Where do you want it?" I asked.

His dark, almond-shaped eyes widened and his glowing pupils made a quick adjustment. A moment later his cock began to droop just a bit. "I will wait," he said contritely. "But not forever."

It was my intention that he probably *would* end up waiting forever, but that was a discussion for another time. I turned back to my console and flew the ship into the dock on Statzeel, settling it down gently on its three landing pads with nothing more than a slight bump that wouldn't even have spilled a cup of coffee. You know, sometimes I amaze even myself!

"Ha, ha!" I exclaimed. "Slicker'n snot!"

"That is two times now that you have used the word 'snot,'" Cat informed me. "What does it mean?"

"Mucus expelled from the respiratory passages," I said absently as I went through the shutdown sequence, attempting to focus solely on the task at hand. My goal was almost in sight; I couldn't afford to get distracted and slip up now. "Slick means that two surfaces can move easily across one another with very little friction—usually with some form of lubrication. You know, like slime?"

He didn't comment further, but I knew he would remember. Like he said, he didn't forget things easily— and I would imagine that any wrong that had been committed against him would be the very *last* thing he would ever forget. I knew I certainly wouldn't want him holding a grudge against me, and I might even find myself feeling a little sorry for some Nedwuts if he ever got ahold of them. Paybacks are hell, you know.

I sent Cat out to pay the docking fee and get the regulation list from the port authority while I got ready to venture forth onto a planet where I could only be a slave. It griped my cookies to have to do such a thing, but there was no help for it. I just plain had to, that's all. I got in the shower and washed off the remaining stench of Orpheseus Prime but balked at dousing myself with some of the local perfume that I had gotten from the smuggler; it was sickeningly sweet and I certainly didn't want to spend all of my time on Statzeel wondering if I was going to throw up at any moment. I mean, being chained up was bad enough, so I hoped it wasn't a requirement. I'd have to check the regulation list to be sure.

I spiked my short hair in what I considered to be a provocative style—I'd seen plenty of prostitutes around the galaxy, and big, spiky hairstyles seemed to be almost a part of the uniform. To complete my toilet, I stuck my face into the make-up port—which I had never used before, by the way—and pressed the "Exotic Beauty" button. It took only a second or two, but I must admit, the transformation was quite astonishing. I didn't look half bad, I thought, peering at my reflection in the mirror. Not as pretty as Ranata, of course, but not too bad. The nice thing about it was that until I stuck my face back into the port, the makeup job would stay put. Don't know who invented that one, but whoever it was must have made enough on it to pay for the retirement of several generations of his or her family. Just wish I'd thought of it, myself.

The makeup job might have been okay, but the clothes were something else entirely! The shoes weren't too horrible—at least I didn't have to wear three-inch heels—and they were comfortable enough, though gleaming satin slippers weren't my usual choice when it came to footwear. The dress was made of a very sheer, flowing, peach-colored fabric that reached to about mid-thigh and had a matching sash tied at the waist. It was unfortunate that I didn't have the big boobs to fill it out at the top, but aside from that, it seemed to fit me well enough. The collar and chain were quite decorative, as well, for they also matched the dress and were encrusted with gems—a lot like something you'd put on a French poodle, which, come to think of it, I was now no better than.

This would *definitely* take some getting used to! I wondered if I was even allowed to speak in public. If not, I could end up in some very hot water real quick, because if you haven't figured it out by now, let me tell you that I am not, and never have been, the quiet, demure little lady that my mother had probably envisioned when I was born. After the disappointment she must have suffered with me, it was no wonder she'd waited another ten years before being brave enough to try again for a better daughter. Of course, Ranata had been well worth the wait. She was perfect.

The collar and chain only opened with a small, intricate key, I noted, and I presumed that the males carried these in their vest pockets at all times so they could release their slaves from time to time without having to search for it. I figured the women had to be let loose once in a while. I mean, surely they didn't expect the men to accompany their slaves to the ladies room! Then again, maybe they got off on such things. Like I said, some places have some really weird customs.

I will admit that it was with some trepidation that I waited for Cat to return. I shuddered to think what his reaction would be to see me in this get-up—I mean, he'd been hard enough to control when I was wearing my flight overalls; what on Earth would he do when he saw me wearing a dress that you could see right through?

The answer was quite simple. His jaw dropped.

For a moment he just stood there, not saying a word. Then that persistent cock of his pulsed once and bloomed from its foreskin like a Tedrellian primrose at dusk. If I'd thought he'd been aroused previously, it was obvious to me now that I'd only seen him moderately excited before, for his cockhead not only developed the ruffled edge I'd seen on it earlier, but it also spurted a clear, viscous fluid that seemed to come from the point of each serration on the thick corona of the glans. I noticed something else, too; he had muscular control of his penis and seemed to be able to point it in virtually any direction; he snapped it up and hit himself in the stomach with it and then moved it in a circular motion while I stood there watching. I stared at it, thinking that turning him down had been perhaps the biggest mistake I'd ever made in my whole life. What was it he'd said about giving me joy unlike any I had ever known? I may have doubted it then, but I sure as hell believed it now!

"Holy shit!" I exclaimed. "You can't go out in the street like that! We won't be able to get ten feet outside the port without scores of women kneeling at your feet just to get a look at you!"

"No," he replied seriously. "The men will all be looking at you, my lovely master."

I grimaced. "Yeah, right!" I said skeptically. "I doubt it! You obviously haven't seen my sister. She's the beauty of the family." I stared hard at his penis, wondering how in the world we could ever even begin to attempt to blend in with the locals with that thing right out in plain sight. "Are you sure you don't want to go and jack off or something before we go out?"

"Jack off?" Not surprisingly, he didn't understand the slang.

"You know," I said, mentally groping for the right description. "Masturbate—bring yourself to climax?"

"Why would I do that?" he asked, sounding quite surprised. "My desire is for you, not for myself."

What a novel perspective! "Really? You mean you never do it to yourself?"

He shook his head. "I do not! In fact, I cannot, and if I did, it would diminish the experience of being with a woman! My desires have been…delayed for many years. I would not gratify them in that manner now, not when you stand before me with the scent of your desire filling my nostrils and the sight of your body filling my eyes. I have touched you and tasted you, my lovely Jacinth, and now I can see you. To end it, I must have you."

"Do you mean to tell me that you're gonna stay like that from now on until—?"

He nodded. "Until we mate. You may threaten me with your weapon all you like, but it will not diminish."

"Well, piss! So much for being inconspicuous!" I paused for a moment to collect my thoughts. "I don't suppose you noticed any other raging hard-ons out there, did you?"

He got the "raging hard-on" idea without any explanation whatsoever. "Yes," he replied. "There are many men in this state."

I threw up my hands in a gesture of capitulation. "Okay, then, I give up. Put my leash on your wrist and let's get going, Cat. This is gonna be interesting, I can tell."

And it was. I haven't mentioned it before, but the inhabitants of Statzeel appeared surprisingly human; the only difference I could see—and I could see nearly all of the anatomy of every person on the street!—was that they had six fingers on each hand instead of five and that their noses seemed sort of flat. Skin tones varied, as did height and weight, but they all seemed at least moderately attractive with not a dog in the whole bunch. Which was a good thing since I had a cat! I know: Har-dy har, har! I can't help it if my sense of humor was going wacky; I was under a good deal of stress.

Cat did seem to attract a fair amount of attention, but nothing like the stares that were directed at me, and, oddly enough, most of the people staring at me were women.

"Psst, Cat!" I whispered to him. "Have I grown horns, or what?" For the best I could tell, I was dressed just like everyone else and even the make-up job wasn't too far off, though maybe I *had* gotten a little carried away with the hairdo.

"Perhaps it is because you are human," he suggested. "If humans attract this much attention here, then your sister should be easy to locate."

"True. I just wish they'd stop staring, though! It's giving me the willies!" I waited to see if he would ask me what "willies" were, but decided that, in this case, it was probably self-explanatory since I'd have been willing to bet that he probably had a decent case of the willies, too.

We continued to make our way toward the marketplace and I noted that, while there were many women without chains, every man I saw had a woman with him. The women seemed to outnumber the men by at least five to one, which were great odds if you happened to be male. I'd have bet that none of these guys would have any trouble whatsoever getting laid four or five times a day....

I decided that those women without collars were probably the "worker" females and the "pleasure" females were the ones that the males had to keep on a leash. I couldn't wait to find Ranata and get her to explain all of this to me. She would undoubtedly be one of the pleasure types, and I hoped she wasn't too unhappy with her male, because many of them appeared to be every bit as belligerent as the one I'd seen offworld. I saw three men standing together arguing about something or other when the females suddenly stepped between them and began caressing their genitals. The argument ceased and the men smiled and continued their discussion in a much more pleasant frame of mind.

There were young boys with their mothers or with other males of their own age, but every male who appeared to have reached puberty had a female chained to him. It was downright bizarre!

We went up to one of the vendors and Cat asked who we needed to talk to about setting up our own stall. The man pointed out a large female chained to a much smaller male at a window in the building across the plaza, and, having thanked him for the information, we headed in that direction.

I haven't described our surroundings yet, but suffice it to say, it was a tropical paradise, even in the town. Everywhere you looked there was green, riotous growth and brilliant blooms of every possible hue. Songbirds with vibrantly colored plumage flew from flower to flower, and large, hovering insects that reminded me of butterflies—only much larger and more spectacularly colored than anything I'd ever seen on Earth—sipped nectar, as well. The animals that roamed about the town were all sleek and shining and looked sort of like a cross between a dog and burro, with long, waving tails and big, floppy ears. Then, as if all of these creatures weren't amazing enough, I got the surprise of my life. They had horses.

Nothing like the scruffy, scrubby, pathetic-looking beasts of burden that you saw on many other worlds, oh no! These were big, beautiful, and gleaming with robust health. Even on Earth, they would have been remarkable. I hoped that Ranata had one, for she had been horse-crazy almost from the time she was born. They were all being ridden double by a man and a woman, and apparently had no difficulty whatsoever carrying the extra weight. They were simply awesome!

I tore my eyes away from them as we approached the building, noting that even the buildings themselves were beautiful, seeming to blend in with the flora to the point that they might have been made of leaves themselves. Perhaps they were, or perhaps the plants were just growing on the walls; it was difficult to tell. The man inside nodded and smiled at us, and I noted that while he certainly seemed friendlier than most of the males I'd observed, he was also a good deal older than any I'd seen so far. Maybe they got nicer with age, and it was only the young bucks who were so mean.

"Good day, my friends!" he said, beaming at us. "How may I help you?"

Cat hesitated for a moment as if he were waiting for me to speak, but then recovered quickly, stating that he would like to sell some goods in the market. He wasn't terribly specific about what those goods were, and I could have kicked myself for not having coached him better, for other than the ointment I'd used on him, he had no idea what I had in the hold of my ship.

Fortunately, it didn't seem to matter, for as long as we signed a statement that nothing we were selling was illegal, they didn't give a damn what we sold. We were charged a small fee and then directed to an empty booth. The currency was standard credits, I noted, and the rate of exchange was about on par with that of other planets in the region. So far, so good, I thought. Now all we had to do was find someone else who'd seen another human female in the area. I hoped for the sake of simplicity that Ranata was the only one, but the way things had gone during my search, I knew I couldn't really count on anything being quite so easy.

Cat and I went back to the ship and loaded a few cases of various commodities on the load-lifter and went back to our stall. While we were setting up shop, I noticed that I was still attracting the attention of most of the females, and I couldn't quite figure it out until an older woman with two young daughters in tow took me aside for a private word, which, I might add, was a bit difficult since I was still chained to Cat.

"He looks dangerous!" she whispered. "He should have two!"

She moved off without further explanation, and, I'll admit, I was still as much in the dark about the whole subject as I'd ever been. Two of what? And why did Cat look any more dangerous than any of the other men around, many of whom, from the best I could tell, were surly, rude, if not downright nasty! Cat, on the other hand, was polite and reserved in his dealings with the denizens of Statzeel. Granted he had some rather spectacular features and some very sharp-looking teeth, but he wasn't mean! Maybe it was his penis that was so scary. I wouldn't have said so myself, but it was certainly more interesting than any of the others I'd seen, all of which were pretty typical, at least by human standards.

We spent most of the day in the marketplace, but if Ranata was there shopping, she never passed our way. The trouble was, with Cat and me having to stay chained together, I couldn't just go off looking for her and leave Cat behind to man the booth. It would appear that we were either going to have to wait for information to come to us, or we were going to have to come up with a different search tactic. Besides, I was getting tired. We'd spent a whole day on Orpheseus Prime, flown to Statzeel, and were going through another day without sleep. Well, Cat had been unconscious for a while, but I certainly hadn't, and I was wearing out.

Being chained together was more exhausting than I would have thought, too, for anytime Cat gestured with his left hand, I got jerked in the neck with the collar. It required standing very close at all times, and, needless to say, Cat's erection never wavered. I wondered if it hurt him, but I'll have to admit that I never asked since I didn't want to draw any more attention to it than was absolutely necessary. Besides, as sore as my neck was getting, a little pain in the dick was something I figured he had coming to him. It was late in the afternoon when, exhausted and extremely hungry, we closed up shop along with everyone else, and after taking everything back to the ship, went out for dinner to see what information we could obtain in that way.

The food wasn't too bad—I'd eaten a lot worse, believe me!—but if you've never tried to eat a meal across the table from someone who has hold of your leash, let me tell you, it can be a bit awkward! Cat did his best not to choke me to death while I was eating, but just having a chain across the table made for some close calls. Cat seemed to like to drink from a glass using his left hand, and I usually used my right. As a result, my drink got bobbled by the chain several times before finally spilling all over the table. The waitress was very prompt in mopping it up, but after that, I switched to drinking with my left hand, moving my glass out of the line of fire.

Interestingly enough, the waitress said the same thing to me that the other woman in the marketplace had while she was cleaning up the spilled wine. "He needs two," she whispered.

Finally I got brave enough to ask. "Two of what?"

She looked at me as though I were the town fool. "Leads!" she whispered back. "He needs two leads!"

She departed quickly, leaving me as mystified as ever.

"You know, I must be really stupid," I said to Cat. "I've had two women tell me today that you need two of something, but I still don't know what they mean."

Cat replied without hesitation. "I do," he said. "A man remarked to me earlier that he was surprised to see me with only one woman." His lips curled into a sly grin. "I believe they mean that I could satisfy two."

I rolled my eyes. "You haven't even satisfied one yet, so don't get cocky, Kittycat!"

He chuckled softly. "I like it when you call me that," he said. "I have found several ways to make you say it. Perhaps when we mate, you will say that as well."

"What? You *like* being called Kittycat?" I asked in surprise. "I didn't exactly mean it as a term of endearment, you know." I was beginning to wonder about Cat, and I'm sure my expression reflected that feeling. "I mean, it sounds sorta kinky to me. Besides, you say that like our getting together is an inevitability."

He looked at me blankly.

"Okay, which part didn't you understand?" I was going to have to stick to straight Stantongue and leave out the euphemisms and slang or he was gonna drive me frickin' nuts!

"Most of it," he replied. "What is kinky?"

"That's a hard one," I said, spearing my fingers through the hair at my temple before I remembered I was probably messing up my spikes. "It means a sexual preference that is abnormal or deviant in some way, like enjoying tying someone up and beating them, or only liking women

dressed in leather underwear or—oh, I don't know!—
there are a million different things that could be considered kinky. Does that make it any clearer?"

"And liking it when you call me Kittycat is kinky?"
he asked. He appeared to consider this for a moment
before stating firmly, "I would not call it that, myself. I
think it is a…term of endearment." He looked so smug,
I wanted to slap him. "I believe that you like me more
than you will admit."

"Oh, is that right?" I demanded hotly. "Well, if I like
you so much, then why am I not on my knees sucking that
interesting appendage of yours, like half the women in this
restaurant are doing to *their* males, huh? Answer me that!"

His eyelids lowered and I'll be damned if he didn't
start purring again! "I could make you do it, Jacinth," he
reminded me. "Here on this planet, if I pulled your leash
and put you between my knees, you would be expected
to do it, would you not?"

Obviously, I should have kept my mouth shut about
that. Ha! I would just *keep* it shut. He couldn't very well
pry my jaws open, could he?

When I didn't reply, he began slowly gathering up the
chain, pulling it taut until I had to lean forward across the
table. "You look very…enticing in that dress," he purred.
"It makes me want to mate with you very badly. But I will
not force you, Jacinth. That would be too…kinky."

Well, thank God for that!

"You could have kept me in those chains and made
me do anything you liked," he went on, "but you did not,
and I will not do it to you, Jacinth. You will have me
when you are ready. I will be waiting."

I shivered slightly at the deep purr with which he ended that sentence. It was almost a growl, but more than that, it spoke of passion: heated and potent and just waiting to be unleashed. What would this man do if I ever said yes to him? I suppose the answer to that was fairly obvious, for with a lethal weapon like his, he'd probably kill me. I'd just about convinced myself of that when a little voice in the back of my brain told me that I would undoubtedly die smiling—just like every other man and woman in that restaurant!

Now, I'll admit that I'd never been to an orgy before, so I couldn't say from first-hand experience, but let me tell you, the goings-on in that establishment had to have come pretty close—although from what I'd seen in broad daylight, it was rather stupid of me not to assume that the nightlife would the most erotic to be found anywhere in the galaxy.

One of the first things I noticed as I glanced around was that none of the couples chained together sat on opposite sides of their tables the way Cat and I did, and also that very few couples were alone at a table; most were in groups of four or six. Another thing I noticed was that they were all touching each other in some sexual way nearly all the time. If a woman wasn't stroking her male's penis, he had his hand on her boobs or up under her dress, and the sheerness of the fabric made it perfectly clear what was happening under there.

As the evening progressed, the sexual conduct became even more uninhibited. A group of musicians (two males and two females) set up and began playing, which got the people out on the dance floor and then the show *really* began! Now, I've been in a lot of places where the people were all over each other while they danced, but I'd never seen people actually having sex on the dance floor. I certainly did that night! The funny thing was that, dressed as they were, no one had to get naked or remove any clothing whatsoever in order to do it.

I saw men on the dance floor moving their undulating hips in time with the music while their females knelt before them as the men fucked them in the mouth. There were couples at tables who were openly engaging in a variety of positions, but the most favored seemed to be with the women sitting in the laps of their males and rising and falling with the beat of the drums. There were people in groups doing all sorts of things with people who were chained to someone else. Apparently wife swapping was an accepted practice as well.

Their eating habits were pretty erotic, too. Men drank wine by dipping the female fingers into their glass and then sucking it off. One woman—and this was the strangest thing I'd ever witnessed in my life!—was actually sitting on the floor with her plate, using her man's dick as an eating utensil. While it pains me somewhat to admit it, I was getting pretty well turned on from watching all of this, and I was very glad I was on the opposite side of the table from Cat. Those serrations on the head of his cock had to be dripping all over the floor as it was, and if he could pick up my scent out of all the rest of them in the room, he wouldn't have had to ask how I felt about all of it—he would know.

I found out something else about Statzeelian sexual preferences, which was that they seemed to think that prominent noses were really hot, and everyone there seemed to have a fetish for my nose. Now, my nose has never been described as huge—though it was considerably larger than Ranata's—but when compared with the flat schnozzes of the locals, it must have seemed positively enormous. Cat didn't exactly have a cute little button nose either, and more than one woman paused in passing to admire it, which I thought was rather odd when that showy cock of his was waving around in plain sight.

One man stopped beside me, asking Cat if he could touch my nose—a request which nearly had me in stitches, by the way—but Cat seemed to think it was pretty harmless, and gave his permission without much show of reluctance. Of course, what the guy didn't tell Cat was that he intended to do the touching with his penis. He moved closer to me and stroked my cheek with his big, gleaming wet cock before sliding it across my cheekbone to rub the side of my nose. I was laughing, thinking that it seemed pretty strange, though not all that erotic, really—that is, until he stiffened up and shot his wad over the bridge of my nose and hit one of the female dancers in the ass with it. I was still in a bit of a shock, when I'll be damned if several of the other men didn't start lining up for their turn!

After that, two of the women positioned themselves on either side of Cat and started licking his nose, which, I noticed, didn't seem to bother him at all. Of course, I couldn't see what was happening with his dick under the table, but I have no doubt that the damn thing was gushing. They seemed to like his hair, too—which I thought showed impeccable taste on their part—and

once one of them got her hands in it, all the others had
to give it a try. I knew from my own experience that it
felt pretty damn fabulous, and, like his large nose, it was
also a bit of an oddity, for none of the local males had
hair much past their ears, let alone hanging to their
waists in perfect spirals.

Just how we were going to find out anything about
Ranata in a place like that had me stumped, but I
couldn't very well leave unless Cat did, and he was
making no moves to depart—especially not when a
couple of the women discovered his cock. At one point,
he had no less than three women whose males were lined
up to fuck my nose crouched between his knees to get a
taste of it. He *had* to be enjoying that, and the women
really seemed to be getting off on just the taste of him,
apparently enjoying that fluid he was pumping out every
bit as much as a wine connoisseur might savor a particularly fine vintage. More than one woman told me I was
the luckiest girl in the entire universe, and while I
considered this to be a bit excessive, it was also likely
that they knew something about cocksucking that I
didn't. However, not wanting to seek any further enlightenment on the subject, I just nodded and smiled a lot.

I thought I'd seen just about everything that night, but
there was one thing that I didn't see, and that was an
angry, belligerent male. It seemed that as long as they
could have all the visual and direct sexual stimulation
they wanted, they were pretty tame and never failed to
thank me profusely for the use of my nose. After a while,
a new game seemed to have been invented which
consisted of a male rubbing his cock on my face until he

came over the bridge of my nose and his female would then attempt to catch the semen in her mouth. I lost count after a while, but from the soreness of my poor proboscis when we left, I think it was safe to assume that I'd been fucked by every couple in the place that night—even the musicians. I thought the lead guitarist was pretty hot, but then I've always had a thing for long-haired rock stars— though I must admit that I prefer those with larger noses myself. But he really was good. I mean, a guy with six fingers could play some serious riffs!

Chapter Five

WE FINALLY LEFT THE RESTAURANT, AND ON OUR WAY out, we passed the first really odd-looking alien I'd seen since we arrived. Most of the other offworlders were species that I had seen somewhere before, but this one was different. You couldn't tell from looking at it whether it was male or female, but since it was alone, I guessed that it was probably female—though to be quite honest, I wasn't absolutely sure. I suppose it could have been a male traveling without a female, and therefore did not have to have her chained to him, but I'd gotten the distinct impression that this was illegal—though if this particular species was genderless, it would obviously be difficult to decide which sex to pair up with it.

This business of making offworlders chain up their women and dress like the natives was a bit of an oddity among planetary customs. Generally speaking, on most worlds, alien life forms were allowed to dress in their usual manner, and if one obeyed the local laws, very little was mentioned about what you wore. But on Statzeel the style of dress (or undress, as the case may be) seemed to be a large part of the law.

The alien being stopped when it saw me, and its large, red, teardrop-shaped eyes began to glow. It had a rather bulbous head and very pale—almost translucent—skin. It wore no clothing of any kind, and in that respect, it was obeying the dress code by going it one better and dispensing with clothing altogether, which might have eliminated the need to be chained up. I didn't know, and for once, I didn't ask because I didn't even want to look at the damned thing, let alone talk to it! Only about a meter in height, it had long, thin limbs and appendages, and reminded me of some early sketches of aliens that the people of Earth had drawn long before they'd actually met any of them. This was, however, the first alien I'd ever seen that truly resembled those early descriptions, and it looked for all the world like something out of a nightmare, or perhaps the wild ravings of some lunatic who claimed to have been the victim of an alien abduction.

Stopping before us, it spoke to Cat in a thin, breathy voice. "An Earth woman!" it said with a fair amount of appreciation. "You are fortunate, indeed, my friend, for they are highly prized here! You will make a large profit on her when she is sold." The alien then wheezed in what I presumed was a fit of laughter, though it was difficult to tell if it was laughing, or simply had a touch of asthma. Of course, it didn't really matter because it gave me the creeps no matter what it was doing. "The last one sold for over two thousand credits, but she was not nearly so lovely as this one."

My ears pricked up at this. Ranata hadn't been on this planet for very long—six months at the most. I wondered how often Earth women showed up here, though if the way I'd been stared at was anything to go by, it seemed that they were pretty scarce. I hoped Cat would ask the right questions since I still wasn't sure if

I was allowed to speak to strange men unless spoken to—if this *was* a man; it seemed to have no penis, but that sort of thing wasn't always hanging right out there in plain sight; the males of some species could retract them to the point that they appeared to be almost nonexistent. Cat, on the other hand, was quite obviously male.

"She *is* lovely, is she not?" Cat purred in reply. "But she is not for sale."

Dammit, Cat! You're supposed to be asking where Ranata is! Not chit-chatting with the visiting aliens!

"Pity," the alien said, turning those gleaming red eyes on me once more, its gaze raking me from head to toe. "She is a fine specimen."

With an appraising look like that, this thing *had* to be male! I made a weak attempt at a smile and fought the urge to roll my eyes. If this guy had actually seen Ranata, he sure as hell wouldn't be saying such things about me, which made me wonder if the woman he was talking about really was my sister, after all.

Cat nodded in agreement. "Her sister is very lovely, as well. I am told she is here on Statzeel. I would like the opportunity to purchase her, if that is possible."

The little alien shook his odd, oversized head. "I do not believe she would be sold either. Though she might…" Those huge red eyes took on a slightly golden hue as the alien went on after considering the possibilities for a moment. "…be stolen. If," and the golden gleam became more pronounced, "the right price were to be paid for information as to her whereabouts."

Ah-ha! Now we're talking! This might be the creepiest little alien I'd ever seen in my life, but he obviously knew the value of a dollar—or credit, that is—and therefore, could be bought.

Cat pulled Ranata's photograph from the pocket of his vest, along with five credits, and handed them over. "Do you know where she might be found?"

The creature studied the photo, and I could see the golden light of those eyes gleaming off the glossy surface. "This is not one I have seen," it said. "But there are questions I could ask of the right people. For the right price, you understand."

"Of course," Cat replied, as though in complete agreement. "I understand."

"Meet me later tonight in the trees outside the space port." The alien glanced up at the darkening sky. "At moonrise, I believe. I will be there with the information you require if you will also be there with…one hundred credits, shall we say?"

I cleared my throat in an attempt to let Cat know that I would be willing to pay any price whatsoever for information about Ranata. I couldn't tell if he got the message or not, but he nodded anyway.

"I will be there," Cat said firmly.

"Oh, and be sure to bring your lovely toy along with you," the alien said, and I watched, rather perversely fascinated, as those weird eyes returned to their customary red hue. "We wouldn't want to break any laws, now, would we?" This time when the wheezing began again, it was quite obviously in amusement. Still chuckling, he left us to go into the restaurant.

"Geez, I wonder what *that* thing eats! And also why he doesn't have someone chained to him!" I exclaimed.

"If it *was* a 'him,' that is. What a creepy little alien! Have you ever seen one like that before?"

"No," Cat replied. "I have not. Do you believe he is trustworthy?"

"I doubt it, but what choice do we have? I guess I'll give you my pistol just in case he isn't. I'd carry it myself, but I'm not sure where I could put it that it wouldn't show—although I suppose I could hide it in my sash." On the other hand, the sash really wasn't wide enough to conceal Tex adequately, and I hadn't noticed anyone else openly toting weapons either— well, not the automatic pulse pistol type, anyway! There was a little gold ring sewed into the sash for some reason, but the pistol would have looked a bit silly dangling from it. I had seen the occasional male with a sword, but they seemed to be more for show than anything, since the only men I'd seen so far with swords had also been mounted on horses at the time. Perhaps it was a part of the riding habit on this world— you know, the guys just thought it looked cool to be wearing a sword while they were on a horse, maybe as a carryover from an earlier time when swords were something everyone carried all the time, and it sort of stuck when it came to equestrian attire.

Cat gave me the oddest look. "You would trust me with a weapon?"

"Is there some reason I shouldn't?"

"No," he replied. "I am worthy of your trust, but I have not been trusted in a very long time."

"Well, you'd better get used to it, Kittycat," I said roundly, "because I need you! The smuggler I got my information from told me to take someone with me that I could trust, and that someone is you, big guy!"

I emphasized this point with a poke in his stomach, thinking that the odd thing was that, up until I'd actually said it out loud, I hadn't realized just how much I *did* trust him. I couldn't have said just why that was, but somehow it was there: as solid as granite and as immovable as the mountains on Tirellia Minor—and they had some serious mountains on that planet, some of them sticking right out of the atmosphere and into space.

I paused, momentarily struck by the gravity of what I was thinking, and also because it was making me feel slightly embarrassed for some reason. Deciding that the conversation was getting a little too deep for comfort, I figured I ought to lighten it up just a bit. The way I saw it, Cat seemed to be reading way too much into this trust thing—and maybe I was, too. "At least, I *hope* I can trust you!" I added with a chuckle. "After all, you *have* got me on a leash! And speaking of which, I'd like to get back to the ship so I can get this damned thing off for a while. I don't like things around my neck of any kind, and especially not collars!"

Cat didn't say anything else regarding the trust issue, but merely nodded in agreement, and we went back to the ship to await our rendezvous at moonrise. On the way, he seemed to take what I considered to be an unfair advantage, pulling me closer to him with my leash and choosing to stroll along, taking his sweet time when all I really wanted was to get back to the ship as fast as I could so I could conk out for a while. All in all, I thought it was a bit tacky of him to piddle along like that when he had to know I was bushed! Of course, when I told him that, I had to go into this long, rambling explanation of what it meant to be tacky—which if you've ever tried it, you'll know is kinda hard to do. Explaining "bushed" was a little easier.

Back at the ship at last, I left Cat to his own devices, told the computer to wake me a little before moonrise, and plopped down on my bed. I was bushed, beat, tired, exhausted, and totally wiped out—at least I think that about covers it—oh, unless you want to count how sore my nose was. I hadn't bothered to take Cat to task over letting them do that to me, especially since it didn't truly constitute what I'd call sex. I still thought it was pretty funny myself, and he couldn't possibly have known what would happen if he were to let someone touch my nose. Then, after the first one got his rocks off, we probably would have started a riot if we'd refused the rest of them—you know how those Statzeelian guys are when they get pissed.

I didn't even bother to change my clothes, and I fell asleep with the thought in mind that while I probably shouldn't trust Cat, I not only needed to, but wanted to, as well. I'd been on my own for so long and was always so suspicious of everyone, so cynical in my outlook on life and, you know something? I was damned tired of it! It would be so nice to let someone else carry the burden at least for an hour or two, and that someone else was my big, ol' Cat.

The computer woke me in plenty of time for our meeting and raised the lights. Apparently Cat must have been tired, too, for he was curled up at the foot of the

bed, purring contentedly. "Hey, Kittycat," I said, prod-
ding him with my foot. "Time to go and see ET."

"ET?" he murmured sleepily. "What is ET?"

"Short for extraterrestrial—you know, someone not
from Earth."

"Not from my world either," he muttered. He sat up
and yawned, showing most of his sharp, white teeth.
When he stood up and stretched, I noted that his erection
had subsided. I wondered how long it would take for it
to come back.

I got my answer in about thirty seconds. "Well, you
obviously haven't forgotten me," I said with a chuckle.

He shot me a rather withering glance and picked up
my collar. "That would be *your* fault," he informed me.
"You called me Kittycat."

"Hm-m, and that's all it takes, huh?"

He nodded. "I warned you."

"Yes, you did," I said. "Well then, Kittycat, put my
poodle collar on and let's get this show on the road."

"Whatever *that* means," he muttered as he adjusted
my collar and turned the key in the lock. Then I locked
the leash to his wrist and put the key in his vest pocket.

"You should be able to figure that one out on your
own," I told him with a yawn. "I'm too sleepy to explain."

It was a tad chilly out, which woke me up a bit and
made me wonder if the native females had see-through
cloaks to wear at night, or if they just never went out
and about much after dark. I'll have to say, though, that
the sheer fabric had turned out to be much warmer than
I would have imagined, but the dress didn't cover very
much of me and I shivered slightly in the cool night air.

Cat apparently noticed my shiver and put his arm around me while we walked. It might not have kept me all that much warmer, but it felt pretty nice anyway—much better than being jerked along on the end of a leash, for example.

The moon was just starting to peek through the tree-tops when we arrived in the small stand of trees near the spaceport. I hoped the news would be good, but quite honestly, I was preparing myself for disappointment. I had come so far, and the thought that my search might actually be nearing its end was nearly incomprehensible to me.

Not being able to see very well, I allowed myself to be steered blindly through the darkness. Cat didn't seem to have any difficulty whatsoever seeing in the dark, directing us on an unerring path to the little red-eyed alien who was waiting for us there. Yet another reason why Cat was a pretty handy guy to have around.

The little alien bowed as we approached. "My blessings upon you," he said in greeting. "Forgive me for not introducing myself when we met earlier, my friends. I am called Delamar." Bowing again, he peered up at Cat expectantly, obviously expecting us to introduce ourselves as well.

"We are Carkdacund and Jacinth," Cat said with a bow of his own. "Are you male, then?" Cat asked politely. "How is it that you do not have a female chained to you?"

"Oh, I am exempt from such foolishness," Delamar replied with a casual wave of his funny little arm. "As a healer on this world, I would find it very...

inconvenient…to have someone chained to me. And as
to matters of dress," he added with a downward sweep of
the same arm, "I have nothing to conceal."

It sounded reasonable, but I wasn't so sure he'd asked
for that exemption to do any "healing." He just didn't want
anyone else around when he made his little deals, which,
as a trader myself, I could readily understand. The fact that
he wore nothing and had nothing to conceal was patently
obvious. How the heck did his species reproduce? It's
possible I would have asked him where his cock was if I'd
been the one asking the questions, but Cat merely nodded,
seeming to be satisfied with this explanation.

Delamar went on to announce, "I bring you good
news, my friends! The woman you seek is but four days'
journey from here. I can give you her location, but no
more, and for that, I only ask that you pay me fifty
credits. I had hoped to give you more details, but this
was all I could obtain in so short a time."

Cat pulled the sack of credits out of his vest and gave
the whole thing to Delamar. "Our agreement was for one
hundred credits," he said gravely. "I will pay you no less."

The alien nodded and bowed again, saying with
apparent approval, "You are an honest trader, and shall be
rewarded," and then went on to tell us where Ranata was
being kept. "It is a fine house, very large with many rooms.
My information does not include her exact whereabouts
within it, but you should be able to find the house without
difficulty. It is on a high hill to the east." I was riveted by
what he said, no longer distracted by the mystery of the
weird little guy's reproductive equipment—Ranata was
truly alive, and relatively close by! Delamar went on to

describe the topography of the road we must travel and the various landmarks to be noted along the way.

The route we had to take seemed fairly straightforward and Cat nodded, seeming to follow the man's directions; I would have preferred getting the exact coordinates myself, because if all else failed, I could always use the ship's navigation computer to find her—especially if we had to alter our route for some reason. I started to say something, but was stopped short as those red eyes turned to fix their gaze on me.

"Your toy is very lovely," he said. "You must guard her well lest she be taken from you. Are you well bonded to her?"

Just what he meant by that was unclear, but Cat replied anyway. "As well as can be." Which, while it might have been stretching the truth just a bit, was at least diplomatic.

"It may not be enough," the alien wheezed. "But because you have dealt truly with me, I will give you a gift."

"We thank you, but that will not be necessary," Cat began, but Delamar cut him off.

"No, no! I insist!" he said. "My gift will be of great help to you should the two of you ever become separated. What I will give to you will enable her to find you, though you be many miles away."

I figured it was some kind of homing device to attach to Cat, which sounded like a damned good idea, but was surprised when Delamar approached me, instead. "May I play with your toy?" he asked Cat.

I shuddered with revulsion at the thought of this creature touching me. The guys in the restaurant had at least appeared to be almost human, but this thing gave me the creeps. Cat, however, was unperturbed. "As you wish," he replied.

I know I shot him a look that would have sliced a lesser man in two, but Cat ignored it completely. Obviously he was willing to accept the gift from this thing, no matter what it might do to me. Perhaps it was a Zetithian custom not to refuse a gift or something, who knew? But this creepy little alien was quite obviously intending to touch me in some way, and I didn't exactly relish the notion.

"You must be close to her, and you may wish to stand behind her for support," the alien suggested to Cat. "She may become…unsteady."

I started to open my mouth in protest, but those red eyes seemed to capture my gaze and hold it tightly. Standing transfixed, I found that I could not speak or move, and it terrified me as nothing had in a very long time.

"Do not be afraid, little toy," Delamar said in that breathy voice of his. "You will not be harmed. Though you may feel some…odd sensations."

The red-eyed alien reached out with his slender little fingers and took my face in his hands. I suppose if I'd thought about it at all—which I hadn't—I would have expected them to feel cold, but they were surprisingly warm. I was dimly aware that Cat had moved around behind me and was letting me lean against him, but all I could see were those big, red eyes gleaming out of the darkness. My body responded to the alien's touch as though a relay had been flipped and I felt a fiery sensation snake its way from each of his hands on my face down to the pit of my stomach. There, the two lines seemed to converge before welling up inside me and then wrapping themselves around my heart.

"Earth women are so delightfully responsive," Delamar wheezed. "I have only treated one such before, but this one is even better." He made that odd, laughing, wheezing sound once more and continued holding me until I felt almost faint, leaning back against Cat for support. "Hold her beneath her arms," he instructed Cat, "or she may fall. Some of them do."

I was dimly aware that Cat did as he said, but my focus was still on those fiery red eyes and the havoc being created within my body. I wanted to run, but I had no control over my limbs whatsoever. If I had feared the loss of control that came with sex or alcohol, I feared this even more, for it went well beyond that kind of surrender; it was a total annihilation of the senses and was a far more intense sensation than any mere touch of a hand on my cheeks could normally induce.

It went on for several minutes and as I stared into that pale, luminous face, Delamar's eyes began to change, first slowly going from red to purple and then on to blue. When they turned a deep aquamarine, his mouth opened and a long, forked and whip-like tongue protruded and steadily grew in length until I felt it reach out to touch my lips, teasing them apart. I wanted to scream but was still unable to make even the slightest sound as his tongue delved into me, sliding down my throat.

The alien's tongue moved inside me and I felt sure I would gag on it, but didn't, for some inexplicable reason—and I'd been known to gag on much less. I watched, helpless and transfixed, as a round ball seemed to form in his mouth only to be squeezed down within the long tube of his tongue in a pulsatile, propulsive movement until it reached the tip and suddenly filled me with a warm gush of fluid.

The little shit is poisoning me! I thought angrily. I'm being poisoned and my stupid Cat is standing there like a gullible idiot and not only letting it happen, but is actually holding me for the little bastard!

And then his tongue pulsed inside me once more and a sensation the likes of which I had never felt before— or since, I might add—took me in its grip and sent my whole body reeling. It was so strong I thought I would pass out from it as it welled up inside me like a ball of fire before finally erupting to inflame every fiber of my being. I watched helplessly as the little alien's eyes gradually returned to their customary red color and his tongue slid out of me, whipping back into his mouth like a sucked up piece of spaghetti.

"Wonderfully responsive!" he wheezed. "Such a delight to treat!"

The little asshole was making himself sound like a doctor treating someone with an upset stomach! I was probably about to die, and the rotten scumbag was patting himself on the back! I was as angry as I'd ever been in my life, but I still couldn't move a muscle. And Cat! I had trusted him, and he'd let me down, big-time!

"Just hold her there for a short time," he instructed Cat. "She will recover quickly and will feel no effects by morning, but will sleep very soundly tonight. To imprint her with your scent, she must now taste you."

Cat looked at him questioningly.

"Kissing her is the most effective means," Delamar said. "Then she will be imprinted with your scent and will be able to locate and track you over great distances. You may find this useful in your quest." He smiled again. "I wish you luck and joy in all of your endeavors, my friend. May the pathway to your destiny be a smooth one." And with that, he bowed once more and disappeared into the night.

So, the little shit had poisoned me with his creepy snake tongue just to turn me into a raging, Cat-seeking bloodhound! I was gonna kill my damned Cat, I thought grimly. The alien had asked if I was well-bonded to Cat, too. What the devil did that mean? Had the poison bonded me to Cat in some way? And if so, was it permanent? Were Cat and I stuck together forever? The guy hadn't said that it would do anything but enable me to track him, but, as a trader, I knew that a lot of things about a deal weren't always immediately obvious. After all, he'd been sort of sketchy about the details, and we had absolutely no proof that it would actually work. Hell, it might even end up killing me! I was of the opinion that Cat should have asked for a lot more information before agreeing to this "gift," and I was mentally kicking myself for not speaking up while I still could. As it was, I wasn't a bit happy and I fully intended to wring my damned Cat's neck, and I would do it, too, just as soon as I could move my arms again.

Then he kissed me.

He made damned sure I knew what he tasted like, too, sliding his warm, sensuous tongue inside my mouth, kissing me quite soundly until I probably could have followed his scent even without alien intervention. Oh, yes, and he'd had the same effect on me as he had when he'd kissed me before, too. Intoxicating, overwhelming, mind-numbing….

In a daze from Cat's kiss, as well as the alien poison, I was unable to do anything to prevent Cat from picking me up and carrying me back to the ship. I couldn't recall ever having been quite so helpless in my life, and we were almost there when I finally began to be able to move a little on my own. "Gonna kill you, Cat!" I muttered as I punched at his chest with a hand that could barely make a fist, "gonna fuckin' kill ya!"

"No, you will not," he said, completely unperturbed by my threats. "You are just angry right now. You will…get over it."

"Way to go, Cat, that's a fuckin' idiom!" I mumbled. "You're learning! Now if you'd just use one fuckin' little contraction there might be some hope for you."

"Open the hatch," he said, completely ignoring my babbling tongue as we approached the ship.

Obligingly I put a hand out and fumbled with the thumb-lock. Needless to say, my arm felt like a wet noodle and it took me a couple of tries to get the lock mechanism to disengage. "See whatcha let him do ta me?" I grumbled. "Can't even unlock the goddamn door." Despite my current level of ineptitude, I finally got it right and the hatch slid open with a hiss, and Cat carried me inside. Having deposited me on the bed, he just stood there for a moment, looking at me. Peering back at him through eyelids that had suddenly grown quite heavy, I noticed something odd about him. "Whazat?" I asked, pointing at his sleeve.

Cat raised his arm, inspecting his sleeve, which now appeared to be stained with a slimy, aquamarine-colored fluid. It reminded me of the color of that smarmy little alien's eyes when he—

"E-e-w-w!" I exclaimed, feeling suddenly nauseated. "It's that alien's goddamn poison spit! Oh, God, that is so gross! I need to get in the shower, Cat! It's probably all down my—" I sat up, reeling like a drunkard and looked down at my dress. Aquamarine slime had spilled all down the front of the peach-colored fabric and had run down my right leg and a drop or two of it was clinging to my pretty little satin slipper. My stomach heaved at the sight of it, and I knew if I didn't get it off of me quick, there was going to be an even bigger mess before long. "Oh, yuck!" I groaned, clapping a hand over my mouth as I heaved again. Cat picked me up once more and carried me into the bathroom. "The sonic shower first, then the water," I croaked. "I may stay in the bathtub for the rest of the night! I probably need my stomach pumped, too. My God, this is making me sick!"

Cat didn't say a word, but, instead, grabbed the nearest towel and thrust it under my chin, neatly catching the rather colorful vomit which I would undoubtedly have spewed all over the room otherwise. (I had a little cleaner-droid, but it was somewhat temperamental and tended to baulk at having to clean up messes like that!) Then he pulled me into the sonic chamber along with him and hit the activation switch. Within moments, all traces of the alien poison had been vibrated from my body and my clothing, as well as Cat's, but the conviction that I'd been poisoned remained. I was seriously freaked out by the whole episode and I still couldn't even stand up straight without Cat's assistance; my legs were as weak and trembling as the tentacles on a Derillian jellyfish.

"Forget the shower," I gasped as I felt myself falling under a blanket of overwhelming lassitude. I didn't think I could keep my eyes open for another second. "Just put me to bed, Cat."

He pulled off what little clothing I had on and tucked me under the blankets, before disrobing and climbing into bed with me. The last thing I remember was him purring against my ear as his arms went round me and his cock brushed against my thigh. I didn't think the stupid son-ofabitch would have been purring like that if he'd known just how lucky he'd be if I didn't whack his damned balls off in the morning. I mean, for all practical purposes, we'd paid fifty credits for a stomach full of aquamarine slime that I couldn't even keep down, and aside from that, the best I could tell, my sense of smell was no better than it had ever been! To be quite honest, I didn't feel so much poisoned anymore as I felt ripped off!

Chapter Six

I DIDN'T, OF COURSE—RIP HIS BALLS OFF, I MEAN—AND
was quite astonished at how truly marvelous I felt when
I awoke. I didn't think I'd even feel much like castrating
a Nedwut—if one had been handy, that is. Too bad there
hadn't been one around the night before, although I
doubted that I'd have had the strength to do it then, even
though I was pretty well pissed! The most surprising
thing, however, was that all the rage I'd felt was gone. I
felt downright perky and I discovered that I held no
grudge against little red-eyed Delamar whatsoever, and
if I'd met him on the street, I probably would have
hugged him. It was very odd, indeed!

Cat was still spooned up against my back and purring
in my ear. "Mm-m-m," he purred. "I do not believe I
have ever slept so well." He sighed contentedly before
adding, "and that is not just because I am unfettered by
chains. I like sleeping with you, Jacinth. You make me
feel laetralant."

"I make you feel what?" I demanded. He'd never used
anything but straight Stantongue in speaking to me. This
was a word I'd never heard before.

"It is a word in my own language which has no translation," he replied. "Other words may be used to
describe the feeling of laetralance, but they do not have
the exact meaning."

"I'll bet there's an Earth word for it!" I declared. "We've got ten different words for nearly everything—sometimes twenty! Give me some hints."

"It means to feel satisfied and content, but also that the body is relaxed and the mind feels a strong attachment to the one you are with. It is not a feeling one may experience alone; it must be shared."

"How about afterglow?" I suggested. "You know, the warm, fuzzy feeling you get after making love."

He paused to consider this. "No, one does not have to mate in order to feel laetralance. It happens after that, at times, but it is not necessary, and will not always occur even after mating."

"Okay then, how about *being* in love?" I ventured. "Is that what it means?"

"Yes and no," he replied cautiously. "It is being in love and feeling at peace and being contented all at the same time, in body, mind, and spirit."

"Well, you're right then," I admitted. "There *is* no translation. Not into my native tongue, anyway." Which was surprising given the number of words in the English language. "But it sounds like a pretty nice feeling."

Cat purred again. "It is," he said softly. "And I feel it when I am with you."

"Well, that's nice," I said briskly, patting him on the head. "So are you ready to go on a run through the jungle to find my sister today?"

"Mm-m-m," he purred. "Perhaps we could wait a day or two. Just stay here and lie together and mate." He ran his hand down my side to my hip and traced patterns on my skin with his fingertips. I felt his damp penis tickle the back of my thigh and his lips pressed against my shoulder.

I shook my head. "Nope, don't feel like it!" I said cheerfully. Then I remembered that I was supposed to be able to follow Cat's scent now. I took an experimental sniff in his direction. Nothing. Not a damn thing! "You know, I think that creepy little alien lied to us! My sense of smell isn't one bit better than it ever was. Of course," I added, gingerly rubbing the side of my sore nose, "it could be because I got my nose fucked by all the men in that dive we went to last night. I think I've had enough dicks in my face to last me for a good, long while."

"He did say that you would be able to track me if we ever became separated," Cat reminded me. "We have not been separated. He may not have lied."

"Yeah, well, if you think I'm gonna play hide and seek with you just to prove it, you've got another thing coming, Kittycat!" I informed him. "Besides, I'm not so sure whether being able to track you would be such a good thing or not. I mean, you might not want me to be able to find you sometimes." Cat appeared to be doubtful about this. "No, really," I insisted. "You couldn't possibly want me around all the time! I mean, what if you were out with the guys getting drunk and chasing women? Would you want me to be able to find you just so I could jerk a knot in your tail?"

"I do not have a tail," he said firmly. "Nor would I want you to jerk a knot in it if I did, and if you were my mate, I would not be out chasing other women. Such an activity would be pointless if I had you as my mate. But if we were ever separated, Jacinth, I would want you to be able to find me."

"Well, you know, if I'd known it would be so important to you, I could just as easily put a homing beacon on you, instead," I countered, glossing over just how sweet a sentiment that was. And it was sweet—at least I thought so, though I wasn't exactly what you'd call a current expert on such things. "It would have been a lot less risky, and probably would have worked better. And, besides, what about you, Kittycat? You seem to have a pretty good smeller there, yourself. Couldn't you find me, instead?"

"Possibly, but not over a very great distance," he admitted. "I can smell you when you are close and realize that it is you, but I could not do it even from across the plaza on Orpheseus Prime." He sighed as he remembered. "I feared that you would not return to the auction to bid on me. I thought you had gone."

Just how he thought he would have been able to pick my scent out of the stench of Orpheseus I'll never know, and I still was rather amazed that he had been able to do it even when I was standing right there under his nose. Then another thought occurred to me. "You say that as though you were hoping I would buy you! But as I recall, you didn't seem all that twerked up about it when I did," I reminded him. "'I am a slave and a prisoner; I will attempt to escape,'" I quoted him. "If you wanted me to buy you so damn bad, why in the name of sense did you say something like that?"

He shrugged. "I do not know. Perhaps I was not ready to admit that I was attracted to you and would remain with you always, whether you chained me or not."

"Playing hard to get, huh?" I nodded knowingly. "That's such a *guy* thing, isn't it? You can't admit you care about someone, so you just had to wait and come back of your own free will to make a deal with me, instead. Is that right?"

"Yes," he agreed, though he seemed somewhat chagrined to admit it. "But I am here now, and I will do what I promised. I will help you find your sister, but I will not leave you when our search is finished. I will stay with you, always."

Well, this was surprising! Guess I didn't need to be "bonded" to him after all! Of course, you know how it is when a stray cat follows you home; once they adopt you, there's just no getting rid of them. I had thought that he might have other plans for what to do with his freedom, however. "What? You mean you're not gonna go off on some raging personal vendetta against the Nedwuts for destroying your planet?"

"I am but one man," he reminded me. "I cannot fight them all."

"Well, at least you have that much sense!" I said with a good deal of relief, because I sure as hell didn't want him picking a fight with every Nedwut we happened to run across! I'd seen plenty of them in the past and had, fortunately, managed to avoid any serious entanglements with them—at least, up to that point. Of course, I knew that a gang of them had taken my sister and, believe me, I held quite a grudge against them for that; but since they all looked pretty much the same to me, I wouldn't have had any way of knowing if I'd gotten the right ones even if I did manage to bump off a few of them. I wasn't particularly interested in exterminating all of them either. I just wanted the little shits to go back home and leave the rest of the galaxy the hell alone.

I realized then that I was tickled to death that Cat wanted to stay with me, though I couldn't have said why. Perhaps it was just because I'd been alone for so long. It was hard to admit it to him, though, and I knew I certainly wouldn't do it today. I guess I was playing hard to get, too.

"Well, come on, Cat," I said, giving him another pat and getting up from the bed, doing my best to ignore the fact that I was completely nude—and so was he. In another place, another time, we might have been feeling laetralant for a better reason than just a good night's sleep. I mean, even first thing in the morning, he looked good enough to eat, and I'll admit, I wanted nothing more than to curl up with him and rub his tummy while he purred. But I had a sister to find and rescue, and I'd wasted enough time already. Steeling myself, I went on, "We've got to pack up for at least a fourteen-day trip, so get your tail out of bed and let's get started."

"Fourteen days?" he said with surprise. "The red-eyed one said that it would take only four to reach her."

"Yeah, well, if you believe we can get there, find Ranata, and get back here in eight days, you're even more gullible than I thought, Kittycat! Plus the fact that there'll be three of us on the return trip; we've got to be prepared for anything!" I paused, tapping my chin for a moment as I considered the possibilities. "I wonder if we could rent or buy some horses. The way Delamar talked, the road between here and Ranata's house is a pretty good one, but I'd just as soon ride if I could."

The thought of riding a horse again was one very appealing part of Ranata's rescue that I hadn't counted on, and it would be a welcome change from some of the other conveyances I'd had to use in the past. I once rode in a cart pulled by something that looked a bit like an ostrich and the damned thing hadn't had any more sense than a Nedwut on a three-day drunk! As I recall, I ended up walking that time, too, and with a bit of a limp, I might add. In this instance, however, I thought that riding was a terrific idea. What I didn't reckon on was Cat being such a wuss about it.

"I will not ride one of those creatures," he said, sounding about as immovable as a space cruiser with a dead engine.

"What's the matter?" I taunted him. "Afraid you'll fall on your ass? I thought cats always landed on their feet when they fell down."

"Perhaps the cats you are familiar with can do that," he said firmly, "but the people of my world cannot." From the way those black and gold cat eyes of his were glittering, I had an idea that he was going to be rather stubborn about this.

"Be that as it may, I still think we should try to get a couple of horses," I argued. "They would be so much better than a droid to carry our supplies. I mean, I've got a pack-droid, but the damned thing is so obnoxious, I've never used it much and would prefer not to take it with us on a journey where any stealth might be required— although I suppose I could power it down to keep it quiet if we needed to."

"It is…noisy?" Cat ventured.

"You're damned right, it's noisy!" I exclaimed. "Whatever idiot programmed the stupid thing thought it would be simply grand to have a droid that could not only carry all of your supplies, but would also sing hiking songs to you while you walk. I've yet to figure out how to disable the music feature, so mostly I leave it in the hold."

I'd tried to sell it once, but the potential buyer had been rather annoyed by it as well. That was one deal that I should have been a bit dishonest about, just as the crook who'd sold it to me had been. He told me it would stop singing after the first standard mile, which, like a fool, I believed. What I didn't realize was that he knew he would be long gone before I'd ever walked that far with it, the slimy little Croanot! I've been suspicious of every one of those creepy-crawly little bastards ever since! Of course, the fact that they look like big, fat, greasy spiders should have been my first clue not to trust one of them. You want to talk about a species that will totally gross you out: it's a Croanot! Ugh! They give me the creeps every time I think about them!

I put my local clothing on again—trying not to think about all the slime it had been covered with the night before—but also packed a pair of flight overalls, a couple of shirts, several pairs of shorts, and some decent boots as well. I thought perhaps if we got far enough out of town, no one would see us, and if we got off the road just a bit, we might be able to avoid most of the other travelers anyway. Sticking to the road would be unnecessary if we were dressed the way I usually did, but I had some serious qualms about going through the jungle in that flimsy little Statzeelian get-up. It wouldn't even protect me from sunburn, let alone the poisonous plants and nasty insects that were bound to be indigenous to this world. Statzeel might have seemed like a tropical paradise, but I'd never been on a single planet yet that didn't have its fair share of things that it was prudent to avoid.

I tried not to look when Cat got out of bed, but, dammit, I'm only just so strong! It wasn't like I hadn't seen him naked before—and probably more times than I'd seen him dressed—but he still kinda took my breath away. I gave myself one brief glimpse of him and resolutely turned my back on him to get started on the packing.

He didn't say anything about it, but I wouldn't have blamed Cat for being a bit miffed that every other man in the bar had managed to get off on me except him. Maybe that was why he let them all do it, thinking that it might get me in the mood—I don't know, because he never said. He *had* kissed me, though, and despite the fact that he could have done anything he wanted with me, he hadn't taken advantage of my nearly comatose state once my transformation into a so-called bloodhound was complete. Of course, making love to a wet rag might not have been what he had in mind, and I had a feeling he was just waiting for nightfall to roll around again to make another move. He seemed to be a patient, but determined, fellow, and perhaps he thought that being out in the jungle might bring out some of my more basic animal instincts. However, if he thought I was going to just up and give in to him out there in the jungle, he had another thing coming! I was a little tougher than that—or so I believed. Besides, I thought he deserved a little punishment for putting me through all that crap with Delamar. I would probably end up fucking him at some point, but not until we found Ranata and had her safely stowed in my ship and were well on our journey home. I needed to stay sharp, and I *knew* what sex does to me!

In the end, Cat proved to be more stubborn than the proverbial mule; we wound up taking the damned pack-droid with us after all. And I had to admit, it was quite useful, even if it was irritating. I filled it full of stuff we could sell if need be, just to give us a better cover, and though we kept to the road as we left the town, fortunately no one questioned us about our destination. Traveling salesmen were pretty much the accepted norm on most worlds, anyway, and I doubted that we would be the only ones out there on the road. Medicines were the easiest things to carry, and you always met someone with an ache or a cut or two along the way who hadn't brought along a first-aid kit.

"Who knows," I told Cat cheerfully. "We might even make a profit out of this trip!"

Actually, I'd already found something I could turn a tidy little profit on, and that was the fabric from which the Statzeelian female clothing was fashioned. There were plenty of worlds where the inhabitants liked to be able to show a little skin now and then, and the fact that this stuff was actually able to keep you warm at the same time was something that I felt would sell very well on many planets. I'd already seen bolts of it for sale in the marketplace, and planned on picking up as much of it as I could before we left.

Another thing I had in the hold which I hadn't thought to bring out the day before was the sunscreen that they make on Frituna Five. It would last a full month with one application, and with all the fair-skinned women I'd seen out and about, it might turn out to be a hot item. I used it myself on a regular basis and had never gotten a sunburn on any planet yet. Of course, I'd never put it to a really good test because I usually didn't have this much skin hanging out—well, okay, I *never* had this much skin hanging out!—but it kept my nose from getting burnt. Cat seemed to think my suggestion that he put it on his dick was a good one, but then teased me into putting it on for him. I did my best to seem nonchalant about it, but I'd have been lying if I said it wasn't doing anything for me, and it obviously got him going because his cock started gushing fluid from the corona as soon as I touched him. Honestly, he was so wet it's a wonder the sunscreen even stayed on him long enough to do any good!

I put some on Cat's face, too, which got him purring again. Between his purring and the pack-droid singing "I'm Happy When I'm Hiking," it's a good thing we weren't trying to be sneaky about getting to Ranata's house—well, at least not yet, anyway. There would come a time when we'd have to be very careful because I certainly didn't want one of those ornery Statzeelian males coming after us when he found out we'd stolen the Earth woman for whom he'd shelled out two thousand credits! He was bound to be a little pissed.

Cat and I marched along the road with our singing droid, and I was forced to admit that I was enjoying myself—well, the scenery, anyway—for it was just about the most beautiful planet I'd ever visited. The plants, animals, and insects we'd seen in the town were just a small sample of the fabulous wonders that were out there in the jungle. Every plant seemed to be trying to outdo the one next to it when it came to displaying big, showy flowers, and the birds and the sky were as brilliant as the blooms. We passed a clearing of sorts along the road where the meadow was covered with blue and purple flowers, looking for all the world like a field of Texas bluebonnets. We probably hadn't needed to bring along any water either, because about every mile or so, there was either a stream running alongside the road or a waterfall. There were the cutest little monkey-like creatures as well, and I saw several of them regarding us solemnly with their huge, round eyes from their perches in the trees.

While we were still fairly close to the town, we met quite a few other travelers, most of whom were either on horseback or in a horse-drawn vehicle of some kind. I thought it was interesting that a planet advanced enough for space travel would stick to such outmoded forms of ground transportation, but it did add considerably to the local charm and appeared to be much more enjoyable than walking—a fact that I brought to Cat's attention on a fairly regular basis.

Poor Cat! He hadn't had to walk very far in his Statzeelian boots up until then, and I could tell they were hurting his feet because he got slower and slower as the day went on—to the point where he was actually limping. I kept waiting for him to complain, but he never did. Finally I got tired of watching him suffer and made him stop.

"Boots too tight?" I asked.

"Yes," he replied in a rather clipped and irritated tone of voice. "But I have no others."

"No shit, Cat!" I remarked dryly. "You were stark naked and barefoot when I bought you! Why didn't you tell me they didn't fit? We could have checked into getting some others before we left town, you know! But, have no fear, my dear Cat, for relief is at hand! I brought my Shoemaker in a Box with me. I never travel anywhere without it—well, not if I'm planning to do much walking and have the droid to carry it for me, that is. I've made more money off of this thing than just about anything else I've got."

If I sounded excited enough to fire off my sales pitch, you must forgive me, for this little gizmo was one of the slickest inventions I'd ever run across. I'd found it on Taalus Geled, and what you did was, you took off your old shoes, set them down in front of the box, and then a beam of light scanned them. Then you scanned your foot (and leg if it was tall boots like the ones Cat was wearing) and put your old shoes or boots in the box. About thirty seconds later you had a new pair, just like the old ones, only they fit you perfectly. All you had to do was add a bit more matter to the box if you needed a larger size or if the ones you had were full of holes. Any sort of matter would work, although adding some sticks of wood seemed to make shoes that held up the best. If you wanted a different style, there were a number of selections to choose from and you just scrolled the control to the ones you liked and pushed the button. I have no idea how it works, but with something like that you could, theoretically, recycle the same pair of shoes forever. I'd done a booming business with it while I was hanging around Orpheseus waiting for the right slave to show up in the auctions there. Pretty cool, huh? Anyway, I doctored Cat's feet and made him some new boots, and we continued on our way. Cat still limped a little bit from time to time, but I think he was just faking it so I'd rub his feet.

We passed no towns along our path, nor were there any inns along the road, though there were other roads that crossed ours from time to time. It seemed odd to me that there would be no such amenities so near a space-port, but there's just no accounting for differences in local customs. I assumed that any travelers along the road just camped out wherever they happened to be at nightfall and, fortunately, we had come prepared for that eventuality. My main concern was keeping the nocturnal beasties away and, while the droid had an anti-predator feature that worked by emitting a high-frequency sound that would keep them at bay, I hadn't counted on the fact that Cat could also hear it. It just about drove him up the wall, so I had to turn it off.

Fortunately, that first night out wasn't too bad as far as any bugs or critters were concerned. I had some repel-lent which seemed to work well enough—though it had been manufactured on an entirely different planet and was, therefore, intended to repel different species of insects—and we were able to sleep outside next to a gently flowing stream. Cat hadn't been very talkative that day—mostly because his feet were hurting him, and then there was all the droid's singing, which made conversation difficult at best—but that night he seemed inclined to be loquacious. Stretched out on his pallet beside me on the bank of the stream, I could see him clearly in the moonlight—which was bright, by the way, since Statzeel had two moons—and if I'd been asked to come up with a more romantic setting, I don't believe I could have done it. Aside from the sound of the flowing water, there were insects and other chirping critters out singing their nightly chorus to the moons and stars, and, for some reason, it got me to thinking about what the past few years of my life would have been like if I hadn't had to go chasing Ranata.

Actually, I'd been thinking about it for the past several hours of our journey. Perhaps it was weighing on my mind because my quest seemed to be reaching the final stage at long last, and I knew that after this, my life—as well as Ranata's—would undergo a significant change. All the searching, the bribing, the interrogating—even fighting when I had to—all of that would now come to an end. That I was getting tired of it all didn't matter because a mission such as that tends to give your life a purpose which, once it is removed, makes that life begin to seem empty, or even pointless. It had been a tough six years, perhaps, but it hadn't been without its moments of exhilaration and excitement. The ups, the downs, the thrill of the pursuit that had kept me going, the promise I made to my father: all those things that had become so much a part of me were soon to be put behind me and laid to rest. When I thought of all the things I would have missed, all the strange places I wouldn't have visited, all the odd creatures I would never have seen, it almost seemed worth it. That I would never have met Cat was a given, and I hoped that, despite her suffering, Ranata might come to feel the same way some day; eventually seeing that this ordeal had been an integral part of her life, shaping and changing her into the person she now was. It goes without saying that it can be rather difficult to see the bright side of six years of slavery, but if she was lucky, she might even begin to see that, though the past could never be changed, she might have grown stronger because of it.

The sister I remembered had been so young, so carefree, so certain of her allure and her own rosy future, and, while her ordeal might have changed her for the better, it was also distinctly possible that it had broken her completely. As I neared the end of my quest, I realized that I was afraid of what I might find.

Taken by the Nedwuts, she had been sold and traded many times over, hop-skipping across the galaxy like a rare commodity that couldn't seem to remain in any one pair of hands for long. Greed at the price she would bring continually outweighed what it might have been worth for someone to keep her. There were other possible reasons for having been bought and sold so many times, of course—she might have been rebellious, or simply failed to please and then been passed on to someone else for a few credits. I'd been able to discover some of the prices she'd sold for, and it wasn't always a huge sum, her value seeming to have fluctuated considerably over the years. One previous owner had reported that she was more trouble than she was worth. He hadn't gone on to explain why, and refused to answer any more questions when I pressed him to discover the reason. I suppose it might

have been that she was too weak or sickly, for she had
never been strong. Not like Cat, who had been a warrior
before being enslaved. He might not have been broken by
all of the whips and chains, but how had she fared?

Oh, I'll admit I was afraid to discover what had been
happening to my sister over the past six years, but,
surprisingly, I was also encouraged by what I had seen
on my short sojourn on Statzeel. Of course, just what
would happen once we found her was anyone's guess,
but, for some reason, the urgency to find her was beginning to fade. This might have been due to the fact that I
had not, at least thus far, been witness to any mistreat-
ment of the women of Statzeel, nor had I seen any
women who appeared to be unhappy or downtrodden. I
couldn't imagine that slavery could ever be acceptable,
but I hadn't witnessed any public floggings, or, come to
think of it, much of anything in the way of crime. It was
a peaceful planet from what I had observed, and though
the men did seem to get pissed pretty easily, the women
were always able to calm them down.

This, alone, might have explained the sudden drag-
ging of my feet, but there was another reason as well,
and one that had been a thorn in my side all of my
adult life. You see, that other reason was that I still had
a pretty good idea that when we finally did find
Ranata, Cat would be as taken with her as any other
man, and I would be cast aside in her favor. I had no
way of knowing just how steadfast and true Cat would
turn out to be, and I wasn't so sure I wanted to put it
to the test. That Ranata might not want Cat never
occurred to me.

I never told Cat about that fear, hadn't even admitted to myself that I was keeping him at arm's length because of it—this reason outweighing the loss of control which I generally avoided. I knew I wasn't beautiful or alluring; never had been and never would be. The Exotic Beauty the makeup port had painted on me was a sham and I knew it. I couldn't shake the sneaking suspicion that Cat was acting the way he had been only because I just so happened to be the one who was there to set him free and be kind to him. It wasn't like he was in love with me or anything. He'd said he would stay with me, but he didn't have to—after all, he was free to do as he wished. I didn't own him, didn't have any claim on him whatsoever, and had no reason to believe that he would continue to stay with me forever. If my past track record was anything to go by, he probably wouldn't, for no one else ever had, and while I might have been alone out of necessity to a certain extent, it was not completely by choice.

I suppose I could have hired a first mate to help me out, but I'd never met anyone I trusted until I met Cat. Perhaps it was because he'd been a slave and had come back to me after I'd set him free that made me trust him so much, or it could have been something inherent within him, though I couldn't have said for sure. I did know that I liked being with Cat, and I didn't think it was just because he was company after I'd been alone for so long. Sure, I trusted him, I was attracted to him, but to stay with someone forever required love—at least that's how I saw it. Did I love him? Did he love me? I didn't know the answer to either of those questions, but what I did know was that I would most assuredly miss him when he was gone.

That night as I lay on my pallet while night fell, listening to him tell me of his homeworld and its people, I knew that he understood why I hadn't given up the search for my sister long ago. He understood what it meant to lose someone dear to him, and what a loss that must have been! I couldn't begin to fathom how he must feel, knowing that he had not only lost his entire family, but the entirety of his species as well.

When I asked him about it, he replied, "I do not know that I am the only one. I have never seen any others, but that does not mean that they do not exist."

Rolling over to face him, I gazed up at his intriguing face, now bathed in soft moonlight, and thought about what a loss it had been to the galaxy as a whole to be robbed of a species as beautiful and unique as this one must have been. It was a crime beyond measure, but no degree of punishment meted out to those responsible could ever restore Zetith and its people. In this case, the finality of death went far beyond the usual boundaries, for when a single person dies, generally speaking, there are offspring left behind to carry on. But not this time. Not with Zetith. And, not having a mate of his own kind, Cat would possibly never even be able to produce any children of his own. The sadness of this fact was almost overwhelming to me.

"That's true," I agreed, "but, as far as you know, you're the only one. You could search the galaxy for the rest of your life and never find anyone else, Cat! It's got to be hard knowing that."

"If it is hard, it is because I know that it could have been prevented. It was not a truly natural disaster. That is what I find difficult to accept."

I did, too, but for a different reason. "You said it was an act of war, but also that the planet itself isn't even there anymore. Why would anyone destroy an entire planet? Most wars are fought to gain control over a disputed territory, so it just doesn't make any sense to destroy a planet as well as its people. It's as if they intended to exterminate your race, and didn't give a damn about the world you lived on. Of course, I don't understand why anyone would do that either. I mean, who could hate an entire civilization enough to do such a thing?"

"The Nedwuts?" he suggested. "They were the ones responsible."

"Yes, but you didn't even know what Nedwuts were until I told you, Cat! They weren't the ones you were actually fighting, were they?"

"No," he replied. "But we were besieged by more than one enemy." He paused there, sighing sadly before continuing. "We were a strong race, but we could not fight them all."

"But why, Cat?" I demanded. "Tell me why!"

"There were many theories," he said. "But we never knew for certain, though their hatred of us was very strong."

I'd heard of people who didn't care for cats, but this was carrying it a bit too far! Then again, genocide was nothing new; this was just one of the few instances where the attempt to exterminate a race had come very close to succeeding. Then there was the abuse of Cat himself, both as a Zetithian and as a slave. I didn't understand that, either.

"You know, I'm surprised those scumbag Nedwuts

haven't had anyone try to wipe them out, too. If there was ever a race that needed killing off, it's that one!"

Cat smiled knowingly. "You have reason to hate them, even as I do, but would you do that, Jacinth? Would you kill them all for what a few of them have done, giving them no opportunity to change, not even allowing those who might have been innocent to go on living?"

"Well, probably not," I admitted. Then I thought about how alone Cat was, how abused he had been, and I wasn't quite so sure…"I don't know how you can be so damned noble about it!" I grumbled. "Honestly, Cat! You ought to ditch me and go after them!"

"We have spoken of this before, Jacinth," he chided me. "I am but one man against many."

"True, but there are plenty of them around that you could pick off one by one, you know."

"But I must travel to find them," he said reasonably. "And I find that I do not wish to travel anymore."

"Well, what *do* you want to do, Cat?"

Lips curling into another smile, he began to purr.

I couldn't help but laugh. "Walked right straight into that one, didn't I?"

His purr was a low rumble as he rolled over and pushed himself up onto his hands and knees. Crawling toward me, he said, "I have made my wishes known to you, Jacinth. It is for you to decide."

Looking up into his glowing eyes, for a long moment there I had a hard time remembering why my answer had always been no. Then, slowly, the reasons for my reluctance took shape in my mind once again. Fear of rejection, fear of that loss of control, fear of

losing myself to another. Those fears put walls around
me—solid and impenetrable walls. I wanted him,
wanted him to love me, wanted to feel free to love
him—without limits, even—but I was too damned
afraid to admit it, and was absolutely terrified of taking
that first step.

Ranata had been in love many times as a teenager
and she had flitted from one boy to the next with no fear
of losing either her heart or herself. Why was I so afraid
to do it? What was wrong with me? I wasn't afraid of
anything else; why this? Why couldn't I not give a
damn? Just have fun with Cat and not get into a sweat
over the details?

Then I realized something. I couldn't be nonchalant
about it, because it *did* matter to me. It mattered so much
that a little fun and games wouldn't cut it. I wanted it
all—probably could have had it, too. But I'd let him go.
He could have been my slave forever. I had owned him
once; he'd been mine, and, stupid me, I'd given him
away. I reminded myself that as his owner I could have
made him pretend to love me and to let me love him, but
I couldn't truly make him do it. It's no secret that love
cannot be commanded or bought; it can only be given,
and must be given freely.

"What are you thinking, Jacinth?" he asked, peering
into my eyes as though seeking the answer there.

"That I'm a coward and an idiot," I replied with
brutal honesty. "I could have you and yet I keep
pushing you away."

"You are neither a coward nor an idiot," he said,
reaching out to touch my cheek. "You are brave and

very wise, and you have given me something which no one else has ever done."

With just a simple touch of his hand, I could feel my body beginning to tremble—and I *never* tremble! My voice was a bit shaky, too, and I didn't even know if I'd be able to speak, but I managed to croak, "What's that?"

"You gave me my life, Jacinth," he replied. "It did not belong to me until you gave it back."

"No, I didn't," I argued. "You could have been free long ago. You could have escaped from slavery somehow. At some point in all this time, you could have escaped."

He shook his head. "There was no reason for me to escape because I had nowhere to go, Jacinth. My people were all gone, and my planet destroyed. There was nowhere that I even *wanted* to go. But that has changed now, and I have said that I will remain with you always. Why do you doubt it?"

"I have no idea," I whispered. "Maybe it's because I'm just too jaded and cynical for my own damn good."

"You said you needed someone you could trust," he reminded me. "And that someone is me. If you do trust me, then you must believe me as well. I will not lie to you, Jacinth, but I have nothing to give you and no way to prove that what I say is true. I have nothing but myself. You gave me my freedom; now I am giving it back to you."

"But you can't do that!" I protested.

"I am a free man," he stated firmly. "I am free to do whatever I wish."

"But I don't want a slave, Cat!" I sputtered. "Slavery is an...an abomination!"

"Then you must take me as your lover," he said, leaning closer. "Or you may take me as your friend. But either way, I will remain your slave."

I was astonished. I didn't know what to say. I mean, what *can* you say to a man who has just given himself to you? Thanks, but no thanks? Sorry, but you're on your own now, kid? I couldn't shrug it off; I couldn't say something funny. In fact, I couldn't say anything at all.

So I kissed him.

I might have made the first move, might have taken him by surprise, but Cat seemed more than willing to follow it up with some moves of his own. I'm not sure he was expecting me to do that, but he pulled me into his arms with very little hesitation and began kissing me in earnest. Ever since that time, whenever I think of love, or someone else utters the word, the image of that night lying on the banks of a creek in the middle of the Statzeelian jungle is what flashes through my mind. The soft night air, the rushing stream, the sound of Cat purring while his lips touched mine in a soft caress—oh, yes, these are the things that I remember most vividly. In my mind I can still see his jet-black curls catching the moonlight, can still feel the strength of his arms as they encircled me, can still savor the taste of him on my tongue, can still feel the heat of his body and the passion of his kisses.

I knew for certain then something I had always suspected, which was that I had never been loved before, and, God help me, I would never know it again—not like this, and not with anyone but my Cat. This wasn't momentary or fleeting; no, this was eternal and forever, and I was hopelessly lost. And you know what? I didn't care.

Oh, not that I didn't care that I had fallen in love at long last; it was simply that all of my fears no longer held any power over me. They had all crumbled into dust only to be swirled upwards into the air and dissipated as though they had never been. I knew now that I was in love, and probably had been from the moment I'd laid eyes on him. I believe I even said it aloud, though the words may have been drowned out by the chirping of Statzeelian crickets or the loud purring of my Cat. I'm sure I said it with actions at least, for I held him close to me like the precious jewel that he was, caressing his body with a worshipful touch. I was in heaven, a perfection of feeling marred only by a sharp sting on my right ankle where some insect must have gotten past the repellent I'd used.

I drifted on in a haze, kissing Cat, feeling his hands on me, and being kissed in return. I felt his hair tickling my arms as I reached around him, felt his warmth until my skin became suffused with a numbing heat. The sound of the crickets increased, swelling to an ear-shattering intensity before dropping down to a soft hum and then fading out completely. When I next opened my eyes, it was to look upon the bright sunshine of a new day.

Chapter Seven

THE FIRST THING I NOTICED WAS THAT CAT WAS NO longer in my arms, but was already up and bustling about, apparently working on getting breakfast ready. The next thing I noticed was that he was making more noise than he usually did, and also that he seemed, well, pissed.

Rolling over, which took a great deal more effort than usual, I felt a stabbing pain in my ankle where I'd been bitten the night before. I tried to sit up to take a look at it, but realized that at some point during the night, the marrow of my bones must have been removed and then replaced with a lead core, because I felt too weighted down even to move. My head felt easily three times its normal size, and if I'd ever been hungover like that before, I sure as hell couldn't remember what I'd been drinking at the time! It took a couple of tries to get the saliva going enough to work my swollen tongue loose from where it was stuck tightly to the roof of my mouth. Just the simple act of opening my mouth made my head swim and though I'm quite sure I said the word "Cat," I'm also just as certain that it came out sounding more like "A-a-th-h."

Cat ignored me, going right on with his cooking. Well, I think he was cooking, but it sounded more like he was just beating pans together to make enough noise to annoy me. Which it did.

"A-a-th-h!" I repeated. "Elp ee."

He ignored that, as well, so I followed it up by taking as deep a breath as I could and letting out a high-pitched "E-e-e-e-e-e!" Which, of course, got his attention. With eyebrows alarmingly vertical and a glowering, golden glitter in his eyes, he slammed down the pan he was holding and advanced toward me with a menacing step. Yep, no doubt about it, he was pissed about something!

Towering above me, he let out a growl and spat out, "What?" in a manner which made me want to knock his feet right out from under him—which, of course, I couldn't have done, at least not in my current condition.

I managed to swallow with some difficulty and tried to talk again. It came out a little better this time, but not by much. "Ug ite," I said, attempting to point to my foot with a nearly immovable hand. "Urths."

I must have been better at pointing than I thought because, with a sharp, exasperated snort, he shifted his gaze toward my feet.

The change in his expression from irritation to concern was so swift and complete, it was downright comical to watch. I would have laughed out loud if I could have, but that was something else I couldn't do, so I didn't bother to try.

Kneeling, Cat took a closer look at my ankle and then acted decisively, scooping me up in his arms and carrying me to the water's edge before laying me back down to dangle my foot in the soothing coolness of the flowing brook. Sighing with relief, I closed my eyes again, as hot tears began to pour down my cheeks. This was turning out to be one helluva trip, I thought grimly. It was no

wonder nobody had tried to stop us from going to find
Ranata, for they all must have known full well that this
damn jungle would chew us up and spit us out before we
ever even got close. Reminding myself that we had
passed other travelers coming from the opposite direction
didn't help very much, because, quite obviously, they
knew a few things about surviving a trip down this road
that we didn't. Should have consulted the local tourist
guide, I decided. Too bad it was too late to buy one now.

Cat came back with a cup of water and held it to my
lips. "Drink this," he said.

I did my best, but most of it wound up running down
my neck. Though I might not have swallowed much of
it, it still tasted pretty good, and I could already feel the
swelling in my tongue beginning to subside. I lay there
thinking that it was a wonder I hadn't occluded my
airway completely during the night and died in my
sleep! Wouldn't that have been the ultimate irony?
Having come so far to find Ranata and being this close
to actually seeing her again—and finally falling in love
on top of that!—only to die from an allergic reaction to
a damned mosquito bite! I could just see the inscription
on my tombstone:

HERE LIES CAPTAIN JACINTH
"BAD LUCK JACK" RUTLAND
ALWAYS A DAY LATE AND A CREDIT SHORT
MAY SHE REST IN PEACE AT LAST

Rest in peace. Now there was a lovely thought! I
certainly wanted peace and I could definitely use a rest!
And I wanted to do it with my Kittycat. I didn't think it
was too much to ask....

"I thought you had grown tired of me and had fallen asleep out of boredom," Cat said sheepishly. "I apologize for my anger."

I managed a weak smile. "Sthupid Cat! Tol' you I love you, dinnt I?"

He smiled back at me. "Yes, you did. I should have remembered that."

"Kithssed you, too, dinnt I?"

Nodding, he replied, "Kiss me again, Jacinth."

Shaking my head, I said, "Not now, tongue too thick." I must have been getting a little bit better, because that part came out pretty well.

"I do not care," Cat said firmly. "I would like to kiss you, and then I would like to bathe with you in this water, if it is not too cold."

"M-m-m, no, not too cold. Feelth good."

Cat pulled off his boots and slipped out of his shirt and breeches. Then removing my peachy dress, he lifted me into his arms again, kissing me deeply.

"Y'know something Cat?" I murmured. "You look better without clothes than anything I've ever seen. It's a cryin' shame you ever have to get dressed."

"But I am your slave," he purred. "You may dress me any way you wish—or not."

"Oh, yeah, that's right. I keep forgetting. Well, you do look damn good in those boots. All you need is a sword and boots, I think. And maybe a big, wide belt to hang your scabbard from."

"And you, my lovely master," he said, sliding me down into the water. "You I would wrap in flowing...what do you call the fabric from which this dress is made?"

"I have no idea," I replied, "but I'm gonna buy some before we leave here. I'll make a fortune on it." My limbs still felt sort of heavy, but I was at least able to stand up in the water, which at its deepest point, came about to mid-thigh. My ankle still felt stiff, though. From my personal perspective, the longer this bath and breakfast took, the better. In fact, staying put the whole day didn't sound too bad at that point. "Don't suppose you brought any soap, did you?"

Cat grinned. "Yes, I brought soap," he said, holding it up. "And a cup. I am going to wash you, Jacinth."

"What's the matter, Kittycat?" I teased him. "Do I smell bad?"

"No," he replied with a slow shake of his head. "You smell of desire. My only wish is to have a reason to touch every part of you."

The morning sun was streaming down in beams through the open spaces in the canopy above us, heating the morning dew to a steamy mist. It was already getting hot, and promised to get much hotter as the day progressed, but, quite truthfully, most of the heat I was feeling had more to do with the look in Cat's eyes than it did with the sun.

"Is that what you wish?"

"Yes." He was purring again. I wondered if he had any idea what the sound of that did to me. I should probably never tell him, I decided. Wouldn't want him to know too much…. There were other things I should probably never tell him, either, like how much I liked his hair, for example. The soft breeze had picked it up and was wafting it enticingly across his chest and around his shoulders, making me long to capture it in my grasp.

"Don't ever cut your hair, Cat," I said suddenly. "I want to wash it every day for the rest of my life."

"If it brings you joy," he said with a sly smile, "I will let it grow until it reaches the ground."

"No," I said. "Just until it's down to here." To demonstrate what I considered to be the best length, I cupped his balls in my hand. "Yes," I went on with a firm nod. "That would be absolutely perfect."

Cat took my hand and moved it up to his cock. "Not here?" he inquired with a mischievous glint in his eyes.

"There's nice, too," I conceded. "And it will pass there," I said as I squeezed his thick penis, "before it reaches here." Taking his nuts in my hand again, I gave them a gentle squeeze and told him to give me the soap. "I want to wash my big slave kitten."

Cat shook his head. "No. I will wash you first."

"We're not gonna fight about this, are we?" I demanded.

He smiled. "We will wash each other."

Leading me over to where a large, flat slab of rock jutted out into the stream, he set the soap down on it and then filled the cup with water. We took turns getting each other wet and then we got into the soap. I honestly cannot say which felt better: his hands on me, or my hands on him. Either way evoked sensations within me that I hadn't known I was capable of feeling. The tight muscles of his thighs felt hot and slick as I ran my lathered fingers down his legs, back up again to his groin, and then across his chest. Gripping his hard cock in my hand, I slid back and forth on him from the root to the head and back again, delighting in the sound of his appreciative purr. The soft skin of his scrotum was velvety smooth beneath my touch, and his own fingers began to trace slippery circles around my nipples, spiraling in toward the sensitive center until he had teased them to a level of engorgement which went far beyond mere arousal.

Moaning softly, I gave in to the sensation and leaned back against the rocky ledge, spreading my arms out across it for support. "Is this what you meant when you said you would give me joy unlike any I have ever known?"

Cat shook his head. "No," he replied. "That comes later."

I nodded mutely. It was going to get even better, and—stupid me!—I had been resisting this. What a fool I was! What an absolute *fool*....

Taking advantage of my position against the stone, Cat moved closer, using not only his hands and fingers, but his whole body against mine, much the way he had just a few days before when we had been about to crash into this jungle planet. Even though his moves then might have been similar, the effect of his hot, soap-slick skin against my own was intensified and had me aroused nearly to the screaming point. I honestly could not imagine that I could ever experience anything to compare with what he was doing. Until he turned me around, that is.

I lay half-sprawled across the boulder with my head pillowed on my arms as Cat doused my back with a cupful of water and then leaned into me. I'd almost forgotten just how much muscular control he had over his dick, but when it began sliding up and down between my buns and all over my ass, I remembered. As he reached around me with both arms to tantalize my nipples again, I felt that thick, soapy shaft slide between my thighs and heard myself—me, now!—begging him to keep going.

"Tonight," he purred. "We will wait until tonight. I want you thinking about this all day. I want your desire to consume you."

"It already is!" I gasped. "Please, Cat!"

"No," he replied. "You would not be able to travel afterward, and we must continue on our journey. But tonight, I will give you my love, and you will know joy."

He was either the cockiest bastard I'd ever met in my life, or the sexiest; I couldn't decide which.

Despite such a lovely beginning, we had a really shitty day after that. As we hiked deeper and deeper into the jungle, the humidity increased by about three hundred percent, and the bugs got even worse. I didn't know what kind of super mosquito had bitten me the night before, but it made me extremely leery of anything that hummed or buzzed or flew just a little too close for comfort, and I was wearing myself out swatting away anything that moved in my direction. To top it all off, it was hot as hell without so much as a breath of air moving, and I began to realize why there were no settlements of any kind along that road. The air itself was so thick and heavy with moisture that even walking didn't create much of a breeze. You would have had to run to create any kind of wind at all, which would have just sucked the life out of you that much faster.

It would have been considerate of someone to have built some kind of shelter at one of the clearings, but I suppose that would have been expecting too much. Of course, I now understood why everyone else rode horses in order to get them through this damned jungle as quickly as possible. I was beginning to believe that Cat's insistence that he wait for nightfall to do his thing had been a big, honking mistake, too, because as hot and miserable as I was, trust me, sex was absolutely the last thing on my mind! On the other hand, slapping him silly for refusing to ride a horse was becoming an increasingly favorable option with every step I took.

Then the pack-droid broke down.

Now, I realize that, other than the fact that it could carry things and sing, I haven't described my droid in great detail, but suffice it to say, it was essentially a big, heavy cabinet with storage compartments on three sides and ran on a caterpillar tread. On the front end it had a detachable humanoid component that could walk alone and help you carry stuff, but I didn't know if that part was strong enough to pull the bulkier section. Of course, in this particular instance it wouldn't have mattered if it could or not since it was the caterpillar drive that was locked up anyway. The damn thing wouldn't budge a centimeter and since I wasn't about to leave it behind and carry all that shit myself, I dragged out some tools and got to work.

It goes without saying that satin slippers and peachy see-through dresses are not the best attire for attempting to repair a caterpillar drive, so I stripped them off and put on a tank top and a pair of shorts, essentially working in what was normally my underwear. Cat hadn't mentioned it as yet, but I knew he had to be dying from the heat in the get-up he was wearing. I'd worn boots like that myself, and I'd have bet a space cruiser that his feet were swimming in puddles of sweat, but he didn't complain about it any more than he had when the damned boots were rubbing blisters on him the day before. Must have been a slave thing, I decided, since a slave could probably complain all he wanted and no one would give a damn whether he was uncomfortable or not. Of course, considering what had happened to me the night before, he might not have wanted to expose any more skin than was absolutely necessary— though the way that shirt was clinging to him like a second skin, I had an idea that one of those nasty critters could probably bite him through it anyway.

"You really ought to take off that shirt, Cat," I remarked. "I've got plenty of sunscreen and insect repel-lent, you know."

He smiled seductively. "If I remove my shirt, will it increase your desire?"

"It might if I was feeling any at all right now!" I declared. "Honest to God, I don't think I've ever felt less like getting nailed in my entire life!"

"Then I will take it off," he said, chuckling softly as he stripped off the damp garment. "It is necessary for you to want to be 'nailed.'"

"Heard that one before, have you?" I said dryly. "That's probably about as universally understood as 'fuck,' wouldn't you say?"

"Perhaps," he agreed. "But it is also…self-explanatory."

"True." I lay down on my back, scooting underneath the droid between the two sets of tread, and took a look at it. If I was lucky, it might be something simple like a loose bolt or just a little something jammed in there. Then I saw what the problem was and immediately began cussing like an Arconian sailor—who have coined some of the more colorful expressions in the galaxy, by the way—ending up with a growled and heartfelt "—and fuck me swingin'!"

"I will try it if you like," Cat said doubtfully, "but I believe it would be…difficult."

"Very funny!" I snarled. "For your information, that was an expletive, not a request."

"The problem with the machine is a bad one?" Cat ventured, leaning down to peer under the droid.

"You bet your sweet ass it is!" I said. "There's a big, fuckin' rock stuck up in here and it's shifted the belt off the pulleys. This is gonna be a real bitch to fix." And, of course, it would have to happen when I was already hot and nearly exhausted! That bug bite had taken the wind out of my sails a bit, too, and I'd already had to stop and remake my shoes twice to accommodate the swelling. The Derivian ointment was helping, of course, but it still hurt like the devil whenever I touched it. "Shit, shit, shit!"

"I will help," Cat said simply. I thought it rather odd that he didn't get mad about crap like this, but could get royally pissed when I fell asleep on him while he was kissing me. I suppose a blow to his vanity might have hurt more than a little bad luck, but then, his having been a slave for a number of years, I suppose a little hard work didn't scare him very much. Ordinarily, it didn't bother me, either, but, like I said, I wasn't exactly feeling a hundred percent that day.

It took us a good two hours to get the rock out. First, we tried prying it loose, and when that didn't work, Cat had to break it apart using a hammer and chisel. This in itself would have been hard enough to do even without having to work in the hot, confined space underneath the droid, but Cat kept his cool—a lot better than I did.

Before tackling the belt and pulleys, we took a break for lunch and just sat in the middle of the road leaning up against the droid instead of looking for a spot to picnic. As you might expect, the damned droid had picked a really rotten place to break down, for not only was it in the densest stretch of jungle we'd passed through so far, but there wasn't a creek anywhere in sight. I would have given a million credits for a swim at that point, but the way our luck was running, any creek we swam in around those parts probably would have been full of the Statzeelian equivalent of piranhas or electric eels.

I, for one, had been around enough to know that you couldn't always trust the water, no matter how innocent it might appear, and if I hadn't been in such bad shape that morning, I doubt that I would have taken a bath in that stream with Cat at all. I'd once had a really bad experience in a swimming hole on some planet or other—I believe it was Ractoul Zeta, if memory serves—and had nearly been nibbled to death by ducks. I know it sounds ridiculous, and they looked perfectly harmless—quite pretty, in fact—but they were a carnivorous lot and just wouldn't leave me alone! They chased me out of the water and I actually had to resort to spraying them with a wide stun beam to stop them. I got my revenge by cooking and eating one of them, but I don't mind telling you I've been a bit leery of ducks ever since.

Despite the fact that Cat had claimed that he would eat anything I gave him—though I *had* noticed he had a bit of a sweet tooth—for once, he seemed to take exception to the food we had on hand and tossed his leftovers into the jungle instead of stowing them back in the refrigeration compartment on the droid. It could have been the heat that was affecting his appetite, because it *was* hot as hell, but I still considered it to be a bit wasteful myself. I mean, I never threw *anything* away unless it was either stinking to high heaven or sprouting a mold or fungus of some kind. However, in this particular case I didn't see much point in picking on him about it, especially since we were only about two days away from reaching Ranata, and also because I was inclined to agree with him. Twenty-year-old Andrellian marching rations were pretty awful, but I'd gotten a really good deal on them, and they would keep you alive and on your feet—if you could chew them, that is. I decided I would make a point of stocking up for the return trip in the town before we stole Ranata back.

But to get there at all, we first had to get the droid up and running again. I had a crowbar, and we tried to lever the belt back onto the pulleys, but that sucker was built pretty tough, and it was beginning to look as though we would end up having to take the whole damn caterpillar drive apart just to get the belt back on. We were about to give up and do just that when I remembered that I had a machete on the droid somewhere, and I thought that with Cat pulling on the belt with the crowbar and me using the blade of the machete to guide it back into place, we might just be able to do it.

It still took several tries, and we had to switch places because my arms weren't quite long enough to reach inside the drive with the machete, but finally, with a loud snick, it popped back into place. I just stared at it in disbelief for a moment there, so I didn't start rejoicing right away. Then I noticed that Cat was being awfully damned quiet, as well.

"Cat?" I began. "Are you…."

"Do not move or make another sound," he said, cutting me off rather ominously.

Of course, having issued such a command, he got my curiosity fully aroused and, silly me, I stuck my head out from underneath the droid. The first thing that ran through my mind was that the next time he said something like that, I should probably listen to him, and, second, that there was no going back now, because they had seen me, too.

Cat stood, machete in hand, facing down a pack of five of the meanest, nastiest-looking beasties I'd seen since we landed. In fact, I'd have to say that these guys pretty much took the cake even when compared with some of the ornerier critters I'd seen on other worlds. They had apparently already eaten the food Cat had thrown out and seemed to think that we either had more, or that we might make a tasty lunch, ourselves.

"Holy shit, Cat!" I exclaimed. "Didn't anyone ever tell you not to feed the bears?"

I said bears, because that's about as close as I could come to what they looked like. All the other animals I'd seen on Statzeel had seemed pretty tame to me—domesticated, even—but these things looked like a cross between a bear, a saber-toothed tiger, a wild boar, and a Drell. Shaped like bears, they had teeth and jaws like the prehistoric tiger, grunted, and had cloven feet like a boar, and I say Drell-like because they had dreadlocks all over them and were probably about as rude as Drells, too. Fortunately, they weren't quite as big as your average bear, being more along the lines of a large dog.

"Where is your pulse pistol?" Cat asked, calmly ignoring my question.

"Well, I don't have it on me, if that's what you're asking," I replied grimly. "If you haven't got it, I'd say that it's probably in the lock-up on the other side of the droid."

Cat nodded. "Climb up on top of the storage unit," he directed. "Try to get to it from above if you are able."

"I'll give it my best shot," I said. I did my best to move slowly, but obviously it wasn't slowly enough, because one of the little buggers circled around to face me, effectively trapping me underneath the droid; there was simply no way I could have crawled out and climbed up on the droid quickly enough to avoid being attacked. I couldn't get out by backing up and going out the other end, either, because the detachable helper-droid was standing there—which I had, unfortunately, powered down to save the batteries while we were working on the drive belt, or I could have simply told it to move out of the way. Making a mental note to never, ever, turn the damned thing off again unless I was stowing it in the hold, I yelled: "I can't get out, Cat! They've got me trapped under here!"

"Stay there, then," he said. I could hear him moving around to the open end of the storage unit. The pack inched along with him, apparently, because by the time I could see his boots, I could see them, as well—all five of them. They were standing there snapping their jaws and grunting, seemingly waiting for Cat to make the first move, when all of a sudden, two of them lunged forward. One went high, aiming for Cat's throat while the other went low, taking a snap at his right leg and tearing through the leather as if it had been made from the same flimsy material as my dress. Cat parried the attack of the first creature with the machete, drawing blood and making the thing squeal in anger. Kicking the other one out of the way, Cat repositioned himself as they withdrew for a moment and milled about as though taking the time to consult with one another and reevaluate their opponent.

Moments later, they began their next assault, returning in a group of three this time. As Cat fended off each of them, they seemed to rotate their numbers, for when one retreated, another took its place, always leaving two held in reserve while the other three were on the offensive. It was an effective strategy, prompting me to grudgingly admit that they were a little smarter than the average bear. I crawled up as close to the outside as I dared, hoping to get a dig into one of them with the pointed end of my crowbar, but Cat had taken up a

position just far enough away that I wasn't likely to get
one unless they were to break through his defense.

And it was quite a defense! Honestly, if I hadn't been
so scared, I might have been sitting there admiring his
form and footwork. The boy definitely knew how to
handle a sword, and he moved with all of the fluid, but
deadly, grace that one might expect from a feline sword-
master. If the animals' aim was to wear him out before
going in for the kill, it was becoming increasingly
obvious that they just might wind up giving up the fight
before he did.

They might have been a determined bunch, but Cat
had a longer reach, and soon had all of them bleeding
from a variety of wounds. Cat, himself, had a scratch or
two on him, but he fought like a machine—working
steadily, parrying, thrusting, and spinning easily to face
each new opponent. Oh, yeah, he was a warrior, all
right, and he was absolutely magnificent to watch in
action. With a wide-legged fighting stance, his hair
flying and blade flashing, he was the embodiment of
every hero from Agamemnon right on down to—well,
depending on what planet you happen to be from, just
about anyone else you'd care to name. I caught a
glimpse of his expression a time or two as he spun
around to take on another beast and saw that he had a
rather satisfied smirk on his face. This was what he did
best, it seemed, and, in spite of the danger, he appeared
to be enjoying himself!

Finally, having fought with them long enough to take
their measure and find the weak spot in their attack, he
took them out, one by one, right straight through the

throat with his blade. Then, turning toward me in triumph, he reached out a hand to help me up and then yanked me into his arms for a kiss.

"Oh, way to go, Kittycat!" I murmured against his lips. "You are one truly cool cat!"

Taking a long lick on the side of my neck as though he planned to eat me alive, he said, "I believe we will be eating well tonight."

"Want a little roasted beastie, do you?" I inquired curiously. Then it occurred to me that this whole thing might have been deliberate. "Is that why you threw out your lunch? To use as bait?"

"No, my lovely master," he purred. "I would not put you in such peril. If I had known of these beasts, I would not have done such a thing. It is my duty to protect you."

"Well, I'm all for that!" I agreed. "And speaking of which, since you're the one wearing the pants, you need to carry the pulse pistol—all the time! Obviously, we should have been a lot more cautious on this trip that we have been so far. I suppose it would have been asking too much for that damned Delamar to warn us. Of course, I think every word he told us was a lie, anyway, so his information probably would have been pretty useless." I took a deep breath and surveyed the area. The dead tiger-bear-pigs were scattered all over the place, and the droid was just sitting there in the middle of the road. "Well, then, Kittycat, I guess that's that! What do you say we pack up our droid and get the heck out of Dodge?"

He just looked at me and laughed.

"Another old Earth expression," I explained, "essentially meaning let's get going before more of the bad guys show up and we have to do this all over again."

"I believe that would be…prudent," Cat agreed.

"Yeah, and it would be 'prudent' not to throw out anymore bait for those damned bear-pigs!" I said dryly. "You know, I ought to jerk a knot in your tail for that, Kittycat! We could have gotten killed!"

"I do not have a tail," he reminded me again.

"I know," I remarked, "but it sure would be fun trying to find it."

Chapter Eight

THE SUN WAS SINKING LOW ON THE HORIZON WHEN WE stopped for the night and, since we were still in the deepest, creepiest part of the jungle, we opted to sleep in a tent this time. My tent, having the Auto-Erector function built right in, went up quickly and the droid built us a fire to roast one of those critters Cat had killed. Of course, if I'd had any idea just how many truly hideous insects our campfire would attract, I'd have never agreed to cook the damn thing. As it was, I sprayed so much repellent around that Cat started sneezing.

"Sorry, Kittycat," I apologized, "but I have no desire to get drugged into a stupor by another bug bite!"

"And I would not want you to," he agreed. "I want you awake and filled with passion."

I'll have to say, the way he was looking at me almost made me forget what a lousy day it had been. It also made me curse that damned mosquito even more, because the night before we had been in such a beautiful, idyllic setting, whereas tonight we would be stuck inside a stuffy tent with God knows what buzzing around outside. Cat had said he wanted me awake, which shouldn't be too hard since I doubted that I would sleep a wink because of all the bugs, but being filled with passion wasn't something I was sure I could manage at that point. No, the way I saw it, he'd missed his golden opportunity that morning in the pool. It would serve him right for making me wait, I thought irritably, because I just wasn't in the mood!

Our roast beast took forever to cook, too, and I felt like I was plumb starving to death by the time it was done. It didn't taste too bad—at least not once I'd doused it with a healthy dose of Tiranian hot pepper sauce. Cat didn't seem to like the hot stuff very much, possibly because he hadn't eaten anything with much flavor while he'd been enslaved; so he ate his plain, but I thought it tasted pretty gamey myself.

It was well after nightfall when we finished our dinner, and by then, the onslaught of insects had reached the point that I was about to lose my sanity altogether. I know it was just a few bugs, but honest to God, when one of them makes your foot and tongue swell up like balloons, the last thing you want to see or hear for a while is another skeeter!

We decided to leave most of the cleaning up until morning, and, having doused our campfire, got inside the tent together. I hadn't said anything to Cat about feeling so out of sorts, but he might have guessed it. Of course, that didn't stop him from trying to change my mind, chiefly by nuzzling me and rumbling like a mountain lion on the prowl. But I was tired and dirty and sticky with sweat, having spent a fair amount of the day groveling in the dirt underneath the pack-droid in my underwear. Aside from that, my back and my feet were killing me, and that roast beast wasn't setting so well on my stomach. I didn't feel the least bit sexy or pretty or alluring or any of those things I wanted to be feeling the first time I made love with Cat; it simply was not the right time!

The trouble was, despite what I was telling myself, Cat could smell my pheromones or whatever it was that he called my "desire"—and it had him hard as a rock and he would *not* leave me alone!

"Cat, I swear, if you don't get away from me, I'm going to get Tex out and shoot you!" I warned him. I was sweating like a horse at the end of a mile and a quarter and the damn bugs were dive-bombing the tent to the point that I didn't think I could take much more before exploding.

"But you want me," he began. "How can I not—?"

"I said, back off!" I growled at him. "Don't touch me!"

Cat retreated to the other side of the tent, but I could still hear him purring, even over all the buzzing against the tent from the insects. Curling up on my pallet with my back to him, I tried to shut out the incessant noise and Cat's purring the best I could, but then he tried again, spooning up against me from behind and licking my ear.

"Please, Cat, I don't want you to think I don't want you, because I do. But right now, I'm tired and hot and dirty and I just can't do it."

"I do not mind that you are dirty," he said, "and I like it when you are overheated with desire." He paused then, tracing a fingertip down my side and over my hip. "I believe you have been thinking too much, Jacinth, and now you are afraid."

"Hell, yes, I'm afraid!" I exclaimed. "We're out here in the middle of the jungle, it's been one life and death ordeal after another today, and you, well, you're the one who wouldn't do it this morning, who insisted that I think about it all day to increase my desire. Well, Cat, it backfired on you! I was ready and willing this morning, but right now, I just want some sleep!"

"And do you believe that you will be able to sleep with large insects hitting the tent all night?"

I sighed, stretching my shoulders as I felt my spine popping in several places. "Probably not," I conceded. "And I *need* to sleep! I feel like I've been rode hard and put up wet, as the saying goes."

"Jacinth, do you love me?" he asked.

I rolled over to face him, and though the tent was so dark I couldn't see a hand in front of my face, I could see his glowing eyes. "Yes, I do, Kittycat," I said gently. "I love you dearly. You're my big, strong, brave hero, and even if you weren't, I'd still love you with all my heart."

"Then if you will be awake, and if you love me as I love you…" His voice trailed off in the darkness, and suddenly, I felt his breath on my face as he moved closer. "Kiss me, then, my lovely master, and we will spend this night, and every night hereafter, together. Forever."

"You won't fall in love with my sister and run away on me, will you?" I blurted out. Having actually said that aloud, thus exposing my worst fear, was evidence that I was pretty well near the breaking point.

"No," he replied. "I will not fall in love with your sister and run away. I will be with you, and only you, until you are old and your life has reached its end."

"Oh, Cat…" I sighed.

It was very dark, and his eyes must have been closed, shutting out their light, so I don't know who moved first, but a moment later, his lips were melting into mine and suddenly I didn't give a damn that I was tired or dirty or

scared or irritated. I didn't even have to remind myself
that I'd called myself every kind of fool that very
morning for resisting him so long, because I wasn't
going to resist anymore. I was going to shut down the
thinking part of my brain and simply *feel*.

And when I put my hands on him, he felt so good it
made me want to cry, but no more so than when he put
his own upon me. He was kissing and caressing me, but
he was also massaging me deeply, pushing away the
pain, the exhaustion, and replacing it with the soft glow
of desire, paving the way for the heat of passion. I did
the same to him, kneading the muscles of his back, his
shoulders, his chest. I couldn't get enough of him.
Reaching lower, I took his backside in my hands and
pulled him closer.

The chorus outside the tent fell silent as the wind
increased and a cooling, soothing rain began to fall,
pattering lightly on the roof of our tent, sending a wave
of soft air swirling over us. I relaxed completely then,
and as I did so, I could feel the need for Cat building up
inside me. He'd been right, of course. My desire for him
had been there all along; it had simply been buried under
all the baggage I had been carrying with me throughout
my life. But now, I laid it aside for a time. I would pick
it up again, perhaps—but not tonight. Tonight I would
think about nothing but my love, my Cat.

I focused solely on my feelings, how it felt to take Cat
in my arms, how it felt to kiss him, how it felt to caress
his body until he groaned with pleasure. I even knew the
precise moment when the warmth of desire gave way to
the heat of passion, and soon, every cell in my body was

on fire, clamoring for him to help me find my release. Every erogenous zone I possessed, from lips to nipples to clitoris, was aching with need.

"Please, Cat," I whispered.

I didn't have to ask him twice. Purring even more loudly than before, he rolled me onto my back, nudged my legs apart and nailed me with that big, ruffled cock. The sensation of relief was as instantaneous as it was overwhelming; I felt as though my overheated flesh had been plunged into a lake full of cool, crystal-clear water.

Then he began to move and the pleasure began to build. Where there had previously been frustration and even pain, there was now pure, mind-numbing ecstasy. The scalloped edge of his cockhead seemed to fold back on the shaft as he thrust in, but the out-stroke fanned it out again, raking the sensitive membranes of my G-spot as I gasped in awe. He filled me up completely, stretching me to the limit, but I was so wet and slick from all the lubrication that poured out of both of us that his cock moved with a smooth, nearly frictionless glide which brought me quickly to climax.

And another, and another, and another. Oh, sure, I'd had a few orgasms in my time, but this just went on and on and on! Cat had been denied relief for some time, but it certainly didn't make him come any quicker. I wasn't counting, but I think it must have taken a full hundred strokes for him to finally release with a loud roar, reminiscent of the sound he'd made when he'd attacked his former master.

Cat collapsed on my chest, his hair fanned out over my body and his cock still lodged deep within me. He wasn't moving, but I could still feel something. Something that teased me inside like nothing else ever had: it was as though that ruffle around his cock was moving back and forth, sweeping against the most sensitive parts of my body and making my orgasm continue on for an unbelievable length of time. I was forced to admit that this was one man who hadn't been pulling my leg when he'd said he'd bring me joy unlike any I had ever known before. I should have listened to him, should have surrendered long ago....

While it might have been true that there had been something different about him that I'd seen even when he was standing there on the auction block in chains, unfortunately, mistrusting men of any species had become second nature to me over the years. They had been the source of most of my own misfortunes and those of my sister as well. Many of them were liars who had taken advantage of my single-minded pursuit of Ranata, telling me exactly what I wanted to hear—for the right price, of course, and I had paid good money for bad information many times. The red-eyed alien, Delamar, had simply been the most recent recipient of a bribe from me, and it remained to be seen whether or not he had been a liar, too. Oh, yes, dishonest, scheming, and deceitful men had littered the path I had followed from Statzeel all the way back to Dexia Four where Ranata was first taken. This one, however, I should have believed, because he hadn't been lying or boasting; his claim had been true—no brag, just fact.

Chapter Nine

I WENT TO SLEEP AS QUICKLY AS I HAD THE NIGHT before—and without the benefit of any mosquito venom, I might add—and slept every bit as soundly. Cat had been right about that, too, because, while I'm sure I could have gotten up and started off on a long hike if I had to, I sure as hell didn't want to! No, I wanted nothing more than to curl up and sleep with my purring Cat until morning gave way to afternoon.

When I awoke, I found that I *had* curled up with my Cat, for my head was pillowed on his stomach and I could feel the steady rise and fall of his breathing, hear his stomach growling, hear his heart beating, feel him purring. It was a gentle reminder that I was not alone, but had been lying in slumber with a living, breathing man. Not that I hadn't slept with him before, of course, but this was different, and the reasons for that were perfectly obvious.

Then I became aware of something else. Something was licking me on the cheek.

My first thought was that some unknown jungle beastie had gotten into the tent during the night. I knew that it couldn't have been Cat doing it since I was facing toward his feet and my arm was resting on his leg, so his head had to be lying in the other direction. Then I decided that it really didn't feel like a tongue; it was too smooth and slippery, and, generally speaking, tongues tend to be a little rough. With a significant amount of trepidation, I opened my eyes just the tiniest little bit to see what it was. It was Cat all right; and he was awake, apparently, for his stiff cock was right up in my face and he was stroking my cheek with the ruffled head.

"Well, good morning to you, too, Kittycat!" I said dryly. "Trying to tell me something?"

"Perhaps," he replied, letting out a loud purr. Curling his hips, he pushed it harder against my face before sliding the head across my lips.

I groaned and rolled over onto my stomach with my head pillowed on my arms. "Oh, please, Cat!" I pleaded. "I've never liked that sort of thing! It makes me a little sick just thinking about it. I know every woman on Statzeel seems to think it's the greatest fun ever, but cocksucking has never been one of my favorite pastimes."

"They *did* seem to enjoy it," Cat agreed. "I never asked them to do it to me, and it did not seem to me that the other males made them do it either. It was…voluntary."

"Oh, what do a bunch of stupid slave women know?" I protested, raising my head to look up at him. "They've probably all been bred to enjoy it."

"Possibly," Cat said. "But I did not have to be bred to enjoy it, Jacinth. Perhaps you will find my cock to be more to your liking than that of other males."

"I gotta tell ya, Cat," I began, eying said cock rather doubtfully. "I don't think that thing will fit in my mouth. In fact, I'm surprised it fit anywhere else either."

"It is more…flexible than it appears," Cat informed me. "But you do not have to take it all in your mouth. Just lick me."

I put my head down and groaned again. "Well, all right, if you insist," I said reluctantly. "Maybe just a taste…"

Apparently that idea found favor with Cat, for when I raised my head from my arms, it was right there in front of my face again, and it was dripping with moisture. I stuck out my tongue rather gingerly and licked the edge of the corona, catching a bead of fluid as it was about to fall. It didn't taste like much of anything, not even salty or sweet.

"There!" I said. "Are you happy now? I certainly hope so because I am not, and I repeat *not*, going to suck you off! I—" Gasping as a powerful orgasm hit me right in the pit of my stomach, I exclaimed breathlessly: "Holy shit, Cat! What the devil was that? Well, I mean, I know what it was, but why did—hey, listen, what's *in* that stuff?"

"Something that you like very much, it would seem," he replied, sounding rather pleased with himself. "Have some more." His cock pulsed and another wave of fluid flowed from the points of the corona.

This time I took a firm swipe of it with my tongue, and as before, moments later, I got hit with another climax. "Whoa, momma!" I said excitedly, my entrepreneurial spirit taking flight. "We've got to bottle that stuff! It would sell like hotcakes on any planet in the galaxy!"

Cat was more cautious. "It may have to be fresh in order to work correctly."

"Details, details," I grumbled. "Why don't you just shut up and give me some more."

Cat pumped out another dose and I sucked his whole cockhead into my mouth. He was right: it *was* more flexible than it looked—didn't taste bad, either. Sort of like hazelnuts, actually. I went on for a few minutes, noting that the orgasms did not abate, nor did there seem to be any upper limit to the number of times it could happen.

"That's amazing, Cat!" I said rather breathlessly. "I think I could do that, well, several times a day at least, and not get tired of it."

"So you are not made ill by the thought of doing it?"

"No, not really," I admitted. "In fact, you even taste good! By the way, what do you call that drippy stuff that sets off orgasms?"

He shook his head. "It does not have a name," he replied.

"Oh, come on! You've got to be kidding me! Something that good has to have a name!" Then another thought occurred to me. "Hey, are you the only one to have that effect on women, or did all of your men have it?"

"We were all capable of producing the same fluid, though I have heard that some men were more…effective than others."

"And you're the only one left," I muttered ruefully. "Gee whiz, Cat! You guys would have been very popular on Earth—or probably anywhere else you went."

"With women, perhaps," he replied cautiously. "My race was destroyed by men."

"Jealous men, too, I'll bet." I took another experimental lick and waited. It took about thirty seconds and then another orgasm blossomed into full flower. "That is just so cool!" I exclaimed. "Hey, what does your cum taste like? Well, you probably wouldn't know that, would you? What I mean is, does it do anything to women?"

"My cum?" he repeated.

"Yes, bird-brain! You know, your semen."

He still appeared to be mystified.

"Oh, come on, don't tell me you've never heard that one before! Semen is the correct term, of course, but cum is one of those words that's used almost universally—that and about fifty other euphemisms I could name—and that's just in the English language. There are about a bajillion others, too." Obviously I was going to have to get as technical as I had when explaining the word "snot." "What I'm referring to is the, um," I paused, searching for the right word. "well, you know, the fluid that carries your sperm. What do you call it?"

The light seemed to dawn in his eyes. "Snard," Cat replied promptly.

"That's all, just snard? You don't have any other words for it? No slang?"

"No," he replied evenly. "There is no other word for it in my language."

"That's odd, why not?"

"No other word is necessary."

"Well, you're probably right about that," I admitted. "I'll have to say this about your people, you are unique in that respect. Everyone else has a whole slew of things they call it. Well, snard it is, then. Could you give me some? I want to see if it does anything."

Cat grinned. "It makes children," he said.

"I know that!" I said witheringly. "I want to find out what it tastes like, and if it causes orgasms, too. So go for it, Cat. Let me have it. Fuck me in the mouth until you come."

"Come where?"

"In my mouth, you idiot! I want you to come in my mouth. You know, ejaculate some snard into my mouth so I can taste it." I couldn't believe I actually said that. First time for everything, I suppose.

Cat was purring like crazy as he crawled up over me and slid his big, ruffled, hazelnut-flavored cock into my mouth and began fucking. From his pre-cum alone, I was having an orgasm about every thirty seconds as I sucked him. And when he finally ejaculated, I had an even bigger, more intense orgasm, followed by a strong sense of euphoria. Unlike the other fluid, his "snard" was slightly sweet and had a sort of creamy texture. Then I realized that I had nothing to compare it with because I'd never done that with anyone else before, so I couldn't have said it was any different from that produced by any other species—well, in flavor, at least. I was fairly certain that the orgasmic effect was quite unique, and it did make me sort of sleepy, which was probably why Cat hadn't wanted to do it in the morning. I wasn't completely incapacitated, however—at least not to the point that I couldn't travel. I didn't want to, of course, but that didn't necessarily mean I couldn't.

He did something else which seemed rather unique. Looking at him at essentially point blank range, I was able to observe then what I had only felt the night before when he had climaxed inside me. The scalloped edge of his cockhead began to undulate after he ejaculated, moving in a steady wave around the circumference of his shaft. It was fascinating to watch and I remained transfixed until it subsided.

It goes without saying that all of this explained why he'd been so popular in the restaurant that night, and also why all the other women had thought I was so lucky to have him. It was no wonder he'd had three women devouring him at once; what was surprising was that there hadn't been more of them! I was beginning to think that the collar and leash thing was a damn good idea after all, though it was a miracle I'd gotten out of there with him still chained to me!

Ranata and her rescue were totally forgotten as I rolled Cat over onto his back and lay with my face between his legs and gazed up at that fabulous cock, inhaling its heady aroma and having orgasm after orgasm as the ruffle continued to ooze small droplets of slippery fluid that slid down the shaft and onto my waiting tongue. I was becoming totally addicted and intoxicated and I figured that at some point one of the orgasms would probably just kill me.

Eventually, however, Cat decided that he'd had enough of being teased and got up and nailed me again. Of course, I understood now why I'd had so many orgasms the night before, for, apparently, the same effect could be had from either oral or vaginal contact with his coronal fluid. I decided that it must be absorbed directly through the mucous membranes and go straight into the bloodstream causing an orgasm as soon as it reached the brain. The only limiting factor seemed to be the absolute refractory period required before I could climax again.

It was no wonder that his planet had been destroyed! No male in the known universe could possibly compete with the men of his species when it came to pleasing females, and, apparently, I had the only one—or at least one of the very few!—of them left alive. Talk about your hot commodities! And I had only paid five lousy credits for him! I mean, he would have been a steal at five hundred! That deal would have to go down as absolutely the best bargain I'd ever made in my life—maybe even better than the hundred credits I'd paid for the Shoe-maker in a Box!

Finally, we got around to getting up for breakfast, although I have no idea why, because I wasn't the slightest bit hungry and could have stayed there in that tent with Cat for the rest of the day, never caring if I so much as tasted a morsel of food ever again—or ever found Ranata. Sex of any kind tended to cloud my judg-ment, but sex with Cat had turned me into some kind of nymphomaniacal wonderwoman.

No, at the moment, the quest for my sister didn't seem like such a pressing matter. I reminded myself once again that I had yet to see a single female here that seemed even moderately discontented. Perhaps Ranata was happy—just as happy as all of the other women seemed to be. It could be that there was a good side to this slavery thing after all. Bondage had been a turn-on for many people throughout recorded history, and though this particular society may have carried it a bit further than most, I had to admit that it seemed to work

for them. Maybe Ranata's owner wasn't too much of an
asshole, and maybe she actually liked him—or even
loved him. Of course, I seriously doubted that she had a
man with a cock like Cat's, but maybe she liked sucking
on him just the same.

After breakfast we headed for Ranata's house. As we
walked along, I found that I truly liked having Cat no
more than a chain's length away from me—although we
were usually even closer than that. Cat either held my
hand or had his arm around me for most of the journey
that day, and I didn't even get annoyed by the pack-
droid's singing. It was then that I decided that whoever
designed the damn thing must have been in love—who
else could stand it?

We seemed to be coming out of the depths of the
jungle at last, though with the rain of the night before,
the humidity had dropped considerably and, as a result,
the heat was more tolerable. The road was a little muddy,
though, and I converted my slippers to something a bit
sturdier. By midday, the trees along the road had thinned
out quite a bit, and we stopped for lunch alongside a
meandering stream bordered with cool, grassy banks
that even the jungle didn't seem to encroach upon. We
built a fire and feasted on grilled tiger-pig as though we
hadn't a care in the world. It was peaceful and idyllic,
and I was beginning to understand what Cat meant by
feeling laetralant, for I seemed to be experiencing it
myself for perhaps the first time. We were no longer two
virtual strangers on a rescue mission; we were two
newlyweds on our honeymoon, or on a journey to visit
my sister whom my new husband had never met. The

idea that such a journey might be fraught with danger was the farthest thing from my mind, so when a pack of Nedwuts came down the road, I was completely unprepared for their attack.

I had brought Tex and his companion, Slim, the pulse rifle, with me, but the rifle was on the pack-droid and Cat still had Tex in his pocket. I had no idea how good he might be with a pulse pistol, but as good as he was with a sword—and he *had* been a soldier at one time—I had to assume that he was at least somewhat familiar with a variety of weapons.

As it turned out, I needn't have worried. Cat had the pistol in his hand before the Nedwuts even saw us, warned by all the racket they made coming down the road. We could have tried to disappear into the jungle, but by the time I thought of it, it was too late; they were riding hard and came upon us pretty quickly. Unfortunately, they had their own weapons in hand as well.

There were six of them, all mounted, all armed to the teeth, and all snarling at us. I hadn't seen any of them in the town, nor had I seen any other signs of trouble except for the occasional crabby native male, and it seemed out of place for such ugly, hateful creatures even to be present on such a beautiful planet. Then I remembered that those tiger-pigs had been pretty nasty, and it made me wonder if the Nedwuts liked them as pets. If that was so, then they were bound to be unhappy, since the roasted carcass of one of them was still hanging on the spit above our campfire. They were already breaking at least two laws, for they were all males and not one of them was chained to a female, nor did their clothing meet with the planetary regulations. And that they were pissed off was quite evident, though I don't know which of us provoked them more, an Earth woman, whom they must have known was very valuable on this particular planet, or Cat, who belonged to a race that the Nedwuts believed to have been exterminated—by some of their own kind, no less.

"Well, what have we here?" the leader snarled, reining in. "A Terran and a Zetithian! Both very rare and very valuable. I think we should take them. Don't you agree, boys?"

All of the others nodded and snarled. Of course, if the little bastards thought they could get the two of us without a fight, they had another thing coming! Then I remembered something which might prove to be highly significant, for the last time I'd changed the setting on my pistol was when I'd been threatening Cat with it, and had set it to the lowest possible stun. Nedwuts, on the other hand, were pretty tough and required the highest stun setting, and even that didn't always stop them. If Cat fired and didn't slow them down enough and then had to change the setting, they'd have time to get off a few pulses of their own. Under ordinary circumstances, I would have made a run for the rifle on the pack-droid, but since I was chained to Cat, there wasn't much hope that I'd get there without messing up his aim at the very least.

I took my eyes off of the Nedwuts for one second to get a look at Tex, but as it turned out, I needn't have worried. Good ol' Cat didn't mess around, it seemed, for he had Tex set to kill.

I studied the group carefully as the first Nedwut dismounted and started toward us, while the others followed his lead. He and the one coming up on his left appeared to be the two dominant gang members. I was standing there, trying desperately to think of a peaceable way out of this situation, when Cat methodically began picking them off. He wasn't hiding the fact that he had a pistol aimed at them, so I guess the Nedwuts hadn't reckoned on my Cat being the type to shoot first and ask questions later. After the two in the forefront were down, the remaining four didn't hang around to discuss their future plans in committee, for they all made a hasty retreat back to their horses and took off at a gallop, kicking up the proverbial cloud of dust as they rode away.

"Well, gee whiz, Cat!" I exclaimed. "Why didn't you just kill all of them? They're bound to come after us, you know. Once they regroup and have time to think about how mad they are and choose a new leader, they'll come back. Not that I blame you for killing a few of them, you understand, but this could make the rest of our journey a little dicey."

Cat gave me a sidelong glance with his glittering eyes. "I could have killed more of them, but we only needed two horses."

"Oh…yeah," I said, considerably taken aback. Cat was pretty good at plotting strategy, it seemed. I was beginning to wonder if he'd been more than just a foot soldier. "Good point! So, what, are you saying you're willing to ride, now?"

"If our enemies are mounted, then we should be as well," he said reasonably.

While this sounded perfectly logical to me, it had also been just as logical for us to have been riding horses to begin with! "Now, wait just a doggone minute here!" I said. "You were pretty damned adamant about not riding before. Mind telling me why?"

Cat didn't answer right away, and it appeared that he was going to be every bit as stubborn about telling me why he wouldn't ride as he had been in refusing to do so at all.

"Come on, Kittycat!" I cajoled. "What's the matter? Afraid of the big, bad, horsies?"

Cat's eyes narrowed as he directed a rather scathing look at me. "I am not afraid of them."

"Well then what was the big deal about riding one?"

Cat must have been pretty well irritated at my line of questioning because he actually growled at me! "I did not wish to ride while wearing these...clothes."

"Well, why not? Everybody else does!" Then it hit me. "You didn't want to ride with your nuts hanging out, did you?"

"No," he said, biting off the word. "I did not."

"Well, for heaven's sake, Cat!" I exclaimed. "How the hell do you think it's gonna feel for me to ride without wearing any underwear? I mean, my bare butt is gonna be in the saddle! At least you have pants on!"

Cat appeared to consider this. "I had not thought of that," he admitted. "Perhaps it would be permissible for you to wear other clothing when you ride."

"I didn't notice any of the natives wearing anything different, although they may have had on a divided skirt. I'll admit, I was a little too overwhelmed at the sight of horses at all to pay any attention to what the riders themselves were wearing. Anyway, I'm willing to try it. I can always put on my overalls or a pair of shorts and hope no one sees me. But you, well, I think you'll just have to get over it."

While we were talking, the pack-droid proved its worth once more. The robotic section detached itself and went off to catch the two horses that were straying near the camp, taking advantage of the opportunity to graze on the tender green grass growing along the banks of the stream. It was surprising that it didn't frighten them, making me wonder if the droid had worked with horses before and knew how to approach one without scaring it. Of course, knowing how to catch a horse was one thing, keeping up with one was another. I'd never done anything more than walk with the droid before, myself, so I had no idea if it could keep up with a galloping horse—or even one moving no faster than a trot.

Cat and I dragged the two dead Nedwuts off into the underbrush and packed up what gear we had out and then went to mount up, which required taking our chain off. I hoped we didn't meet anyone else on the way, though the best I could tell, we were more than halfway there, and we could probably get off the road if we saw anyone else coming. The trouble was that a road through the jungle isn't exactly what you'd call a wide open and highly visible space; other people might come upon us before we realized we weren't alone anymore. We would have to keep our eyes peeled.

I was surprised to find that whatever material the saddles were made of was actually quite comfortable to

my essentially bare behind, and we set off at a brisk
trot—fortunately in the opposite direction from the one
that the Nedwuts had taken. The pack-droid kept right on
singing, but it also kept up with us without any apparent
difficulty. I was starting to feel downright kindly toward
the damn thing, although if it picked up another rock, I
would have considered junking it now that we had
horses to ride.

Cat rode a horse like he'd been on one (or something
like it) before, and let me tell you, the vision of Puss in
Boots on a big, black horse was nothing short of breathtaking. Aside from that, I was tickled to death just to get
the opportunity to ride a horse again myself. The
Nedwuts had each had a pulse rifle in a scabbard
attached to their saddles, so we were now much better
armed than we'd been before. I must say, it felt pretty
good to be riding toward the place where my sister was
being kept with Cat and horses and that much firepower.
It made me feel as though we were nearly invincible.
Ranata was as good as rescued, and could ride double
with me on the way back—or maybe I should ride with
Cat so we could wear our chain again. Either way, we
would be on our way home and it would be very good to
get back to Earth. My ship could make the trip almost
non-stop if we didn't push it too hard. The fuel cell was
good for another twenty years, but we might make a few
stops along the way, just for fun. I laughed to myself as
I tried to remember the last time I'd been anywhere just
for the fun of it, because I couldn't come up with one—
not in recent memory, anyway. I'd had plenty of money
before Ranata was taken, but I realized now that I'd

never enjoyed any of it. Aside from my ship, I didn't have much to show for it and had never simply taken a vacation. There had always been deals to make and things to sell, and taking a vacation all alone didn't hold much appeal for me.

But now, I would have my sister back and I would have Cat, who had promised to stay with me forever. Life would be better now: it certainly couldn't be much worse, and certainly no more lonely. And I *had* been lonely and alone for most of my life. Ranata had gone with me on a few trading runs from time to time—the most noteworthy of which being the time she was taken—but mostly, I'd been on my own. There was another factor to be considered, though, for being alone had at least one advantage, which was that I'd seldom had to worry about anyone's safety but my own, and one of the few times I had, I'd managed to lose my little sister.

In this particular episode, I have to admit that I had been far more concerned about Cat being taken by the Nedwuts than I would have been for myself. At least on this planet, I might have been a valuable commodity, but only if I were alive and well, and they would have taken care to keep me all in one piece in order to sell me. Cat, on the other hand, belonged to a race that the Nedwuts obviously wanted eliminated entirely, so I had no hopes that they would merely sell him into slavery on another world. Like he said before, if any Nedwuts had known of his existence, he probably would have been hunted down and killed long ago—a thought which made it that much more imperative to get him back to a region of space where Nedwuts weren't welcome. Earth, for example, wouldn't allow any of them to land, and with good reason. Of course, once it became known that they were responsible for the destruction of Cat's planet, they might not be welcomed anywhere. I say welcomed, though if the truth be told, they were barely tolerated on most planets. This information could possibly get them banned from setting foot on any decent planet in the galaxy. Or so I hoped.

We made good time on horseback and reached the outskirts of a small village before nightfall. I tossed Cat the end of my leash as we approached and we slowed to a much more sober pace, riding closely beside one another, something which got my blood singing just a bit. His, too, because the closer I got to him, the more aroused he became.

We found a stable for the horses and a hotel for ourselves, which was nice since I didn't exactly relish the notion of camping out again with those damned bugs dive-bombing the tent all night long, even though they had thinned out a bit as we left the jungle behind and approached the town. Besides, I really wanted a nice, quiet, comfortable place to spend the night with my Cat, especially now that I knew how fabulous sex with him could be. In fact, I was considering getting started right away, but Cat thought we should hang out with the locals for a bit to see if we could get more information about Ranata. This close to where she lived, he reasoned, at least some of the people might have seen her out and about and be able to tell us something.

We found a safe lock-up for the pack-droid and went out for dinner. I told Cat he'd better not plan on staying out too late, or I was gonna end up doing him in the restaurant. I thought he looked ever so slightly smug when I mentioned that, although, seeing as how everyone else did it, why couldn't we?

The eatery in the village wasn't nearly as posh as the one near the spaceport, but two things remained the same. One: the food was good, and two: there was sex of some kind or another going on at every table. They didn't have a live band, so there was no dancing; but that didn't seem to slow anyone down, and the style of dress was essentially the same as it had been in the larger city. Once again, Cat and I attracted a fair amount of attention, but at least no one thought that fucking my nose would be a fun thing to try. I sat next to Cat this time after I discovered that sitting across the table from one another as we had been before was an open invitation for others to wander over and try their luck. Sitting next to him, no one bothered either of us, although some people did stop by our table to chat.

During the course of our conversations with the other patrons, we discovered that there was another human female besides Ranata living nearby. I wondered if I should attempt to rescue her as well, but, you know, the more I hung around with the people of that planet, the less I believed that anyone needed rescuing. Everybody we saw or talked to seemed very happy, indeed. I had to admit that I wasn't feeling quite so uncharitable toward them myself, even if one of them did have my sister, because they were all very nice. I'd realized after a bit that the females were as free to talk with anyone as the males were, and I got into a conversation with a couple of them who were on their way back from the ladies' room—this was one time, it seemed, when it was permissible to let your woman go it alone and be off her leash, something I hadn't noticed when we were out before. I did notice the occasional female leaving her man in the company of another woman while she was gone, though, and no one seemed to mind sharing their mates with others, trusting souls that they were. I, myself, wasn't quite so generous, and I wouldn't have dreamed of leaving Cat alone with one of them. They might decide they liked multiple orgasms, too, and chain themselves to him—assuming that they could get the key from their own males, of course.

I was coming back from the restroom when I saw that Cat had struck up a conversation with an older male from some other world. He seemed to know of Cat's species and had been anxious to speak with him.

"It was a terrible tragedy!" the man was saying. "I've never found any others of your kind since then, and I have traveled through space for many years. It could be, my friend, that you are the only one left."

"The Nedwuts made certain of that," Cat replied, "for it was no accident that the asteroid struck my planet. It was an act of war."

The man appeared much stuck by this statement. "If that is so, we should let it be known throughout the galaxy! I will spread the word as much as I am able, for the Nedwuts are hated by many, and this would provide good reason for banning them from space travel."

"If it could be enforced," I put in as I approached. "The damned Nedwuts are everywhere!" I regarded the man with interest. "How is it that you know so much about

Zetith?" I asked curiously. "I've been in space for some time now, and I'd never even heard of it until I found Cat."

The man smiled at my ignorance. "Oh, it happened many years ago, of course, but Zetith was a very distant planet, so far from here that most who travel in this region of space have never even heard of it. Until now, it was simply a planet which was destroyed by a terrible accident and has, regrettably, been mostly forgotten. I'm afraid that it is little more than a legend now, having been so far away and with so few of its people left to remind us of them."

"Well, we have Cat now," I said, smiling. "And anyone who meets him will remember him, if not his planet, don't you think?"

"They will," the man replied gravely. "Zetith should not be forgotten, especially not now that the truth about its destruction is known. It was a heinous crime that should not go unpunished. I will do my best to see that it is done." He smiled at me kindly. "You, however, have another responsibility, my dear, for you must take great care of him. He is very precious."

I smiled at Cat, who seemed to be rather embarrassed by this discussion. "I know," I said. "Very precious, indeed."

I didn't know who this guy was, of course; he could have been nobody, or he could have been someone people would actually listen to. I had no way of knowing, but just hearing him say that was comforting. I would love to get rid of the Nedwuts, if only for the sole purpose of ensuring that they never bothered Cat again. I started to tell our new friend that we had, in fact, killed a couple of them that very afternoon, but even though it had been in self-defense, I had no idea what view the laws of Statzeel would take on such a matter. The way I saw it, it was probably best not to mention it. If one of the other Nedwuts filed a complaint about Cat killing a couple of them, we might have to answer some questions, but those guys didn't exactly strike me as having been law-abiding citizens, so I rather doubted that they would go to the authorities. I, myself, had no desire to explain that we were here to take my sister back home. I had an idea that getting kicked off the planet might be the least of what we'd get for doing that!

Having heard what Cat had been telling the man, I realized there was a great deal of Cat's life that I had left unexplored. I knew virtually nothing of his youth and, other than his having been a soldier and then captured, I realized I knew very little about his life before he became a slave, and even less about what came after.

"How long were you a slave, Cat?" I asked gently.

Cat smiled grimly. "The Cylopean was not my first master," he replied. "He was merely my last. I have been enslaved since I was seventeen of our years, and I am forty years old now—or so I believe. Years are of different lengths on different worlds, but I have been a slave for a very long time."

And had at least one scar to show for every year of his servitude! My poor, poor Cat! "They never broke your spirit, though, did they?"

"No," he replied, smiling at me, "for I always had hope. Hope that I would find a good and kind master who would love me. Someone much like yourself."

"Aw, now you're sweet-talking me again, Cat!" I complained. "You don't have to butter me up anymore! I already love you."

Cat smiled and said nothing further, but he began purring in my ear.

"So, how long had it been since you had sex?" I asked curiously. "Since before you were a slave?" If that were the case, it was no wonder he'd been so horny when I bought him!

"Not that long," he admitted. "But since before I was bought by the Cylopean—perhaps five years."

I gave a low whistle. "Whoa! Want to make up for lost time?" It had easily been longer than that for me, but that was my choice, and as much as Cat seemed to like it, it must have seemed like a very long wait, indeed!

"If that means what I believe it does, then yes, I do," he replied. "If you are willing."

"Oh, I'm willing," I assured him. "In fact, I'm more than just willing! Just in case you haven't noticed, you've got me hooked on you now, Kittycat."

He purred loudly enough that a woman at the next table glanced up at him with a worried expression. She relaxed again when I leaned in and kissed Cat gently on the lips.

"Ever do it in a public restaurant?" I whispered seductively in his ear.

"No, I have not," he replied. "But I believe I would like to."

"Mm-m, good answer."

Chapter Ten

I WANTED TO FEEL THAT SAME SENSE OF RELIEF WHEN Cat thrust inside me that I had on the previous night, but I was afraid that being close to him and touching him would somehow diminish the intensity of that feeling, so I moved away from him ever so slightly and let myself just look at him. His dark spiral curls were gleaming in the dim glow from the candle on our table, and a similar fire glittered within the pupils of his dark, smoldering eyes. I reached out and pulled back the edges of his shirt and vest, revealing his chest, and I leaned down to lick his nipples, forgetting for a moment that I was only intending to look at him, but he was simply impossible for me to resist. I sighed as I thought about all the things I hadn't done with him yet: hadn't gone swimming with him in a cool, sparkling lake, hadn't held his hand on a beach at sunset, or made love with him by a flickering fire. I wanted to do all of those things and more, and I wanted to do them with him and him alone.

My desire was becoming more and more intense with each passing moment as the sun went down and darkness fell in the world outside the cozy little restaurant. I glanced down at his cock to make sure it was ready for me, but I needn't have wondered for it was already thick and hard and the coronal fluid was flowing profusely across the apex of the head and down the shaft. Some of it had already dripped onto Cat's breeches, and I thought it was simply a crime to waste any of it. I considered asking some of the other women to help me, but only for a moment, for I'll admit to having been a bit greedy where Cat's fluids were concerned. I wanted them all for myself.

Reaching down, I touched it with a fingertip and brought it up to my lips. As before, an orgasm followed shortly thereafter, rolling over me in waves of pleasure until it subsided and I was able to relax again. I would wait for a while, I decided, instead giving Cat as much pleasure as I could before indulging myself further. After so many years of slavery, I felt that he deserved all the pleasure I could possibly give him. I would devote my life to his enjoyment, I decided, for his joy was my joy. His smile would be my source of delight. His climax would bring me to greater heights knowing how he had suffered before I found him. And if he wanted sex in a public place, well, by golly he could have it, and I would make as big a show of it as I possibly could.

"Mm-m, Kittycat, you make me so hot!" I murmured. "I like to feel you purring when I touch you."

"And I like it when you touch me, Jacinth."

"Well, that's good, because I'm finding it harder and harder to keep my hands off you all the time. In fact, if we hadn't been set upon by Nedwuts, I probably would have pounced on you there by the stream. It was a lovely place, wasn't it?"

"Yes, it was," he agreed. "But not so lovely as you."

"Aw, you're sweet-talking me again!" I said accusingly. "You don't have to do that, you know. You've got me now. I don't need to be convinced anymore."

"But I like sweet-talking you," he purred. "It makes you smile, and I like the way you smile."

"Mm-m, kiss me, Kittycat," I urged him. "Make all the women in this joint pea-green with envy and all the men wish they had even half of your charisma."

Cat took a deep breath and shook his head. "Do not make me seem too…charismatic? Is that the right word?"

"Yes," I replied. "You're pretty good with languages, aren't you?"

"I have been required to learn many languages in my lifetime."

I nodded. Who knew how many planets he'd been on in that length of time? "So, tell me, Cat. Why can't you be too charismatic?"

"I believe it was one of the reasons my planet was destroyed," he explained. "Possibly because the females of other worlds found their own men wanting once they had been with one of us."

If I hadn't been with one of them myself, I would have been chastising Cat for sounding too cocky, but I had no doubt whatsoever that he was telling the absolute truth—though when I'd asked that same question of him once before, he'd hedged a bit.

"Why are you telling me this now, Cat? When I asked before why your planet was destroyed, you said only that there were theories."

"This is my own theory," he replied, "though others shared it. It seems a weak reason for destroying an entire race, but it is the most logical. We were not a warrior race; we did not make war on other planets. It is the only explanation that makes any sense at all. I did not wish to tell you before because you had no such experience with me."

"Afraid I'd think you were bragging?" I asked with a chuckle. "Maybe I would have thought you sounded a little too cocky, but that doesn't mean I wouldn't have believed you. No, my only question is why you've never been the slave of a female."

"Oh, I was," he replied.

"Well, it beats the shit out of me to explain why any woman you ever belonged to would sell you to someone else!" I declared, thinking that they all must have either died smiling or gone completely wacko from the continuous orgasms. "Did they at least keep you happy? Is that why you never tried to escape to freedom?"

He shook his head. "There was nowhere for me to go, Jacinth. When you freed me, I could only follow you, for I had no home to which I could return. But you, my lovely master, you have made me feel as though I have a home with you." The tone of his purr deepened and the glow in his eyes grew softer. "I will never leave your side, for you bring me hope and joy and contentment." He toyed with my leash, easing me closer with it. "This chain we wear keeps us together, but it is not necessary. I would follow you if you ever left me behind, just as I did on Orpheseus. Having seen into your eyes and inhaled your scent, you became a part of me, and I would seek you out whether you be across the room or across the galaxy. We belong together now. Parting from you would mean my death."

"And the other females you've been with?" I asked hoarsely. He was making me feel pretty special, but my skeptical nature resurfaced briefly. "They didn't have this bond with you?"

"No, they did not," he replied. "Only you."

If he was lying, I didn't ever want to hear the truth. "I love you, Kittycat," I whispered, kissing him softly on his full, sensuous lips. "I don't think I would die if you ever left me, but I certainly wouldn't have much of a reason left to live." Ranata had been my reason for living for so long now, I'd almost forgotten that my life could have any other purpose, but I was beginning to remember.

"Then kiss me again, my lovely one," he purred. "Mate with me now and we will show these other fools what it means to love."

My arms entwined themselves around his neck as he shifted me into his lap with his hands firmly grasping my hips. I sighed as I centered his pulsating cock at my entrance and then slid my heated, wet core down over him. Once again I felt that sense of relief, of needs and desires fulfilled, and the promise of better things yet to come. Cat's dark eyes glowed with passionate desire and his nostrils flared as he inhaled my scent.

"Do I smell like someone who loves and desires you?" I murmured.

"Yes, my lovely one, you do," he replied. "Do not change your scent as some women do. You are like wine to my senses, just as you are."

Sighing, I threaded my fingers through his long, luxuriant locks and my lips melted into his. My weight held him deep within me as my legs hung over the sides of his chair. I had nothing to push against to move him inside me, but I knew I didn't need to, for Cat could control his cock like no other male that I knew of— dancing within me without even appearing to move a muscle. Then his coronal fluid began to take effect, and the orgasms began.

I discovered something else about Zetithian males just then, for, apparently, when a female climaxes, it affects them in some way because Cat responded to my squeezing on him with a wave of the serrated ruffle on his cock. I hadn't felt it before because he'd always been actively driving himself into me, but this time, I felt every subtle move he made. The nice thing was, I could sit still on him, kissing him and enjoying the way he purred without having to move if I didn't want to, but I must admit that he seemed to like it very much when I did. I loved the way I could play with his hair, kiss his lips, and caress his chest with my fingertips, and the orgasms just kept coming whether I did anything or not. It was automatic and required no effort to maintain—an ecstasy without price.

"Mm-m, Cat!" I sighed. If I'd been any more content and sated, I would probably have just fallen asleep and slid off onto the floor. We're talking bones to jelly and muscles to mush here. "How on Earth did your people ever get anything done when they could be doing this all the time?"

"Beats the shit out of me," he purred. He paused for a moment before adding: "That was an Earth expression, Jacinth. Are you proud of me?"

"Oh, yes, Kittycat," I said as I lazily licked the side of his neck and teased his earlobe with my tongue. "I'm very proud of my big, brave, sexy, wonderful, intelligent, and very handsome tomcat. Very proud, indeed. I think I'll keep you."

He smiled, showing his sharp, white teeth. "I will give you my snard now," he said, as his breathing became deeper and his face reflected the ecstasy yet to come.

"I don't believe I've ever heard anyone put it quite that way before," I observed. "Actually, a Terran would say, 'I'm coming.'"

"Okay, then, I'm coming," he said reasonably, but the inflection on the last word made me realize that he wasn't just whistling Dixie! Still, he'd also done something else that I'd never yet known him to do.

"Cat!" I exclaimed excitedly. "You used a contraction! I never thought I'd see the day!"

"Sh-h," he said. "I'm coming." His head fell back as his eyes closed and his lips parted in a deep, purring sigh. No roar this time, just an expression of fulfillment as his cock pulsed one more time.

I felt it then, that warm gush of sweet cream that filled me up with his love, followed by the wave of that ruffled corona. It felt intense and intoxicating just as it was, but I wanted to taste him again. I slid off of him and eased down onto the floor between his knees, taking his fabulous phallus in my hand and licking it clean as I had an even more powerful orgasm which caused my own fluids to gush down my thighs and splatter on the floor before splashing back upon my skin.

Cat and I had been having such a lovely time together that I didn't consider that the other patrons might actually notice what we were doing. I'd seen all kinds of openly sexual activity out in public before, and didn't think what we were doing was all that remarkable—I mean, it certainly felt remarkable to me, but I wasn't so sure it was all that obvious to the casual observer. When I glanced up at Cat, however, I was surprised to discover that we not only had an audience, but a highly appreciative one, as well—and also that a good many of them had gathered around to watch. I had been so totally focused on Cat that I hadn't noticed the crowd growing in size. Well, okay, so it wasn't a huge crowd—it wasn't that big a place to begin with—but there were at least a dozen people standing relatively close and actively watching. And that didn't include the score of others that were observing from the comfort of their own tables—or, as in the case of some of the females, the comfort of their own male's prick. Plain and relatively boring pricks, I might add.

"Damn!" I whispered forcefully. "You're absolutely right about being too charismatic, Cat! I'd better get you out of here before the other men decide you're too much of a temptation to their women!" I climbed back up into Cat's lap intending to slide his perpetual hard-on into my waiting pussy. "On the other hand, maybe I should just hide that thing before they get any ideas."

"Where were you planning to hide it?" he asked with a crooked little smile.

"And here I was thinking you were pretty smart!" I said scornfully. "Where do you think I'm gonna hide it, Kittycat?"

"You are not tired of me yet?" Cat purred.

"No," I replied, settling down on his cock. "When I get sick of feeling the earth move, I'll be sure and let you know."

"And is that the only reason you love me?"

"Poor Cat!" I said consolingly. "What's the matter? Are you afraid I think you're only useful as a life-support system for your dick?"

I had never heard Cat really laugh out loud before, but that idea seemed to strike him as being quite funny. He had a nice laugh, too—one I thought I would never tire of hearing. He probably hadn't done much laughing for many years either. I was curious about him, and wanted to know about his previous life, but I feared that he might not wish to remember some of it. I doubted that his whole life had been unpleasant, but the times of fun and love and laughter had to have been few and far between.

"I hope I am more to you than that," he said.

"Oh, you are," I assured him. "Much more! My life hasn't been nearly so hard as yours, Cat, but there hasn't been much in the way of love or laughter, especially since I've been chasing my damned sister across half the galaxy! I have a feeling that things will be different from now on, though." I sighed deeply. "Cat, we know where she is, and no one seems to be volunteering any information about another Terran in the area, and I don't want to make it terribly obvious that I'm trying to find her, just in case someone decides to rat on us to whoever her man is. Let's go back to our room and get some sleep. I find that having an audience doesn't do a whole lot for my enjoyment of you. I prefer to have you all to myself, even the sight of you."

"I believe I like having you to myself, as well," he said. "Mating in public is too much like sharing, and I do not wish to share you with anyone. I wish to be very greedy when it comes to you, Jacinth. You are mine, my lovely master, and I am yours."

We left there a bit later with those words still ringing in my ears. How many times had I cringed at the thought of being owned by someone; how little I had relished the idea that my life might have to revolve around someone else. I had been living my own life for so long that even the thought of sharing it with another had become one of those things that simply never crossed my mind. I had never been one to sit aboard my ship watching the stars flying past and wishing that I had someone there to experience it with me. Never dreamed of being in love and caring for a man. But I did now. It was so odd!

Our room was small, but comfortable, and I went to sleep in Cat's arms after making love one more time and feeling…well…laetralant. And, like he said: there truly is no translation. It was a feeling I'd never had before meeting him, but I thought I could get used to it, and I would do my best, if I could ever just find my damned sister and go home!

The next morning, we were about to pack up and be on our way again when I realized that to allay suspicion, we should probably act like traders and set up shop somewhere—at least for the day. Besides, I kinda liked the little village and wouldn't have minded spending several days there—if we'd had the time. You know: set up the droid in the marketplace, sell a few things and generally relax a bit. Having Cat around sort of made me feel that way, I guess, for you know how relaxed a cat can be. There's something about the way they curl up and purr that makes you want to do the same thing. Of course, after all the trouble we'd had while traveling down the jungle road, I'll admit I wasn't too twerked up about the idea of riding in, nabbing Ranata, and then heading back into the jungle right away.

Not wanting to run back through the jungle was reason enough for sticking around, but also, as I believe I may have mentioned before, the closer I got to finding Ranata, the less urgent I felt about actually doing it. If what I'd seen on Statzeel so far was any indication, I had a pretty good idea that she was most likely safe and sound and had undoubtedly given up all hope of being rescued years ago. And, since she couldn't possibly have known that I was so close, a few more days wouldn't matter—at least not from her perspective. I mean, I was anxious to find her myself, but the only real fear I had at that point was that I might arrive at her house only to discover that I'd been chasing someone else for all those years!

Just hanging around for another day or so sounded so appealing, and the more I thought about it, the less I wanted to hit the road again. So we kept our room at the inn, got the droid out, and set up shop in the market square. We did a lively business selling sunscreen, first-aid ointment, and massage oil—which was very popular with the locals. Cat seemed to get the hang of being a salesman, and even showed some of the customers where his recent wounds had been and went on to explain just how well the Derivian ointment had worked for him. Fortunately, he didn't use the piercing in his cock as an example, or he might have started a bit of a riot. Of course, the fact that it was completely healed by then and he didn't even have a scar to show for having had his cock pierced would have made it seem like a false claim anyway, but I didn't relish the idea of any woman getting close enough to him to smell or touch him, and I certainly didn't want to let anyone taste him! Hell, just having them looking at him was bad enough. It crossed my mind to collect some of his coronal fluid and sell it—giving the occasional free sample to arouse interest, of course—but I wouldn't have wanted to have to explain where it came from, especially given what had happened to Cat's planet because of the stuff. Of course, there wasn't a doubt in my mind that it would sell—and also that the number of sales would subsequently bankrupt the entire community—if Cat could keep up with the demand, that is.

I did a booming business with the Shoemaker in a Box, and with the money we made from that, I bought Cat a sword. And man, oh, man, did he look cool with it hanging from his sash! My only hope was that he wouldn't need it to fight off any more of those tiger-pigs on the way back to the ship. I asked one of our customers about them—the scratches Cat showed her were the ones they had given him the day before—and she told me they were called swergs. She said there had been efforts made from time to time to exterminate them, but that section of the jungle being as dense as it was, they had never been very successful in getting rid of them. I agreed that they needed to be eradicated, the nasty little beasties! Damn things were barely even fit to eat! I might have been able to sell their hides, though, because their dreadlocks were sort of pretty—well, they might have been, if Cat hadn't carved them up so badly when he killed them. We'd have to be sure and shoot them with Tex if we ever decided we wanted to sell the skins.

I had my first direct experience in dealing with one of the local assholes that afternoon. The damned bastard actually accused us of shady dealing and called Cat a liar when he told how he'd gotten scratched up—said nobody could fight off five swergs all alone using only a machete. He didn't believe my Shoemaker in a Box could have fixed Cat's boots either, and swore we'd simply bought him a new pair somewhere else. He was so obnoxious, he even got Cat's dander up just a bit, and for a minute there, I thought they were going to get into an honest-to-God fight! Cat had his new sword, of course, as well as my pulse pistol, so I had no doubts about who would win the fight; but I also realized that roughing up one of the locals might be a damn good way to get ourselves deported. The man had a cute young chick chained to him, but she seemed a bit distracted and didn't make any of the usual moves to placate him.

It occurred to me then that maybe he had to ask her first, though the best I could tell at other times, it seemed to be practically an automatic response. A quick glance in her direction was enough to inform me that she hadn't intervened as yet because she was too busy staring at Cat's cock and hadn't been paying attention to the fact that her master and my Cat were about to come to blows. Cat and I had our stuff set out on a table and we were both standing behind it, so to get her attention I leaned over and rattled my chain on the table. Our eyes met when she glanced up and I rolled my eyes in the slime-ball's direction and gave her one of those "Do something, already!" looks.

She reacted so fast I'm surprised she didn't pull the guy's short hairs when she grabbed his dick. As for me, I almost laughed out loud when I realized that in stooping down to rattle my chain, I was in a pretty good position to give Cat a few licks, myself. His erection seemed to be missing for once—I guess getting pissed off didn't arouse him in that fashion—so I just sucked in the whole damn thing at once.

I didn't look up to see his face, but his penis responded almost instantly, swelling up to the point that I was forced to either back off or let it slide down my throat. I decided that backing off was the more prudent course of action since I had a feeling I might never be able to swallow normally again if I didn't. A sidelong glance at the other guy was enough to prove that his woman was doing a pretty good job of distracting him, too, and I couldn't believe just how quickly it worked to shut him up—both of them, actually, although Cat had never gotten to the point of being mouthy, anyway; he just sort of glowered at the other man and kept fingering his sword hilt. But still, all in all, it was downright amazing! The funny thing was, that after smiling in a rather apologetic fashion, the girl winked at me. Not wanting to seem stupid, I winked back at her, which seemed to have been the correct response.

I didn't ask anyone to verify this, of course, but after that, I decided that the women here must be just like women everywhere, and that they probably got together for lunch once a week to talk about all the stupid things their men had been up to. The more I thought about the incident, however, the more convinced I became that the man in question had gotten mad at Cat because the girl was looking at his dick and it didn't have anything to do with whether or not he truly thought that Cat was a liar. I really had to get Cat off this planet and into a pair of pants that didn't have a hole in them! That cock of his made all the others seem plain in comparison, and I certainly didn't want to see him end up getting killed because of it.

In the end, Cat sold them some Candalian tooth jelly and they finally wandered off.

"Fuckin' scumbag," I muttered as he and his chick walked away. "You know, I just don't get it, Cat. Why do so many men have to act like that?"

To my surprise, Cat didn't seem the least bit angry anymore, and actually seemed to be mildly amused. "Like scumbags, you mean?" Cat asked, "Or would slimeball be more accurate?"

I thought about this briefly before replying. "Same thing, essentially," I said. "Although I suppose a scumbag would be a slimeball in a sack."

"And which of them is worse?"

"You know, I never thought much about it, although scumbag might be a slightly neater version of a slime-ball. Shit, maybe there *is* a difference, after all."

"So a slimeball is worse, then?"

"Yes, I believe it is," I agreed.

Cat nodded solemnly. "Then he would be a slimeball, I think."

Which gave me a serious case of the giggles. "Oh, Cat!" I exclaimed. "I do love you. You aren't a slime-ball—or a scumbag!—and you're so much fun!"

"And totally hot and sexy?" he prompted.

"Where the devil did you hear that?" I demanded. "Did I ever say that about you? I can't remember."

"No, it was two young girls who were here getting new shoes."

"Those kids said that about you?"

"I do not believe they realized that I could hear them," he said. "But I did."

"Oh, God, Cat! You've even got the teeny-boppers hot after your ass! No doubt about it, we have *got* to get you off this planet!"

"But I like it here," Cat objected, his voice dropping to become more of a purr.

"And why is that?"

"Well, I have only to pretend to be angry, and then you will—"

"Dammit, Cat!" I snapped at him. "He was impugning your honor! Called you a liar and everything! Do you mean to tell me you weren't really mad?"

"No," he replied. "And I am not certain that the other man was either."

I gazed thoughtfully after the couple who had just left us. They had drifted over to the far side of the square by then, but the girl still had her hand on the man's dick, and was stroking it quite effectively—so much so that he ejaculated a moment or two later.

"Son of a *bitch*!" I said slowly and with a great deal of feeling. "You know something, Cat? Maybe these guys aren't quite so stupid after all…"

Cat just shrugged and smiled an innocent little Kittycat smile. He might have been pretending, but at least he'd been honest about it—which still made him better than just about any other man I'd ever known.

"…but I still think you're smarter," I added.

Cat's eyebrows rose ever so slightly, and he tilted his head curiously. "Why do you say that?"

"There's a fine line between being teased and being manipulated, but it makes a big difference in the way another person feels about the one doing the teasing or the manipulating. You don't cross the line the way these guys seem to do. I do what I do with you because I want to, not because I have been forced into it or simply given no other alternative. The difference in the way I feel is that I love the way you tease, as opposed to resenting the way another might manipulate. Does that make any sense?"

Cat nodded. "The difference is love," he said. "Not domination or control."

"You got it," I said, unable to resist smiling at him.

A ghost of a smile played across his lips. "But I am your slave," he reminded me. "You own me."

"No I don't, Cat," I replied. "I love you. There's a difference. I set you free and yet you came back to me. The fact that you did that means more than you will ever know."

"And you could have left me in the dust of Orpheseus," he returned. "But you did not, my lovely Jacinth. You chose to take me with you, and to a man who has been bought and sold many times, that means much."

"Oh, I couldn't have just gone off and left you there, Cat!" I protested. "Not the way you were then! You know, even before the auction I considered buying you just so I could let you go."

"You are fiery and stubborn," he said with a knowing smile, "but your heart is kind, and I love you, and I will go on loving you always."

I couldn't recall whether or not he'd ever said the words before, but it didn't matter one bit because I certainly heard him that time, and I remember it still—as well as the soft, loving kiss that followed.

Chapter Eleven

WE LEFT THE VILLAGE THE NEXT MORNING AND TOOK the rest of the trip in easy stages, stopping for lunch and chatting companionably along the way. I was feeling so much at peace with the world that even the droid's singing didn't bother me—much. It was beginning to seem like background music, though I suppose that the distance provided by being on horseback helped considerably. While we were in town, I'd paid attention to the other riders, and noted that men and women who weren't riding the same horse were never chained together, so I guess they had some sense after all! I hated to think what would have happened to me if Cat had fallen off his horse; I'd have wound up with a broken neck at the very least! I'd also taken note of their clothing, and, as I'd hoped, the ladies were wearing divided skirts when they rode astride. I bought one the first chance I got.

I learned a lot about Cat during that ride. He opened up, telling me about his life before the wars on Zetith— he had *nine* brothers and sisters!—and some of the things that had happened in the years since. His life as a slave hadn't always been so bad, but he'd seen some rough servitude—and most of his scars had come after his life as a soldier rather than during that time, except for the scar on his face which he had acquired in, of all things, a training match with one of his comrades.

"What a letdown!" I exclaimed when he told me. "Couldn't you have come up with a better story than that?"

"But it is the truth!" he reminded me. "You would not wish for me to lie, would you?"

"Well, no, but if I had a scar like that, I think I'd come up with a more exciting story to explain how I got it, like I was fighting to save the life of some damsel in distress, or defending my family, or, oh, I don't know, something more…romantic! Not just that the guy I was sparring with was a klutz!"

Cat heaved a rather exasperated sigh. "What is a klutz?"

"Sorry, Cat," I apologized. "I keep forgetting you don't understand but about half of what I say. A klutz is someone who is clumsy and awkward and does stupid things like hitting his friend in the face with a sword."

"Well, you are right, then," Cat agreed. "He *was* a klutz." He smiled at the memory. "I have not thought about him for many years. He was a good friend. He was killed in the fight in which I was taken prisoner."

"Poor Cat!" I said, tears stinging my eyes. "You've lost everyone you ever cared about, haven't you?"

"No, I have not," he replied. "That will come when I lose you."

I stared at him, aghast. "You won't lose me!" I insisted. "I don't ever want to leave you, Cat!"

"But you may," he said gravely. "The people of my race are long-lived, and it may be that I will live longer than you, and there may come a time when I will have to watch you die. I do not wish for it to happen, but I know that it may."

I'll admit to feeling relieved by this, for having to watch Cat die was something that I would just as soon not have to endure. Of course, the way the Nedwuts tended to view his kind, one of them might end up killing him before I had the chance to grow old with him, and I didn't like that idea at all! The old man had said that I should take care of him, for he was very precious, and I would. I would kill every Nedwut from here to Xenobia, if that was what it took to keep him safe, for he was precious, very precious indeed.

"Well, humans live a lot longer than they used to, but I'll do what I can to keep myself healthy and out of trouble," I promised him. "It's the best I can do."

This seemed to satisfy him to some extent, but I had a feeling he was still thinking about it. It must be hard to live a long life while those all around you did not. I'd heard many an elderly person complain that all of their friends and loved ones had died, leaving them to go on alone. It would be very sad, indeed, though there would also be the possibility of finding someone new. Perhaps the good would outweigh the bad.

It was late in the afternoon when we came upon a much larger village, situated at the foot of the small mountain where we had been told Ranata lived. Cat and I got a room at the inn and stabled the horses and the droid. Those things were quite easily accomplished— much easier than approaching the house where Ranata was, for I had no idea what the protocol was in this civilization for paying a visit. Could we simply go up and knock on the door, the way you would on Earth, or were we supposed to send a message first? Rude or not, that was definitely out of the question, because we didn't want to warn anyone of our impending arrival—I wasn't about to let Ranata be spirited away from me again, not when I was this close. After all the time and distance that had separated me from my sister, the thought of simply riding up a winding road to the top of a hill to see her seemed like the most difficult part of my journey. My stomach was tied up in knots worrying about how the rest of the story would play out. I knew that one wrong move could blow the whole deal, and I also knew that if I made that move, I would never forgive myself for letting it happen.

Actually, I had yet to forgive myself for letting her be taken in the first place. She had been in my charge, and facing our parents with the news that she had been kidnapped—even over the comlink between Earth and Dexia Four—had been one of the most difficult meetings of my life. I had sworn not to rest until I found her and brought her home, and now, here I was within a mile of her, and I was afraid. Afraid to face her, knowing that I had let her be taken to spend the next six years being bought and sold like nothing better than a goat or a camel. Would she have grown to hate me for what I had let happen to her? While I had been searching for her, these thoughts had never entered my head, but now, at the end of my quest, they tormented me constantly.

At Cat's suggestion, we hung out in the common room of the inn for a while, and, though it pains me to admit it, I was leaning toward the idea of drowning my fears in the local brew. I think Cat understood something of my feelings, because he ordered me a drink—a strong one—and insisted that I drink at least part of it. Knowing how much I disliked the loss of control that comes from any form of intoxication, he didn't push me to drink it all. But I did—an act that further illustrated how close I was to the edge.

I found it odd the way something I normally avoided like the plague could enable me to see the world from a totally different perspective. As I sat there sipping my drink, I asked myself what was the worst that could happen when I met Ranata again. Death is generally considered to be the worst possible outcome of any situation, but in this case, I decided that even if she were to kill me, it would be no more than I deserved.

But this was one of those instances where there truly was a fate worse than death, and Ranata had been living such a life. The fairest trade would be to set her free somehow and then take her place, although doing so wouldn't change the past, and it certainly wouldn't earn her forgiveness. I believe what I feared more than death or slavery was that she would blame me for her fate and recoil from me. Of course, if she did that, it would make it hard to rescue her, and I would have wasted the past six years searching the galaxy for her.

No, I decided, she wouldn't do that. I could at least talk to her. She might be resentful, but, if nothing else, surely she would be able to see me as her ticket back to Earth! She'd be able to tolerate being on a ship with me for that long, wouldn't she? I certainly hoped so, because if she couldn't, I'd either have to tell our parents I'd failed, or I'd have to pay for her passage back to Earth on another ship—though such a thing would probably prove to be impossible. Space travel was common, but nonstop flights across the galaxy from Statzeel to Earth simply didn't exist.

No, if she went home, I'd have to take her, and, that being said, there was nothing left to fear, because if she refused to go with me, I certainly wouldn't return to Earth and tell Mom and Dad that! Of course, then I'd be stuck roaming through space for the rest of my life. It wouldn't be so bad; Cat had promised to stay with me, so I wouldn't be lonely. All things considered, it wouldn't be that much different from what I'd already been doing up to that point. I'd simply keep on doing the same damn thing for the rest of my natural life. And it was just my life, so what did it matter, anyway?

I may have failed to mention the fact that alcohol not only makes me lose control, but tends to make me a bit maudlin whenever I drink to drown my sorrows. It never quite manages to drown them, but rather, gives them a boat upon which to remain afloat. I should have known better than to finish my drink. I'd have to warn Cat not to buy me drinks unless I was already quite giddy with happiness; otherwise, I might end up becoming downright suicidal. Still, in my moderately drunken state, I had managed to convince myself that if Ranata wanted to leave Statzeel, she'd have to do it with me. There was no other choice. She could take it or leave it. All I had to do was give her the option.

Interestingly enough, while I was sitting there staring off into space and planning the rest of Ranata's life for her, Cat kept himself occupied by talking with some other people who were more in the mood for conversation. Many were travelers such as ourselves, but there were some local people, a few of whom actually knew my sister. Cat told me later that he hadn't even needed to ask about her or show her photograph to anyone, because one couple had volunteered the information, even referring to Ranata by name. I suppose they mentioned her because they thought that, being human myself, I should be interested in a person who, for all they knew, would be a complete stranger, just because we happened to hail from the same planet. It was logical, especially since we were so far from home. That we might be sisters probably never crossed anyone's mind, and that I was there to abscond with her—well, they'd have hardly suggested that I visit her if they suspected me of plotting such a thing!

I came out of my reverie eventually, and found that I had relaxed enough to notice that it was quite cozy and comfortable there, as befitted a local hangout that saw a regular business. It reminded me of the neighborhood pubs back on Earth in England, where they'd held onto their traditions for over a thousand years. Nowadays, you might be able to hop across the solar system in a matter of minutes, but going down to the pub for a pint of ale was still a popular pastime. The more I thought about it, the more I realized that I couldn't wait to take Cat to such places on Earth and show him what life was like there. I considered it most unfortunate that he had no home planet to show to me, and I seriously doubted that he would care to return to any planet where he had lived as a slave.

It also seemed that I would be able to introduce him to my sister, for, as I said, once the locals noticed that I was human, they all encouraged us to pay a visit to Ranata. Apparently they knew her and seemed fond of her. Ranata and I looked nothing alike, so there was no reason for anyone to assume that there was any connection between us whatsoever.

The thing I found most odd was that none of them referred to her as being particularly beautiful. In fact, one of the men congratulated Cat because his Earth woman was much better looking than the one up on the hill. I figured it must have been my nose, already proven to be popular with the locals, because I certainly didn't have any other feminine charms to recommend me; I mean, I wasn't called Captain Jack for nothing! I was pretty sure Cat only considered me to be attractive because he loved me—for whatever reason. He'd made that one remark about the fact that I reminded him of the women of his world. Being "fiery and very, very stubborn" didn't seem like much of a reason to fall in love with a woman, but what the hell did I know about the mysteries of the male mind? It wasn't as though I had years of great relationships and experiences to draw from, and men were so fuckin' strange, anyway. The customs of Statzeel illustrated that sad fact better than just about anything I'd ever seen before. I mean, any planet where the guys felt that they had to chain their best women to them was pretty damned strange, if you ask me!

Having presented ourselves as traders, as we had in the previous town, Cat and I decided that setting up shop in the marketplace would be the best way to avoid suspicion. It would be expected of us. If we played our cards right, people should get used to us being around and no one would even notice when we packed up and left town with an extra person in our party.

Oh, who was I trying to kid! Of course they would! As soon as Ranata turned up missing, they would know exactly who had taken her, and probably be able to make a decent guess that we'd headed back to the main space-port in the area. We might end up having to steal her away under cover of night, and though the thought of taking off into the jungle after dark held no appeal for me whatsoever, I was forced to admit that it was probably the only way we could do it without getting caught.

We made a few useful business contacts in the pub, especially after I mentioned some of the products I was carrying. The funny thing was, I would never have guessed that there would be such a market for tooth jelly on that planet, and usually, I can make a pretty good guess as to what will sell just about anywhere I go. I found out later that they didn't use it on their teeth— well, not directly, anyway.

So, at the insistence of everyone in the common room, Cat and I saddled our horses and rode up the hill to visit my sister. As we rode along, I decided that the man she belonged to must have been fairly well off to have paid two thousand credits for her, and the well-tended gardens lining the road seemed to indicate a fair amount of disposable income, as well as a decent-sized work force. I could take some comfort in the fact that if Ranata had to be a slave, she was at least living in a nice place—unless, of course, she was the only one doing the gardening!

I'll have to say that during all the years of my search for my long lost sister, envisioning what she must be suffering, it never once crossed my mind that when I finally found her, she would not only be living in comfort, but would be pregnant. At least, the Earth woman who came out to greet us certainly seemed to be, though if she was Ranata, she sure as hell didn't look anything like I remembered her.

I stared at the approaching woman in disbelief. It had only been six years, but, my God, she looked older than I did! I reminded myself that those six years couldn't have been an easy time for her, but surely—

"Jack?" she squealed when she saw me. "Oh my God! Is it really you?" She rushed up and flung her arms around me, hugging me as tightly as her pregnant belly would allow. She'd recognized me, which was a damn good thing because I wouldn't have known her if I'd passed by her on the street!

My once lovely sister was now painfully thin and frail-looking, and her hair, which I remembered as having been a thick, luxuriant gold, was now wispy and pale. The skin around her eyes was etched with fine lines and she walked with a decided limp. I took one look at her and made a mental note to kill the bastard who'd bought her, for of all the people I'd seen so far on Statzeel, she was the only one who didn't appear to be brimming with good health.

"Ranata?" I croaked. "Sweetheart, are you all right? My God, you're so thin! Don't they feed you?" I was horrified at the change that had been wrought in my beautiful little sister. I felt tears stinging my eyes as I gazed at her, thinking that the scumbag who owned her must be starving her into submission. I knew I would enjoy killing him, slowly and painfully, for not only was he starving her, but for heaven's sake, she was pregnant! Didn't he care how the child would fare with her in such a state? Didn't he worry about that? And being pregnant at all would probably put such a strain on her that she might not live to deliver that child! What an idiot!

"Oh, of course they feed me!" she exclaimed in a voice brimming with laughter. "I eat like a horse all day long—and I see you have a horse, too," she added. "You know, Jack, I was so thrilled to get here and find that they had horses! It was almost like coming home!"

Well, this certainly wasn't what I'd expected to hear from her. I was so taken aback, I was speechless. Fortunately, *she* wasn't.

"Come on in!" she urged us, beckoning us across the threshold. "Just tie your horses there in the shade," she told Cat. "Oh, I can't wait to hear how you managed to find me!"

She bustled inside and into a well-furnished sitting room, summoning someone named Alanna. "Bring some food and drink, if you please," she said. "You'll never believe it, but this is my sister!"

I regained my senses enough to frown at her. "Sh-h, Ranata! Don't say that so loud! I don't want anyone to know I'm here for you!"

"Here for me?" she asked in a puzzled tone. "What do you mean?"

"I *mean*," I whispered as soon as Alanna had gone, "that I'm here to rescue you and take you back to

Earth!" I eyed her dubiously, thinking that she probably couldn't withstand the journey back to the spaceport, aside from the fact that pregnant women had no business riding horses. I decided that I was going to have to land my ship closer, somehow, and take her out that way.

To my surprise, the startled look on her face gave way to an outburst of laughter. "Rescue me?" she squeaked. Her laughter kept her from speaking for a long, heart-stopping moment. "Aren't you a little late?" she went on. "I mean, I've already *been* rescued, Jack! I don't need to be rescued again!"

I glanced over at Cat who appeared to be as mystified as I was. Suddenly, I didn't think my legs would hold me up any longer and sat down heavily in a nearby chair. "Already rescued?" I echoed. "What the hell do you mean by that? I've been on your trail for six years, kid! You can't expect me to believe that your knight in shining armor has already come for you!"

"Oh, but he has!" she said, giggling merrily. "Dantonio isn't exactly a knight, but he's such a sweetie, and I love him dearly, as you can probably tell," she added with a gesture toward her unborn child. "He bought me in a slave auction and brought me here several months ago. He's so good to me, you've no idea."

"Well, you're right about that!" I said, agreeing wholeheartedly. "I have no idea what's going on here whatsoever! You're still a slave, aren't you?"

She appeared to be uncomfortable about answering that question for some reason, for she made no reply, but, instead, glanced briefly at Cat. "Who is this you have with you?" she asked, abruptly changing the subject.

"Oh, this is Cat," I replied. "I, um, bought him a few days ago in a slave auction on Orpheseus Prime. The smuggler I got the lowdown on Statzeel from said to take someone with me to this planet that I could trust, so—" I shrugged my shoulders briefly, "here we are."

She appeared momentarily diverted by this. "*You* bought a *slave*? Really, Jack, I wouldn't have thought that of you!"

"Well, shit!" I exclaimed. "You're a slave, yourself, so it shouldn't surprise you that there are a few others around! Besides," I added, a tad bit defensively, "I freed him as soon as I bought him. He followed me home, though."

Ranata smiled. "Strays always did take to you," she said reminiscently.

I wouldn't have said that Cat had been taken with me at all, in the beginning, but I guess I'd been wrong about that. Perhaps I wasn't quite so unlikeable after all. I shrugged my shoulders in reply as the one named Alanna returned with refreshments.

"Well, Cat," Ranata said carefully. "It's very nice to meet you, but would you care to excuse us for a moment? I have something to tell Jack that I really shouldn't mention in front of you. Alanna will show you to another room for a little bit and give you something to eat. Okay?"

Cat nodded agreeably and followed Alanna out of the room, leaving me to wonder just what horrendous tales Ranata was about to regale me with.

"Okay," I said as soon as they were out of earshot, "tell me everything, Sis. You've really got my curiosity piqued now."

"Well, first of all, thank you for trying to find me for all of these years. It may not seem that way now, but I really *did* need rescuing up until Dantonio found me. Before that, it was…horrible." A shadow crossed her face and she shuddered at the memories of things she'd undoubtedly rather forget.

"No problem," I replied. "I came after you as soon as I got a lead, but you always seemed one jump ahead of me. I came close a lot of times, but then, always, just when I got there, you'd already been taken somewhere else and I had to start all over again. It's not easy to find someone in space, you know."

"I'm sure it isn't," she agreed. "And if I had been you, I'd have given up a long time ago. But now that you've found me, I hate to have to tell you this…but I really don't need you anymore."

I was just slightly pissed at hearing this, let me tell you! "But you're still a slave, Ranata!" I protested. "All the women on this wretched planet are! Are you trying to tell me you don't want to leave?"

Ranata nodded. "I'm very happy here, Jack. Much happier than anyone in my situation could ever hope to be. I've been enslaved and abused for years, and I'm not even pretty anymore, but Dantonio loves me and cares for me. I will not leave him."

"But—but the chains, the collars and leashes!" I sputtered. "Dammit, Ranata, it's just not right!"

"You don't understand," she began, "but perhaps

Alanna could explain it to you better than I can. She knows the story much better than I do." She called out for Alanna again, and the older woman returned, smiling. "Tell my sister about the history of your planet, if you please, Alanna. She needs to understand why I want to stay."

Alanna nodded and took a seat near mine. "You must understand that what I am about to tell you is told only in the strictest confidence," she began. "No male of this or any other planet must ever learn the truth."

I didn't have a clue what she was talking about, but I wanted to hear her story, so I agreed.

"Very well," she said, settling her long skirts about her. I noted that her garments, and Ranata's, were made of ordinary cloth, not the transparent fabric that I was wearing. It made me feel sort of naked. Nearly all of the women I'd seen out and about had worn the clear stuff, though I decided that at home, perhaps it wasn't terribly practical. I'd seen some older women who weren't dressed this way, either. It seemed to mostly be the realm of the young and beautiful to be dressed provocatively— just like everywhere else in the known universe. "For you to understand our history, I must explain that our planet was not always the paradise you see now. It was at one time a desolate, war-torn world with very little to recommend it. Our males, as you might have noticed, have a rather belligerent nature."

"No shit," I muttered in agreement.

"Yes, well, they were constantly fighting amongst themselves, and our civilization was very nearly destroyed. It seemed that there was no hope for us as a world to survive another generation, not once the weapons of mass destruction were invented. The planet was almost entirely laid to waste," she said sadly. "Our males killed one another so often that there began to be fewer and fewer of them, and what males there were began taking more than one mate. But still, there were many more widows than there were brides.

"Then, one day, a young and beautiful woman whose husband had died at the hands of an enemy declared that she would not lose another husband. When she took another mate, she chained herself to him and would not let him venture forth without her."

"Wait just a minute there," I said. "You're telling me that the chains were a woman's idea? I don't believe it!"

"Oh, yes, it is quite true!" Alanna insisted. "She did it of her own volition, never dreaming that she had stumbled upon the one thing that might save us all. Her husband lived because she was there to placate him— or his opponent—whenever their tempers got the best of them, which, unfortunately, was quite often. She discovered what many had already known, which was that our males could only be calmed by sexual means. She was accused of being a wanton, for she would kneel before her husband and caress him in public to calm him. Nevertheless, as more women noted that she was able to keep him alive in this fashion, they began chaining themselves to their men as well."

"And what did the guys think about that?" I inquired with a good measure of skepticism. "No nights out with the boys? Come on, now, they had to hate that!"

"Oh, no!" Alanna said. "It began to be the fashion to go about with a beautiful female in chains. The men saw it as a trophy, a symbol of high status, and were all clamoring for a chance to show off their women. The clothing you wear now is a result of that change in fashion. We women knew that our men could be placated with sex—it was the only way to keep them calm, and our style of dress developed out of that need. It became very…functional in that respect. And also, you must understand that slavery was not frowned upon so much in those early days when we first began to travel amongst the stars. As our males became tamed, our weapons technology gave way to exploration and we could travel the galaxy and meet people of other worlds, and not fear that our men would cause trouble wherever they went. Our world itself became peaceful and prosperous as we women controlled the males and kept them from warring with one another. However, because we realized that slavery was abhorrent to so many cultures, we also began an effort to breed docility into them."

"Selective breeding?" This was getting more amazing by the second! "How the hell did you manage that?"

"Only the most docile males are allowed to reproduce," Alanna informed me. "We women have our ways, you know. The wives of the most belligerent males have offspring, to be sure, but the semen is obtained from those males who are more…controllable."

"I've heard of underground alliances before, but this one takes the cake!" I declared. "And the men have no idea that this is happening?"

Alanna shook her head. "It is instilled in our girls from the time they are very young that the fate of our world rests upon their shoulders. Not one of us would ever betray her sisters. And we also control the birth rate of males, making certain that they never outnumber the females, so that each male can have at least four females to control him." Alanna smiled. "After all, there must be someone left free to take care of the children and the home and the business of daily life. If we were all chained to men all the time, nothing would ever be accomplished."

"Okay," I admitted. "That explains a lot of things. But it still doesn't explain why my sister is here and doesn't want to leave."

Alanna smiled at Ranata. "We have encouraged our males to believe that Earth women are desirable as mates—very subtly, you understand, for it must seem that they originated the idea themselves. It was discovered, quite accidentally, that humans interbreed well with many species, and that the male offspring of a human female and a Statzeelian male tended to be less…temperamental. Also, we feared that with so few of the males actually being allowed to reproduce, we might be weakening the genetic structure of our people; therefore, introducing new blood was deemed necessary."

"Ha!" I exclaimed scornfully. "If you think human males aren't belligerent, you should come to Earth once in a while. They're just as ornery as the males on any other planet!"

"Oh, but you have not seen one of our males without

a woman there to control him," Alanna said quickly. "We only allow the very young and the very old males to go about unattended, the others are much too dangerous! Some even require more than one female."

I had to laugh then, for the meaning behind the admonitions that Cat needed "two" of something finally became clear. He must have appeared to be quite ferocious with those fangs of his, and the locals obviously thought he needed more women to control him! I was dying to tell him that, but I also realized that it wasn't possible, for I was now sworn to secrecy along with all the others. It might be best to let him go on thinking that he needed two women because he was capable of satisfying two at a time. I had no intention of ever letting that happen, of course, but he could believe it if he wished.

"Your sister was found on another world in slavery and brought here to breed with our males," Alanna went on. "She will have many male children, but never with the same male twice—and our dear Dantonio will never know that only this first child is his."

Apparently they had this selective breeding thing down pretty pat! "So, what, you all trade semen with your friends?" It sounded a little like borrowing a cup a sugar from a neighbor, or passing around a new flavor of chewing gum.

"Something like that," Alanna chuckled. "We have learned to control many aspects of reproduction. We match them up physically so that the male children will appear to be the offspring of the husband, but many times, they are not."

"Momma's baby, Daddy's maybe?"

Ranata laughed. "That's exactly what I thought when I first heard all of this. Oh, Jack, it's so good to have you here with me again!"

"Yes, well, I'm glad to see you, too, but to be honest, Ranata, you don't look healthy enough to have a baby! You should have waited a bit."

"I'm doing quite well, now," Ranata assured me. "You should have seen me when I first got here! I was a wreck!"

She still looked like a wreck to me, but then I hadn't seen her before. I studied her closely, noting that, at the roots, her hair was much thicker than the long wispy strands which curled around her face, and that her fingernails seemed healthier at the base than at the tip. Yes, she was improving, but a baby on top of that? It seemed much too soon to be placing that added burden on her health. I hoped these women knew what they were doing.

"Well, I'm glad you're better, and I'm glad you're happy here," I said, "but wouldn't you really rather go home where you don't have to wear a collar and be chained to your husband? It still seems an awful lot like slavery to me, whether you women volunteered for it or not! I'll admit, being chained to Cat hasn't been too bad, but having to ask him to unchain me so I can go pee is just a bit much!"

They both looked at me as though I'd lost my mind.

"Why should he unchain you when you are the one who carries the key?" Alanna asked curiously.

"What do you mean?" I asked irritably. "*He's* the one who has a pocket on his vest, not me! It's the women who are supposed to be enslaved here, right?"

"No," Alanna said firmly. "We may let the men believe that, but we have always been the guardians of the keys—from the very beginning. What did you think this ring on your sash was for?" she demanded, reaching out to tug at the one at my waist. "It is to carry your key."

Chapter Twelve

WELL, SUFFICE IT TO SAY THAT, AT THAT POINT, YOU could have knocked me over with a Bregnata feather! It was no wonder I hadn't gotten the real story about this planet, for, as luck would have it, I'd gotten my most of my information from a man!

"And the guys really haven't figured this out, huh?" I hadn't figured it out right away, myself, but then I'd only been here for a few days and the native males had had a considerably longer period of time to reflect upon their situation. However, if they were never alone without a woman in attendance, maybe they didn't have many opportunities to discuss it among themselves.

Cat, for one, had suspected that the males had at least learned to work within the system, perhaps realizing that all they needed to do to get a little action was to get pissed off, but did they truly understand the whole story? Somehow I doubted that, because the conspiracy was too universal, contained too many subtleties, and had gone on for far too long—and the men of Statzeel didn't strike me as the type who would have turned a blind eye to such activities if they'd known about them. True, they might realize that the women were using sex to keep the peace—but selective breeding? Given the nature of the beasts, I seriously doubted that they could have known about that part and still gone along with it. Most men don't particularly like having to raise stepchildren, and this went far beyond that!

Even so, while it might have been fairly obvious to most of the men that their women were controlling them—especially since someone was going down on them anytime they got a little testy—the fact that none of the males had seen the larger picture spoke volumes. "Not too bright, are they?"

Alanna and Ranata exchanged a meaningful look.

"Guess not." I thought about it for a minute, trying to process it all. What an amazing undertaking: an entire civilization kept stable by one gender without the knowledge—or even the cooperation—of the other! It boggled the mind to consider it. Your typical neighborhood grapevine was *nothing* when compared with this! "Well, I've got to admit, I'm impressed," I said. Then another thought occurred to me. "So, what, are you actively recruiting on Earth, or are you just leaving it to chance?"

"So far, we have only attempted to recover those already enslaved, but active recruiting might not be a bad idea," Ranata said reflectively.

I thought it was interesting that she already sounded like one of the natives when she said that. It obviously hadn't taken much to win her over—enough to eat and a nice home and a man they all seemed to be fond of. It was no wonder they had taken women who were already slaves. This sort of slavery was the kind that any former slave would see as a definite step up, and making converts of them would be quite easy. Ranata herself seemed to be very happy and content and quite obviously had no intention of leaving with me—although if I'd managed to find her a little sooner, she probably would have. I was glad she was happy, but I'd have the devil of a time explaining this to my father, since I couldn't tell him the whole truth. These women had kept their secret for a very long time and I had no intention of being the one to blab it all over the galaxy and ruin generations of difficult work—for it *had* been work, no doubt about that!

"Well, if you like, I might pass on the information when I get back to Earth, but it's gonna take me a while to get there. We're not exactly just across the pond, you know." Then I got to thinking that they might be going about this the wrong way. "You know, you could do this a whole lot quicker if you used human males, rather than females—or not even that, just donated sperm. You could produce an entire generation of cross-bred children, and only have to do it once. Though, I have to tell you, if you think you'll be able to set the men free and keep things as hunky dory as they are now, you're probably dreaming. Things aren't this peaceful on any other planet I've ever visited. Your males might have been extreme cases, but believe me, there are plenty of others that would just as soon kill you as look at you. Take the Nedwuts, for example. I'm surprised you even let them land on your planet!"

Alanna appeared somewhat alarmed at this. "We do not!" she said tersely. "Are you telling me you have seen them here?"

"You bet your boots I have!" I said roundly. "A whole pack of them met us on the road from the spaceport and would have taken Cat and me prisoner if Cat hadn't been so obviously willing to pick off a couple of them."

"This must be reported!" Alanna said, getting to her feet. "They are an evil, disruptive race. The penalty for being on the surface of our planet is death, and the Nedwuts know it."

Well, this was a good thing. Especially since, despite my original intention to keep mum, I'd gone and blabbed about it! At least the law wouldn't come after Cat for killing a few of them, though I hadn't been so sure about that at the time. I'd thought he was being a bit trigger-happy, myself, but given what he knew about the Nedwuts, I couldn't really blame him for taking the opportunity to take revenge on them for what they'd done to his planet. I mean, I probably wouldn't have passed up the opportunity to rough up a few of them myself, and I didn't have nearly as much of a grudge against them as Cat had. Granted, they *had* kidnapped my sister, but at least she was alive and well. You couldn't say the same for any of Cat's people.

"There were four of them heading back down the road we took to get here," I told Alanna. "All mounted and armed to the teeth, and trust me, they were looking for trouble."

"They are *always* looking for trouble!" Ranata said as a shadow of fear and revulsion crossed her face. "You wouldn't think I would ever welcome the idea of being sold to someone as a slave, but after being their prisoner, it made my first master seem like a real pussycat."

"Speaking of which, where is Cat, anyway?" I asked. "You didn't chain him up somewhere, did you?"

Ranata rolled her eyes. "Of course not! Though he looks as though he should be. Where did you say you found him?"

"In the slave market on Orpheseus Prime," I replied. "Ain't he cool?"

"He is…different," Ranata said cautiously. "What are you going to do with him now?" She made it sound as though now that I had found her, I would have no more use for Cat. You know, I'd sort of forgotten that my little sister wasn't exactly the sharpest tool in the shed.

I smiled and I believe I actually blushed. "I think I'll keep him."

Ranata blinked and shook her head in disbelief. "You? Keep a man? An alien man? Jack, you don't even like men—of any kind! You never have!"

"Well, I sure as hell don't want to shack up with a woman, if that's what you're getting at." I know I sounded more than a little exasperated with Ranata, but, hey, she was picking on my Cat! "Besides, I *love* Cat! He's…different," I said, echoing Ranata for want of a better explanation, for Cat truly was different—in a multitude of ways.

"Well, he'd have to be, for you to love him!" Ranata said roundly. "You were the most confirmed man-hater I've ever seen!"

"I didn't hate them," I objected, ruffling my feathers just a bit. "I just didn't like them—well, most of them, anyway. Some of them weren't so bad."

"Yes, but you never wanted to keep them around," she reminded me. "At least, not for long."

"True," I admitted. I couldn't just come out and tell her that the main reason I hadn't stayed with one before this was because I didn't like that loss of control I felt when I was "under the influence." I didn't seem to mind it when it came to being with Cat, though. He was…different. Then I realized what the difference was. "I guess I just didn't love any of the others enough to—" I paused as I blew out a pent-up breath, "let myself go and trust them not to take advantage of me in my, um, moments of weakness. Besides, the others always just messed up my mind to the point that I couldn't function. Cat doesn't affect me that way; he's more like…well…a partner rather than a competitor. Does that make sense? I feel comfortable with him."

"Like having a cat curled up in your lap?"

"Sort of, only he's not always a pussycat, he's pretty tough—you should see the way he handles a sword, Ranata! Honestly, it's downright breathtaking! He's very sexy, too, and—"

"Yeah, I saw the tool," Ranata remarked dryly. "That's the most lethal-looking weapon I've ever seen."

"Sis, you have no idea!" I exclaimed. "It's like—well, I can't tell you what it's like because I have nothing else to compare it with; I mean, nothing else even comes close! Cat seems to think that his planet was destroyed because men from other worlds were losing their women to the Zetithians, and I, for one, believe it!"

"Sounds pretty cocky to me," she commented.

"Well, you know, when a claim is true, it's not being cocky to say so. What I mean is, when he told me he would give me joy unlike any I had ever known, he wasn't kidding! Honestly, Sis, if he were like anything else I was trying to sell, I'd let you try him out, but you might decide you like him too much and steal him from me." I chuckled as I remembered how afraid I'd been that I would lose Cat to Ranata, and now that I'd finally found her, I was tickled to death that she had a husband she loved well enough to want to remain his slave. I certainly wasn't going to let her get even a whiff of Cat's coronal fluid—in fact, I was considering not telling her about it at all. "And I have no intention of letting that happen. Like I said, I'm keeping him."

"And I wouldn't dream of trying to steal him from you," Ranata said sweetly. "I mean, I still can't get over your falling in love with him! It's so wonderful, and I'm so happy for you! Mom will be, too, you know," she added. "After all, she gave up on you a long time ago."

"Yeah, like at birth!" I grumbled. "I never was the kind of daughter she wanted. Of course, then she had you, and you were perfect! Too bad I had to go and let those damned Nedwuts run off with you."

"Like you could have stopped them!" Ranata said scornfully. "Really, Jack! Who do you think you are? Some kind of superwoman? Good heavens, there were six of them! You didn't stand a chance! They probably would've killed you if you'd tried to stop them." She paused for a moment, taking a deep, though rather shaky, breath before continuing. "That was the one thing I had to hold on to, Jack. They might have taken me, but at least you weren't killed in the process. Just knowing that you were still alive and free and had your ship and could go wherever you wanted…it's one of the things that kept me sane."

"Well, if it helped you to believe that, I'm glad," I said roundly, "but you couldn't possibly have imagined for even one moment that I'd just let them take you and then go on my merry way! Not after you'd been kidnapped by those bastards! I came after you, Sis, and I've been searching high and low for you—all across the galaxy! And you know," I added reflectively, "it's a damn good thing that humans are so rare out here, and that you were so beautiful, or I'd have never been able to track you down. Talk about your classic needle in a haystack!"

"Needle in a haystack?" she echoed. "What on Earth does that mean?"

I'd forgotten that Ranata had never shared my fascination with ancient figures of speech. Of course, the fact that I'd learned most of them while I'd been searching for her made it unlikely that she'd have heard very many of them, but none of that mattered now that I'd found her. "Something very hard to find," I replied. "The literal meaning isn't important, but it's one of those near impossibilities, Ranata. Not completely impossible, mind you, but damn close to it."

I gazed at her intently, finally beginning to see my own little sister in the face of the woman before me. It was hard seeing her that way, and though I know I might have expected it, the funny thing was, I never had. Oh, I knew she had suffered as a slave, but that she wouldn't have remained the same pretty child I remembered was a thought that I hadn't allowed myself to have. I'd always assumed I would simply find her, rescue her, and then take her home. The notion that she might not only be married to someone, but also carrying his child, had certainly never entered my head. And not wanting to come home! Well, that was the part that was hardest to swallow!

But here she was, happily married and having a baby, though she was in a condition which, while certainly improving, spoke volumes about the shape she'd been in when her husband, Dantonio, had rescued her. To be perfectly honest about it, I was still having trouble coming to grips with the fact that she'd been rescued already and didn't need me. I was even slightly miffed that he'd gotten to her before I did. I mean, I'd been looking for her for six years! What had he done? Probably stumbled onto her in a slave market in much the same way that I'd found Cat. It was too damned easy for him, if you ask me. I'd worked much harder at finding her. He'd simply gotten lucky. It wasn't fair.

Of course, nothing in life is ever truly fair, especially the fate that Ranata had been forced to endure simply because she'd had the misfortune to be in the wrong place at the wrong time. She'd never done anything in her life to deserve such treatment, and I very much doubted that Cat had either. Still, it had happened, and though it might have been selfish of me, I needed to know more.

"Sis," I said, my voice sounding a bit shaky, "what happened to you? I mean, I know where you've been and a little about some of the people who've owned you, but that's about all I know. Can you tell me about it?" I hesitated for a moment, thinking that she'd probably rather

forget about it all than report it—although you always
hear that it's best not to keep everything to yourself.
"You don't have to if you don't want to, but, I—I think
I need to know—so I can make it up to you somehow.
Maybe take some of your pain onto myself—possibly
make it less of a burden for you by sharing it, I don't
know. I don't know if it would help or not, but—" I
was floundering just a bit there, and, fortunately, she
came to my rescue this time, mercifully cutting my
explanation short.

"You wouldn't be the first one I've told, Jack," she
said quietly. "Alanna knows, and Dantonio has heard
my story as well. It would be no hardship for me to tell
it again."

I thought she hesitated just a bit then, perhaps realizing that it might be more difficult this time around.
After all, Alanna and Dantonio had probably been
virtual strangers when she told them her history, and
though they might have been saddened by her tale, I was
her sister, and had known and loved her since she was
born. It might make a difference.

"But, please, Jack," she went on, "just promise me
one thing, will you? When you get back to Earth, would
you clean it up a bit when you tell Mom and Dad? I-I'd
rather they didn't know all of the…details."

"You don't even have to tell me all the gory details if
you don't want to," I said, though considering the size of
the lump I had in my throat, it was surprising that I was
able to speak at all.

"No," she said. "You're the one who's been searching
for me, Jack. You need to hear all of it, don't you?"

I nodded reluctantly. "Yeah, I do. I mean, I don't really *want* to know, but you're right; I need to."

Ranata settled back in her chair, placing her hands on her pregnant belly, though whether it was simply the position of most comfort for her or whether she was attempting to shield her child from having to listen, I couldn't have said. Perhaps it was more comforting than comfortable—almost like holding your unborn child in your arms, somehow—though never having been in that condition myself, I couldn't have known.

"You know what happened when I was taken, of course," she began. "The Nedwuts grabbed me and hustled me out of there before anyone had a chance to react. It seemed like such a spur of the moment thing at the time, but I've often wondered if they hadn't planned it because they had a transport ready and waiting—there was even a driver sitting in it, all ready to take off. I can't be sure, of course, but if that was the case, I think I might have been kidnapped no matter where I was. And while it's possible that being in that place with you might have made it more convenient for them, it's also possible that my *not* being there wouldn't have changed anything."

I smiled at her, thanking her for the sentiment, but at the same time, it crossed my mind that she was probably only telling me this to make me feel better. I started to say, "Just the facts, ma'am," but attempting to inject a little levity into her story would have been tactless. Though, not understanding the reference, she might not see it as a joke anyway. I held my tongue and let her continue without comment. After all, it was her story, and it was up to her to tell it any way she wished.

"If I never see another Nedwut again as long as I live, it would be too soon," she remarked. "They're not only mean and hateful, but they stink, and they liked to get right up in my face and breathe their foul stench at me and tell me of all the horrors they had in store for me if I didn't keep quiet and cooperate. Of course, I didn't cooperate, and they had no qualms about hitting a woman, nor did they seem to consider that anyone wanting to buy me might prefer that I be in perfect condition. By the time I was finally sold, I was so beat-up I'm surprised anyone even wanted to look at me, let alone pay good money for me.

"The man who bought me apparently just thought that having a human slave would be interesting since, slavery not being an Earth custom, it's so rare to find one of us being sold. His name was Jalavar, and he was an Econian merchant. I don't know if you've ever been to Econia, but the people there are more reptilian than anything, and they all gave me the creeps even more than the Nedwuts had—if you can believe that's possible! It was a really nasty planet, too. Hot, steamy, and even the plants were hideous—sort of like prehistoric Earth is supposed to have been, only much uglier! Anyway, it was like a planet where the dinosaurs had not only not become extinct, but had evolved into intelligent beings. Well, I *say* intelligent, and while they might have had brains, they were still a bunch of creeps, and when they got into fights, it was usually to the death, and then the winners ate the ones they killed. It was horrible!"

Suppressing a shudder of revulsion myself, I felt sort of glad that I'd managed to miss out on a visit to that particular planet. "How did you ever get away from there?"

"Oh, Jalavar decided he'd had enough of me after a while, and thought that I would taste bad, so instead of eating me, he sold me to a slave trader who was heading to Dracus Five."

Having heard that, I didn't know whether to laugh or throw up, but, instead, decided to add my own part to the tale. "That's where I picked up your trail," I said. "Having tried, unsuccessfully, to follow the Nedwuts, I started hitting every planet around that had a slave market, but by the time I got to Dracus, you'd already been there and gone. I paid a bundle for the information that you had been taken to Sallonius, only to get there and find out I'd been taken for a ride on that deal! I went back to Dracus and beat the shit out of the little slimeball who finally admitted that he didn't have any idea where you'd gone, only that you'd been sold to an offworlder who, from his description, looked sort of like a gorilla."

"Celarnus," Ranata groaned. "He was the worst, I think, and he wanted to mate with me. Have you got any idea how hard it is to discourage a horny gorilla?"

I considered this for a moment, and, having actually met the guy, I was of the opinion that nothing short of a pulse rifle would have slowed him down. "You could have ripped his balls off, I suppose," I suggested. "That might have made him less, um, amorous."

"Well, I did try that," she admitted. "But it just made him mad."

I couldn't imagine why…. "Pissed him off enough to sell you, did it?"

When questioned, Celarnus had only told me that Ranata's service to him hadn't been satisfactory, but he hadn't elaborated on just what type of service it had been. I'd come up with some of my own—and fortunately nonsexual—reasons why she might not have pleased him, and, therefore, hadn't killed him outright. If I'd known he'd raped my sister, I probably would have. I guess he must have realized that before he said too much.

"Well, yeah, he sold me, all right," she said, "but that was mainly because I didn't get pregnant. He wanted children that looked less ape-like, but when it didn't work out, I was sold to another trader. This one thought I was too fat and didn't feed me."

Ranata had *never* been fat, and I couldn't imagine why anyone would have thought that she was, and I said as much.

"Well, if you'd ever seen the guy, you would have known why he felt that way. He was a Kitnock and they basically look like…well, toothpicks."

I didn't have to think too hard to know just exactly who she meant. "Oh, yeah, I remember him! Tall, skinny guy with a mouth big enough to swallow a watermelon?"

"That's the one," she said.

I nodded. Oh, yes, I remembered him quite well, indeed! "I broke his arm trying to get information out of him," I said, smiling at the memory. "I remember being ever so slightly sorry about it at the time, but now…"

"Oh Jack!" Ranata exclaimed with unsuppressed glee. "You didn't!"

"Yes, I did," I said firmly. "He was a real jerk about it, too. Tried to have me arrested for assault and battery— or whatever they called it on that planet. I bribed the cop and he let me go—probably because he didn't like Kitnocks anymore than I did."

Ranata dissolved into helpless laughter, and for once, I was delighted to be able to report that I'd done such a thing, since it made her laugh. God knows, she'd had little enough reason to laugh over the past six years! Sort of made me wish I had been able to report, truthfully, that I'd ripped the gorilla's balls off. Then something else occurred to me, and, of course, I just *had* to ask....

"By the way, Sis—and you don't have to answer this if you don't want to—but how was sex with the gorilla?"

Ranata made a face reminiscent of the one she'd made when Mom made her try some exotic vegetable or other (I forget just what planet it was supposed to have come from, though it was probably Io because they grow lots of weird stuff there) that was supposed to be extremely good for you, but which, unfortunately, smelled a bit like a wet skunk. "About like you'd expect," she replied. "Rather disgusting, though fortunately it was usually quick. He weighed a ton, but, for his size, he had the tiniest little dick you've ever seen."

Which tallied with anything I'd ever heard about having sex with a gorilla—well, guys that looked like them, that is. I'd never heard of anyone actually doing it with a real one. Then it occurred to me that, along with his sexual misconduct, I just might have another reason to go back there and kill him someday.

"How did you hurt your leg?" I demanded. "It wasn't the gorilla, was it?"

"No," she replied. "It was the next one after that. According to him—his name was Crapenit, by the way—I couldn't do *anything* right, and when I'd finally had enough of being beaten, I tried to escape one night. I have no idea where I would have gone, of course, but I tried it anyway and got lost in the forest and fell over, well, a cliff, actually—though not a particularly high one—and broke my ankle. Crapenit was a real sadist and seemed to enjoy the fact that I was hurt and wouldn't do anything about it, just made me hobble along using a stick for a crutch all the way back to the slave quarters. One of the other slaves helped me wrap it up, but it never healed right."

"Can't they do anything for it now?" I asked. "You know, like replacing the joint or something?"

"Probably," she admitted. "But it really doesn't hurt much anymore, it just healed crooked. I might get it looked at after the baby is born."

I nodded. "You do that," I said. "I want to be able to tell Mom that you're in good shape, you know."

"But I *am* in good shape!" Ranata protested. "Well, the best shape I've been in for a long time, anyway. No, really, Jack! I feel great!"

I was still pretty skeptical about that. "Well, don't take this the wrong way, Sis, but you sure as hell don't look it!"

"You do, though," she said with a warm smile. "You look marvelous."

"Aw, that's just the makeup job," I said with a dismissive wave. "Or it could be that you're just happy to see me."

"Well, you *are* a sight for sore eyes," she agreed.

"You, too, Sis," I said. "You, too."

I got the weirdest feeling in my chest just then, like my heart hurt or something. Guess it was something tugging at my heart strings—either that or I was having a coronary. Wouldn't that be just ducky, I thought. To finally locate Ranata and then go and have a damned heart attack! Of course, I knew full well that my heart was functioning just fine—if I could believe the medical scanner on the ship, that is. No, it wasn't a heart attack, I decided; it was something else.

"Where's Cat?" I asked, suddenly realizing what was wrong with me. I hadn't been apart from Cat since I'd dragged him aboard my ship. All it was, was that I must have been missing him. I'd never loved a man enough to miss him, which was probably why I hadn't been able to identify the feeling.

"He's around here somewhere," Ranata assured me. "I'd better find Dantonio, though, and introduce you two before he finds Cat and freaks out."

"And why would he do that?" I demanded rather hotly. "Cat's a nice guy."

"Well, you know how the men are around here," she said. "One minute they're doing just fine and the next they're so mad you wouldn't think they were the same person!"

"Oh, yeah, that's right," I said. "I was forgetting how testy they are. But you know, Cat has a theory about that. He thinks the guys just pretend to get mad so you women will be playing with their ding-dongs all the time."

"Oh, I don't think that's true at all," Ranata disagreed. "They just have very volatile tempers."

"I don't know," I said doubtfully. "The more I've thought about it, the more I think he might be right. We set up shop in the village and this one guy was calling Cat a liar one minute and then buying some tooth jelly from him the next! What I mean is, if he truly didn't believe the sales pitch and it made him mad enough to nearly get into a fight with Cat over it, then why the hell did buy anything from us at all?"

Ranata was spared from having to reply to this when a man stormed into the room, demanding to know who that long-haired, pointed-eared fiend in the dining room eating cake was.

"Better grab his dick and shut him up before I kill him, Sis," I growled, leaping to my feet and reaching instinctively for my pistol, which, of course I didn't have on me because Cat was still carrying it. As a result, I was forced to resort to either verbal sparring or fisticuffs. "For your information, Bucko, my Cat is *not* a fiend, and I'll thank you not to be saying shit like that about him." Looking back, I suppose I could have stooped to his level and called him a flat-nosed, six-fingered freak, but at the time, "Bucko" was about as eloquent an epithet as I could conjure up.

Ranata's reaction to this exchange was to burst out laughing. "Oh, Jack! Calm down!" she giggled. "This is my husband, Dantonio."

I backed down just a bit, but still eyed him a tad suspiciously. So, this was the punk who'd had the audacity to buy my little sister as a slave! You know, in spite of all she'd told me about her life and how happy she was now, it crossed my mind just then that she might have been brainwashed into believing all that crap. Then I remembered my original intention to kill the bastard, and I still wasn't convinced that it wasn't a good idea—and this was aside from the fact that he had just referred to my dear, sweet Kittycat as a fiend.

"Jack?" Dantonio echoed with surprise. He might have known who I was, or he might not, but either way, he still looked sort of pugnacious to me, and to be perfectly honest, I wouldn't have minded getting into a fight with him—not one little bit! In fact, I was looking forward to it, if for no other reason than to knock some sense into the inconsiderate sonofabitch who had gotten my half-starved sister pregnant. Though as skinny as Ranata was, I was a little surprised she'd even been able to conceive at all—and perhaps he had been, as well. Still, if anyone had consulted me—which, of course, no one had—I think I'd have recommended giving her some time to plump up a bit first. But then, a general lack of consideration for anyone but themselves was one of those things that I had disliked about many of the men I'd met throughout my life. So far, this one hadn't impressed me very much because the way I saw it, he'd done nothing more than to pay for Ranata's affection with a little food and a nice place to live. She hadn't had the opportunity to fall in love with Dantonio and then marry him of her own accord; he'd fuckin' bought her!

I know you're probably thinking that I was no better myself, since I had done virtually the same thing with Cat, but I truly hadn't; I'd never had any intention of keeping Cat as my slave, nor had I wanted anything more from him than his assistance in finding Ranata—at least, to begin with, that is. And in my defense, Cat had been the one sniffing around me and wanting to mate; it certainly hadn't been my idea! I hadn't forced him to, nor had I asked it of him, but I wasn't so sure about Dantonio. He might have forced Ranata, and, given all she'd been through in the past, it probably would have seemed like a whirlwind romance to her. I mean, after you've been raped by a guy who looks like a gorilla, how much worse could it get?

Dantonio and I just stood there for several moments, each of us trying to stare the other down, and I truly believe that if we'd been out in the open, we'd have been circling each other like a couple of angry dogs about to attack.

Fortunately for us—though mostly for Dantonio because I have no doubt that I could have mopped up the floor with him—Ranata had plenty of experience in toning down some rather explosive situations. "Yes," she said firmly. "Jack. My sister. You know, your sister-in-law?"

Dantonio undoubtedly heard her, but his belligerent gaze never wavered. If his expression was anything to go by, it was quite obvious that he had already known exactly who I was and also precisely why I was there. "You can't have her," he said evenly. "If you are here to take her away from me, I will fight you to the death if necessary. She is mine and she carries my child."

My first thought was that, having made a statement like that, the men of Statzeel—or at least this one in particular—really didn't know about the selective breeding program, otherwise he'd never have known for certain that the child was, indeed, his own. Given the possessive manner in which he obviously viewed his wife and child, I would have hated to be the one to tell him that all of the rest of Ranata's children wouldn't share that distinction. On the other hand, I *was* feeling a bit spiteful, and might have enjoyed telling him, if only to make his life miserable. Of course, having been sworn to secrecy made it a moot point, anyway, so I didn't.

Perhaps it was because I'd been listening to the story of Ranata's horrific experiences over the past six years and was, therefore, primed for a fight; but instead of somehow reassuring me that Ranata would be loved and cared for, Dantonio's words only made me realize that if I'd only managed to catch up with her just six months sooner, none of this would have happened. The way I saw it, he, and only he, was the reason I couldn't take my sister home, and as far as I was concerned, he was just another slave owner.

"You should have waited!" I hissed at him. "Just look at her! She's been beaten and starved half to death and what do you do right off the bat? You go and saddle her with a child! What were you thinking? 'My child,'" I said, openly mocking him. "If you want to have any more children, Bucko, then you should have just a little bit more concern for the health of their mother! Hell, she might not even live to deliver this one! For pity's sake, Dantonio! Couldn't you have kept your dick in your pants for a little while longer?"

The absurdity of my last question hit Ranata hard and she began laughing hysterically and keeled over on her couch.

Casting a scathing glance in her direction, I muttered, "Well, no, I guess you probably couldn't have, at that."

Unfortunately, the sound of Ranata's laughter caused my own anger to dissipate rather more quickly than I would have liked. Heaving a world-weary sigh, I realized that after six years, I was getting damned tired of fighting all the time. Besides, it was requiring way too much effort to sustain my anger, especially in light of the fact that Ranata still had the giggles.

"Sorry, Dantonio," I apologized. "I guess I'm still pissed at all of my sister's previous owners. I know it isn't quite fair to be taking it all out on you, but to be perfectly honest, I think I'd like to kill a couple of them—unless Ranata thinks torture would be a better punishment. Maybe you could give me a hand."

Dantonio was still staring daggers at me and I was beginning to think he had no sense of humor at all.

"Nah, maybe not. Maybe I'll just go find my Cat. You know, the long-haired, pointy-eared fiend?" I looked at Ranata and asked, "Hey, Sis, do you suppose there's any cake left? Cat really likes sweet stuff. He might have eaten all of it by now."

"If there isn't," she said warmly, "then we'll bake some cookies."

"Sounds good to me," I said. "Been a long time since I had any cookies. Remember the ones Mom used to make?"

"I sure do!" she said. "And would you believe that nobody here ever even heard of cookies until I showed up?"

"Doesn't surprise me a bit," I said. "Hey, if you don't mind, could Cat and I stick around for a few days?"

"I'd be very disappointed if you didn't," she said. "Stay as long as you like." Smiling mistily, she added, "And, Jack, thanks for coming after me. Honestly, if Dantonio hadn't come along, I truly would have needed you."

Yes, she was the same sweet girl she'd always been. Didn't look it, perhaps, but at least her experiences hadn't left her bitter and vindictive.

"You're welcome, of course," I replied, "but like I said, Sis, there wasn't anything else I could have done. I couldn't have just let you go and then lived the rest of my life knowing that I'd let you down. And thank you, too," I said to Dantonio—who was still not smiling, by the way. "At least I caught up with her this time, even if I was too late." I took another gander at him, thinking that none of these guys ever seemed to smile unless some woman had their hands all over them! No sense of humor at all! "Hey, Bucko, lighten up!" I urged him. "She already told me she won't leave you."

No, she wouldn't be leaving him, I thought rather sadly. Although why she'd want to stay with a flat-nosed and rather insipid-looking blue-eyed blond guy with six fingers on each hand was beyond me to explain. Well, okay, so he wasn't bad-looking, really. It was just that I happened to like Cat better. I mean, Dantonio might have been sort of handsome, but that big tomcat took my breath away!

I left Ranata to talk Dantonio into a better mood—or do whatever it took to make him happy. Of course, it wouldn't take much imagination to come up with the most effective means. Honestly, these guys had such one-track minds, it was downright irritating! I mean, sure, Cat wanted to mate all the time, but he didn't get mad just so I'd do it! He could get to me just by being his own irresistible little self. No, the more I observed and thought about it, the more I was convinced that Cat had been right about them.

I had also arrived at a few conclusions of my own by that time, and it seemed to me that the women could, at least in part, share some of the blame for their men's bad behavior. It was my considered opinion that they were nothing more than a bunch of spoiled little boys, and I thought that the women should just let them stew in their own anger now and then, rather than to be constantly rewarding them for it. As I saw it, these men were very much like the star athletes in colleges who, having been idolized by every female on campus, have come to the erroneous conclusion that they could get away with just about anything. The fact that not every other woman in the world would also welcome their attentions was so far beyond their comprehension that the occasional hotshot sometimes winds up being charged with a rape that he fully believes he did not commit.

It would, therefore, seem to be important that men have someone around to knock them off their high horse now and then, if only to ensure that their arrogant behavior doesn't become intolerable. Cater to their whims too much and they will come to expect such treatment all the time. As I viewed the matter, it was the fault of the females, for a man has only to be handsome or powerful to have women crawling all over him, whether he treats them with respect or not. It can only feed a man's arrogance when the women he's treated like shit keep right on crawling back for more. I didn't get it myself—never had, and perhaps that was why I'd never fallen for anyone before I met Cat.

Poking around the house, I found Cat dozing in a chair in the dining room with an empty plate and glass there on the table in front of him. I stood in the doorway for a few moments, gazing at him fondly and thinking that we could go home now. Ranata was safe and happy and I was free to spend the rest of my life with Cat, doing pretty much whatever we wished. Everything seemed to be turning out so wonderfully, but I'll admit I was still having some difficulty coming to grips with all that had happened, and even more so because my years of searching had now come to an end.

Looking for Ranata had been my whole life for so long now that it seemed impossible that I could simply go back to trading the way I had done before. I would also have Cat with me, which would probably change things considerably. Then it crossed my mind that, as in my sister's case, I might actually have children someday. Of course, the fact that Cat and I belonged to different species might eliminate that possibility, but such things weren't unheard of, and it was just as likely that we would. After all, if humans could cross with Statzeelians—who, as far as I could see, were more alien than Cat was—there might be a chance. For example, Cat didn't have an extra finger; the eyes and teeth seeming to be the chief differences between his people and the people of Earth, as well as his rather unique body fluids.

Having met Cat and loved him, I was of the opinion that a race such as his should not be allowed to become extinct. I would do my part to see that it didn't by having my conception prevention procedure reversed at the earliest opportunity, and then we would see what happened. It was a testament to the way I felt about Cat that I would even begin to consider doing that, especially since I had never been even remotely tempted to do so in the past. Being with him had changed me even more than my search for Ranata had done, for, as suspicious, cynical, and hard as I had become, Cat had single-handedly given me back my heart.

He must have become aware of my eyes upon him, for he began to stir just then, uncurling from his chair to smile sleepily at me. "The cake was very good," he said. "But it has made me wish to sleep."

"I've got no problem with that, Kittycat," I said warmly. "Right now, all I want to do is curl up with you and sleep for at least a month! Now that it's finally over, I'm only just beginning to realize how tired I am! Tired of the chase, tired of the fight, tired of the worry…. Now there's nothing left to do but go home, if that's what we decide to do. Is there any place you want to go, or anything you'd like to do?"

Cat shook his head. "I have been many places, seen many worlds and their people. It would be better to see them again as a free man, perhaps, but I find that I do not wish to return to them. I have never been to your home-world, however, and I believe I would like to see it."

"Okay, we'll head back home then. But not right away. If Ranata's husband doesn't end up throwing a big hissy fit over nothing—like most of these guys seem to do!—I think I'd like to stay here for a while and take some time to just *be*." Gazing at him fondly, I remarked, "You know, I probably wouldn't have any idea what to do, or where to go, if it weren't for you, Cat. I imagine I'd be feeling pretty lost and useless right now if I hadn't found you."

"And I would be the property of someone else and still be in chains," he said. His lips curled into another smile as he added, "and *not* eating cake."

"Well, you're probably right about that," I agreed. "But I'll tell you one thing, though: I'm not the least bit sorry we don't have to sneak out of here in the middle of the night for another run through the jungle! Those damned swergs are probably just waiting for us to come back through there again so they can get their revenge."

Cat smiled. "But I have a real sword now," he said, patting the hilt. "They would be foolish to attack us again."

"They were a bunch of bloomin' idiots for having done it the last time!" I declared. "You know, Cat, I still think that was one of the most amazing feats I've ever seen! They'd have killed me for sure if you hadn't been there. I certainly owe you one for that!"

"No, you do not," he said with a slow shake of his head, "for I could save your life every day for the next hundred years and still I would remain in your debt. You have given me life, and freedom, as well as your love. Killing wild beasts is nothing when compared with that."

"Yeah, well, maybe," I said, feeling slightly embarrassed for some reason. "Listen, all I did was pay five credits for you, Cat! And it wasn't even as much as you were worth!"

"And what am I worth?" he asked, beginning to purr softly.

"You, my dear Cat, are beyond price."

Cat seemed rather pleased to hear that, and, okay, so what if I spoiled him a little bit? Hell, the way I saw it, I could spoil him rotten for the next twenty years or so, and he'd still never get as cocky as a Statzeelian, nor would it make up for all of the horrors he'd been forced to endure. I just hoped Dantonio would see Ranata in the same light and treat her like the precious thing she was, as well. Oh, yes, I would spoil him a bit, but not right now, for just looking at my sleepy Cat was making me want to lie down for a while. "Hey, Kittycat," I said with a yawn, "what do you say we stick those two horses in the barn and see if we can find somewhere to take a little catnap until dinnertime?"

"It is done," Cat said with a purr. "The lady Alanna has seen to it."

"Knew we'd end up staying for a few days, did she?"

Cat nodded. "It is a fine room," he said. His purr grew deeper in tone and his eyes began to glow softly. "The bed is large and very soft."

By this time, I knew that particular expression quite well, and therefore knew that sleep was most definitely *not* what he had in mind! "Well, I hope they don't have dinner very early around here, then," I said, "'cause this is bound to take a while."

After he showed me to the guest room, I decided that he was right about the bed, because it felt for all the world like swimming in an ocean of sheets and pillows, and we sank deeply into its soft, enveloping warmth.

"Oh, Cat," I murmured. "This is the best ever! Here we are, in my sister's house, with no worries, no plans—"

"—no insects."

"Yeah, them, too!" I agreed. "Nasty bugs, making me fall asleep on my amorous Kittycat! You know, that was a nice place, too. We might have to stop there on the way back—if we could find some better insect repellent, that is. I'll have to ask around and see what I can find. If it's good enough to keep *those* bugs away, it ought to work against the bugs on any planet in the galaxy, and we'll get rich selling it!"

"Sh-h," he whispered. "We have one another, so we are already rich."

"Sweet talker!" I chided him.

"Mm-m-m," he purred. "Kiss me, Jacinth, and we will enjoy our wealth."

As I melted into his arms, his soft, sensuous lips nipped at mine, tasting of cake—though unfortunately not chocolate, which, along with horses, was another thing that was unique to Earth. Of course, now that I knew that there were horses on Statzeel, that left chocolate as the best thing Earth had to offer to the rest of the galaxy—which was saying quite a lot. It was popular everywhere, and I'd sold all the chocolate I had in the hold before I'd even left the Terran Quadrant. After that, I still had my own private stash of Maximo Dark to fall back on, and I probably wouldn't have sold it either, but a Dorellian noblewoman offered me ten thousand credits for all ten kilos—which I accepted, of course.

Cat was nibbling at me as though I tasted every bit as good myself. I couldn't recall him ever having done that before; I was usually the one tasting him, which had always been quite enough to send me spinning off into space. This time, however, he seemed to be bent on keeping his coronal fluid just out of tongue range while he devoured me instead. Suckling at my nipples, he drove me into a frenzy of desire before working his way down lower on my body to spiral in for the kill. He took a long time to get there, sweeping his hot tongue across my skin while he continued to tease my nipples with his fingertips. Needless to say, when his tongue finally reached my clitoris, I was about to explode.

But he didn't let it happen right away, and lay with his head pillowed on my thigh, lazily licking me as though he had the next ten thousand years to bring me to climax. I think it took about half that long, actually, and by the time I was getting close, I was pleading with him to put me out of my misery and just give me one little taste of him to send me over the edge into oblivion.

"No," he replied. "You do this alone."

My body was drenched in sweat, the muscles in my legs cramping from the effort it was taking. "Please, Cat!" I begged him. "I can't do it!"

"Yes, you can," he said. "Try." His tongue giving way to his lips, he sucked me, deeply and sensuously as his tongue stroked the underside of my clit with its rough, wet surface. Then suddenly, without any warning, I felt a piercing note drive itself through my body, singing louder and higher until finally shattering me into a million pieces. Not stopping even after I'd reached the highest level of ecstasy, he continued to tease me with the tip of his tongue, keeping my orgasm going for what was surely the rest of that ten thousand years.

I was dimly aware that he moved from where he lay, but didn't know where he went until he buried his thick, hard cock inside me. Groaning aloud with the sheer mindless pleasure of him filling me up and rocking into me, it took a few moments to realize that his wonderful cock syrup didn't seem to be affecting me anymore. What he was doing felt better than anything I'd experienced with him up to that point, but I just wasn't having the repeated orgasms that I'd had before. It crossed my mind to feel somewhat disappointed by this—I mean, it might have been different from the way it usually was, but I was still feeling really, really good!—however, it wasn't until later that I realized I'd never come down from the original climax. Cat was simply maintaining the one he'd given me to begin with—first with his tongue and then with the rest of him. I recalled wondering once before whether or not one of the orgasms he gave me wouldn't just up and kill me someday, and decided that, if so, then this could very well be the one to do it.

Cat had been holding himself up with his palms flat on the bed and his elbows locked, but now he slid his arms beneath my back and stretched his legs out behind him, lying flat on top of me. Curling my hips up to give him the deepest penetration possible, I wrapped my arms around him as he leaned in for more deep, languorous kisses. No longer moving back and forth, Cat now began rotating that fabulous cock inside me while he was lying still.

Yep, I'm just gonna die right here, right now.... My brain was nearly there, it seemed; my body just hadn't caught up with it yet. I could feel Cat purring, could feel his tongue and his penis both penetrating deeply inside me, could feel the weight of his body, but the rest was just one big blur of pure bliss. Drowning in his love and with no control left over body or mind whatsoever, I drifted there in a state of total surrender. I was a part of him now, just as he was a part of me—two separate beings merged into one. When Cat reached his own orgasmic pinnacle and his breath went out with a rough purr before softening to a sigh, I felt as if that breath could just as easily have originated from within my own lungs. It was impossible to believe that we could be any closer—not in body, not in mind, and possibly even not in spirit. If I hadn't been in love with him before, I certainly would be now, and I wanted nothing more than to remain that close to him forever.

Chapter Thirteen

WE SPENT THE NEXT SEVERAL DAYS AT RANATA'S house, my sister and I getting reacquainted and remembering old times—happier times when we'd only viewed the subjects of kidnapping and slavery and torment as having been someone else's misfortunes, and not something that had ever directly affected those we loved. I'm happy to report that Dantonio did manage to loosen up some when he finally realized that we weren't going to steal his bride away in the middle of the night, but he still was a bit too stoic for my tastes. Ranata did seem to love him very much, however, and her growing happiness was a joy to see.

I had, for the first time in many years, the leisure to simply enjoy being alive on a beautiful world. It wasn't Earth, of course, but it was more similar to my homeworld than many other planets I'd visited, and, to be quite honest, it was making me a little homesick. Having my sister there, not to mention Cat, made me feel far less discontented than I would have otherwise, but the time was coming when I knew we would have to leave. I could only assume that our parents were still alive and well, and the trip back would take a few years as it was. I certainly didn't want them to die not knowing what had become of either of their daughters.

Cat and I went out riding almost every day, even going down to the village a time or two to do some trading on the side. We took the pack-droid back up to Ranata's place and kept it in the barn along with the horses, and I must admit, I wasn't nearly so irritated by its singing anymore. What I hadn't counted on was that Cat had finally heard "I'm Happy When I'm Hiking" one time too many. We were on the way back up the road one day when, suddenly, he wheeled his horse around, drew his sword, and smacked the top of the droid's head with the flat of his blade.

I couldn't believe my ears. The damn thing actually shut up! "Holy shit, Cat! Why the devil didn't I ever think of that?"

"Perhaps you were not angry enough," he suggested.

"Not angry enough?" I scoffed. "You'd be surprised just how mad I've gotten at it! That damn thing got me run off a planet one time for making so much noise. There I was, making money hand over fist, and wound up getting deported for disturbing the peace! Honestly, I was ready to nuke it till it glowed!"

Overlooking a few figures of speech that I'd have been willing to bet he didn't fully understand, Cat sheathed his blade and pointed out the fact that I hadn't had a sword at the time.

"Well, no," I admitted. "I didn't. Guess it must have been manufactured on another planet where there were testy men who carried swords all the time."

"I am not 'testy,'" Cat protested.

"Oh, yes you are!" I declared. "Honestly, I've got to get you away from these damned Statzeelians before you start picking up any more of their bad habits."

Cat grinned seductively. "But I do not become angry to entice you, do I, Jacinth?"

"Well, no," I said grudgingly. "You don't do that. Don't have to. But still, it might be time to—"

"—get the heck out of Dodge?" he suggested with the lift of an eyebrow.

"Yeah," I said, laughing. "Something like that. And on the way, you can watch some old movies so you'll be able to understand what that line refers to."

"But we will be alone together on your ship," he reminded me, beginning to purr. "Do not imagine that we will have time for watching 'old movies.'"

And the only thing I could say to that was, "Ooo!"

The next afternoon, Cat had gone down to the barn to saddle the horses for our ride and I was sitting out on the porch chatting with Ranata while I waited for him.

"You know how you were telling me about why Cat's planet was destroyed?" she said, suddenly changing our original subject. "Well, the more I've thought about it since then, the more familiar his story sounds. I think I've heard it somewhere before."

"Probably from the Nedwuts," I suggested. "Cat says they're the ones that did it by redirecting an asteroid so it would crash into the planet. It's odd though, for he says he saw it in his mind, rather than with his own two eyes. I haven't noticed him being particularly clairvoyant in other areas—perhaps it was a dream, although he didn't put it that way. Still, it sounds just dastardly enough for Nedwuts to be involved, though I wouldn't have thought they were that smart, myself. Someone else had to pay them or put them up to it somehow—plus provide the technical know-how! I mean, I know they're cunning, but shifting that asteroid took some doing! Not just anyone could have the wherewithal to pull off a deed like that, and it wouldn't surprise me at all to discover that more than the few worlds that Cat said they were fighting were actually in on it. Cat says they were besieged by men from several different planets, but the Nedwuts weren't in the main battles because Cat didn't even know what they were called before I told him. He'd only seen them in his mind and described them to me. If he'd been out there fighting them, he'd have seen them."

"*Several* worlds?" Ranata said, her voice heavily laced with skepticism. "They couldn't have made that many people jealous!"

I just stared at her as though she were a complete idiot.

Ranata laughed. "You know, Jack, I've really missed that 'flying eyebrow' look of yours! But you're serious, aren't you? He really is that good?"

I nodded. "If the ruffle around the head of his cock doesn't get to you, the fluid he secretes will." Forgetting my original intention to keep that little tidbit of information to myself, I went on, "We are talking continuous, effortless orgasms for as long as that fluid is in contact with a mucus membrane. Honestly, it's a better high than any other drug I've ever heard of." Then I paused, as the answer came to me like a bolt from the blue, and suddenly, all the pieces of the puzzle dropped effortlessly into place.

Someone *had* considered it to be a drug: a drug that would have made all other recreational drugs obsolete, unnecessary, and unsellable. The drug cartels, the black market smugglers, and anyone else who peddled dope to an unsuspecting galaxy had feared they would lose customers, for it was safe, had no side effects that I could see, wasn't physically addicting, and was a naturally occurring substance that the Zetithians were giving away for free—and I had the only known source of it left in the galaxy! *Ho-ly sheep shit*! The old man hadn't been kidding when he'd said that Cat was precious! He was more than that: he truly was beyond price!

Suddenly, a wave of anxiety shot through me as I considered the consequences of my theory. "Where the devil is Cat?" I said nervously. "What's taking him so long?" I felt so strange! I couldn't seem to sit still anymore and, without even realizing what I was doing, I jumped up from the porch and began to run toward the stable.

"Where are you going?" Ranata yelled after me.

Pausing briefly in my flight, I shouted. "I know why Cat's planet was destroyed! And I'm never letting him out of my sight again for as long as I live! That collar and leash thing was a great idea, by the way. I think I'll keep him chained to me forever." I ran around the side of the house, nearly running down Alanna who was working there in one of the flower beds. "Have you seen Cat?" I demanded.

Alanna looked up in surprise. "He is at the stable," she replied, "and should return soon." Noting my concerned expression, she went on: "He will come to no harm, Jacinth. My daughter, Juzette, is with him. As you know, we seldom leave men unattended—even those who are not from our world."

I took a deep breath and tried to calm myself. Of course, Cat was just fine, and my news could wait until he returned. I suppose I could have gone dashing down to the barn right then, but it really wasn't necessary. He would be back. I hadn't lost him. Why would I think that, anyway? As if in reply to that question, a different, more jealous side of my brain put forth a suggestion as to why that thought might have occurred to me. Alanna's daughter was a very pretty girl, and perhaps I *did* need to worry! These chain-happy Statzeelian females couldn't stand the thought of an unchained male running around loose, you know! What if she got a taste of his dick and wouldn't give him back?

The answer was simple: I'd kill the little slut! No way was anyone taking Cat away from me! I might not wish to sell his coronal fluid to the highest bidder, but I wasn't giving it away either! He was mine. I'd paid five fuckin' credits for him and he was mine!

With the utmost reluctance, I told myself I was being stupid and went back to where Ranata was sitting and took a seat, but I was perched on the edge of it, anxiously awaiting his return. Ranata chuckled at my obvious distress. "You see what happens when you begin to care for one of them? You don't want them out of your sight for a moment, for worrying about what they're up to or if they're getting into trouble of some kind. I find that I *like* having Dantonio chained to me. Then I don't have to worry or wonder; I know."

"Well, you're right about that much," I admitted. "When I first heard the bit about the collar and chain thing, I'll have to say, I wasn't too twerked up about it, but now that I've done it for a while, I know exactly what you mean. You can't trust the little buggers for a second, can you?"

"Oh, yes, I suppose we could," she conceded. "They aren't helpless and they aren't—well, some of them aren't—that stupid. But Cat isn't from this world. He's not nearly as belligerent, and is possibly more intelligent."

"Well, I certainly hope so!" I exclaimed. "I can't see taking him for a walk on another planet like that, although I *have* seen a couple of people from Statzeel on another world, and, let me tell you, they got quite a few stares, and not just from me! Of course, those were the only pair I'd ever seen before I got here. Your guys must not get out much."

"No, we've found that it's better to keep them at home," she replied. "If we go offworld, a man must have at least three females traveling with him."

"Sounds expensive," I commented. "No wonder you stick close to home."

Ranata and I continued chatting, and eventually the topic returned to the old days on Earth, and I guess I simply lost track of time, for it had been nearly another hour before I realized that Cat wasn't back yet. He'd had plenty of time to groom those horses, clean the tack, and even clean their stalls before saddling them up! To top it all off, I was feeling more irritable by the second, and even my bones were beginning to itch. Giving voice to my earlier thoughts about what might be going on down at the barn, I found myself asking furiously, "Is Alanna's daughter trustworthy? She wouldn't decide to mess around with him—would she?" He was pretty irresistible as far as I was concerned, but perhaps the locals didn't like cats. Some people just aren't cat people, after all, but Alanna's daughter might have been.

"Oh, of course she wouldn't!" Ranata assured me, laughing out loud at the idea. "He doesn't get angry like one of our men, so she would have no need."

I still didn't believe it—couldn't shake the notion that something was wrong. This time I didn't even reply to Ranata's shout when I took off for the barn. I sped around the house and down the path to the stable, racing through the open doors abruptly enough to startle the horses. I ran through the barn and found ours, both clean and shiny, but the black was still in his stall while the chestnut, who had already been saddled, was standing in cross ties in the aisle. Cat was nowhere in sight, and neither was anyone else. I started yelling for him then, panic rising in my throat like a Resaneden goose dinner coming back up—which, if you've ever eaten such fare, you'd know it tends to do—and I ran out of the barn to search the grounds.

The house was situated in a large clearing at the top of the hill, and while I could see for a great distance in nearly every direction, I saw no sign of Cat. Despite a warning pain which began growing in the center of my chest, I took off for the house again at a dead run and stormed up the steps to the porch. "He's not there!" I screamed at Ranata. "You'd better find Alanna's goddamned daughter, right now, because I want to have a little talk with her! Honest to God, if she's let anything happen to Cat, I'll kill her!" If I'd had time to reflect, I probably wouldn't have let myself get so worked up, but my gut told me that it was not only understandable that I be upset by his disappearance, but also that there was something pretty fishy about it. Something was rotten in Denmark, and I was going to get to the bottom of it if I had to knock some heads together to do it!

I tore through the house, shouting for Juzette and Cat. I have no doubt that the entire household was in an uproar because of me, but at the time, I didn't give a shit. Cat didn't answer me, but Juzette did. "What is it?" she asked in worried accents.

"Where's my Cat?" I bellowed, rapidly losing patience. "You were supposed to be with him in the barn, but he's not there now, nor is he anywhere in sight out there in the yard. You'd better find him quick before I start—" It was then that I realized that I couldn't start shooting, since I wasn't the one carrying Tex—or a sword, either, because Cat had them both. I tried to console myself with the thought that at least he was armed, and if he'd run into one of the local guys in a rage, he would be able to defend himself. He'd handled himself pretty well against Nedwuts and swergs, so I doubted that a Statzeelian could have given him much trouble, especially if he had a female chained to him. Of course, that particular method of peacekeeping might not always work; I mean, surely they must have *some* degree of failure—it couldn't be *completely* foolproof— after all, nothing else was.

Everyone in the whole place turned out after that, and there were at least thirty people in that household:

gardeners, cooks, nannies, housekeepers, horsekeepers, in addition to Ranata and Dantonio and his two other wives who each had two children. All the people who worked there seemed to have their entire family living there with them; it was like a little village under one roof, and every one of them seemed to be present and accounted for—except Cat. Juzette reported that she had gone down to the stable with Cat to check up on her own horse, but had left him there to come back to the house alone. No one had even the slightest notion as to where he had gone. Finally, at my insistence, everyone spread out and searched the immediate area, but we found no trace of him at all; it was as though he had simply vanished into thin air.

I still had enough wits about me to know that such a thing was impossible. Technology had come a long way, but short of a laser blast that could actually vaporize a person, there was no magical transporter beam that could do what the old science fiction writers had imagined. Cat had either gone off somewhere under his own power, or someone had taken him.

The thought that he might have been taken straight to a waiting starship had me scared shitless, but there was no place nearby to land one, and I knew all the sites that the smugglers used—had studied the maps for months, remember?—and there were none that were any closer than a two-day ride to reach. Of course, a land speeder of some sort could take him there a lot faster, but I doubted that anyone could have flown in, nabbed Cat, and then flown out without being noticed—they weren't *that* quiet, and in an area where the primary form of transportation was either horses or on foot, people didn't come and go very quickly.

The thing that kept creeping back into my mind were those damned Nedwuts we'd seen. Cat had killed two of them, and they might have circled back around and managed to be stealthy enough to sneak up on Cat and nab him. Alanna had said she would report them, but if they'd been caught, no one had mentioned it to me. It occurred to me that if the Nedwuts had simply wanted Cat dead, it would have been easy enough to do it from a distance if one of them was a decent sniper; though if that were the case, we'd have found his body. I couldn't imagine that Nedwuts would have bothered to carry him off and hide him, for none of the ones I'd ever dealt with had been all that neat about much of anything.

I felt like I was losing my mind. My Cat was gone and I simply couldn't function without him! Perhaps I shouldn't have let myself get so attached to him, but Cat had promised that he would stay with me forever, though I'd never asked it of him. He'd decided to stay with me of his own free will; had even given himself back to me after I'd set him free. Still, he was a man, and what was I thinking to actually believe him? I knew better than to trust a man! It was why I'd been a loner for so long!

I was better off without him, I told myself. If I couldn't trust him out of my sight long enough to saddle a couple of horses, then what good was he? Besides, I couldn't live like this if I went nuts anytime he was gone for a little while! You see, Jack, I told myself, this is what comes of going against your better judgment and letting yourself fall in love! Honestly, I hadn't felt this panicky when Ranata had been kidnapped! She was my sister, and I loved her, though it wasn't quite the same, but still, I was coming positively unglued and I didn't understand why, *unless*….

Then, from somewhere in the back of my disordered mind, I could hear Delamar asking Cat, "Is she well bonded to you?" I hadn't thought about him for some time now, but what else had he said? That being bonded to Cat—by which I'd assumed he was referring to the bond between master and slave—might not be enough, and then he had given Cat what he had called his gift. A gift that would enable me to track Cat over great distances should we ever become separated. I hadn't believed it, of course; hadn't felt the slightest bit different afterwards, unless you want to count throwing up, which, at the time, I'd considered to be a perfectly normal reaction to that aquamarine slime he'd pumped into my stomach—until now, that is. Unfortunately, what the little creep had failed to mention was that I would feel as though half of me had been ripped away when Cat wasn't right there beside me—which was exactly the way I felt! A very important part of me was gone and I felt empty and lost without him. It was horrible, maddening, and compelling. One thing I knew for sure, I had to find him, or I was going to lose what was left of my mind.

Of course, the creepy little Delamar really *had* lied about one thing, because his "treatment" hadn't turned me into a bloodhound; I had no idea whatsoever where Cat might be located and hadn't even the slightest clue as to the direction in which he might be headed. After about half an hour of frantic searching, I was tearing my hair out in frustration and Ranata was beginning to be concerned for my sanity.

"Look, Jack," she began. "If he's gone, there's not much more we can do about it right now. We'll get help to find him, but you have to calm down." She took me firmly by the shoulders and looked into my eyes. "Just relax. You have to relax, Jack, don't think. Just let your mind drift. Take a deep breath, now. That's it, take it easy. Breathe. Close your eyes and breathe. That's my girl. Just breathe."

Her voice might have been calm and soothing to my troubled mind, but I fought against it anyway. I simply had to find Cat! My dear, sweet Cat! I loved him so much I couldn't live without him; he was a part of me now and I needed him! I felt like I was dying; that pain that had begun growing in my heart from the moment I realized he was gone had now swelled to the point that I thought my chest would burst wide open under the strain. Tears were streaming down my cheeks and I was in such misery that if I'd had Tex handy, I think I might have blasted myself into oblivion.

And then I felt it. I *was* dying; my heart was splitting open and blood was pouring into my chest cavity from the gaping wound. I felt it filling up the space where my lungs should be and I couldn't breathe anymore. It was so ironic, for after a seemingly fruitless and never-ending search, I had found my dear, sweet sister at long last, only to die right before her very beautiful blue eyes. For I *did* die, right there in Ranata's arms.

Chapter Fourteen

I KNOW I DIED, FOR WHEN I WAS REBORN, I COULD HEAR the sounds of weeping from my sister and her family, and Ranata's tears were dripping onto my face. I was cold, too; more chilled than I could ever recall having been before, for the chill went right straight down to the bone— even the marrow had begun cool. The first breath of my new life filled my head with a cacophony of scents, but I seemed to know, unerringly, not only precisely what those scents were, but also exactly where the source of them was located. My eyes were not even open, but I knew beyond a shadow of a doubt that Ranata still held me and that Alanna and her daughter and husband were standing to her right. Dantonio was kneeling behind Ranata with his arms around her. I could smell the fear and the sorrow that flowed from each of them, and I knew those emotions for what they were just as surely as if I'd seen their facial expressions with my own two eyes.

The horses. I could smell them, too—could even judge the distance from the stable where they were still chewing their hay to where I lay in the cool grass of the lawn that surrounded Ranata's lovely home. Then I took another breath and I got a whiff of him, carried to me unmistakably on the wind.

Cat! I could almost see the line of his scent from where I lay. He had passed down the tall hill through the jungle and was east of the town in the wilderness—and still moving away from me—with four Nedwuts! Their path would lead directly to one of the illegal landing zones. They were taking him offworld somewhere, and in space, I seriously doubted that I could track him—at least not with my nose. I had to catch up with them before they reached their ship, or he might be lost to me forever, and I'd spend the rest of my life searching for him, just as I had searched for Ranata. I had to get moving, and quickly.

My eyes opened at last, and Ranata gasped in surprise. "Jack!" she exclaimed weakly. "My God, you gave us such a scare! I thought you were dead! Are you all right?"

I took another breath and could smell the sadness and apprehension emanating from her, a scent that was now becoming mixed with the sweet aroma of relief. Just how I knew what all of these scents were, I have no idea, but it was as though I had been breathing them in all of my life and had simply never been able to label them. I sat up and stretched, noting that the chest pain was gone and not even the slightest hint of soreness remained.

But as I looked around, I noticed that something else had changed. My vision had always been good, but now, it was so sharp I could spot a butterfly on a flower a mile away. The images were so sharp, so crisp that they almost hurt my brain to interpret them. I figured that all of this would take some time to get used to, but I also wondered if the change in me was permanent.

As I turned to face Ranata, she let out a scream loud enough to curdle blood and which probably would have awakened me even if I'd still been dead. "Your eyes!" she whispered hoarsely. "Jack! What's happened to your eyes?"

"Well, I can *see* a lot better, if that's what you mean," I replied, surprised to find that my voice still sounded the same, "but are you telling me they *look* different, too?"

She nodded dumbly.

"They're red!" Alanna whispered in amazement. "The pupils are glowing red!"

"Well, I'll be damned if that little creep wasn't telling the truth after all!" I declared, getting to my feet. "Look, I know where Cat is now. I've got to go after him, but I can't go like this," I said, indicating my little see-through riding habit. "I need some real clothes and my pulse— shit! That's right, I forgot. Cat's got it. Well, I guess I'll have to take that cursed Nedwut's pulse rifle," I grumbled. Of all the times not to have my trusty Tex in his holster, it had to be this one! "My horse," I shouted. "I need my horse!" I ran down the path to the stable with the line: "*A horse, a horse! My kingdom for a horse!*" running through my head. I forget what ancient monarch had uttered those words, but I now knew exactly how he'd felt at the time, because I couldn't get to one quickly enough to suit me. The damned Nedwuts probably had about a two-hour head start on me, and I would be lucky if I caught them before they got to their ship. My only hope was that they might stop for lunch or something, never dreaming that I could track them as well as I could.

The tall chestnut was still standing there in cross ties with his saddle in place, and, after checking the girth, I pulled it as tight as I could with my fumbling fingers. The pulse rifle was still hanging from the saddle in its scabbard, and I took the one from Cat's saddle, as well. I was going in armed for bear—or Nedwut—and I wasn't taking any chances on one of those rifles crapping out on me. I ran through the barn to where the droid was and palmed open the lock, thanking God once more that it hadn't had a key, which Cat might also have been carrying along with my pulse pistol! I threw a shirt and my flight overalls and boots on over what I was already wearing, stuffed some food and miscellaneous supplies into the saddle bags, and then, bridling the big horse quickly, led him outside and leaped into the saddle just as everyone else came down the hill to meet me.

"Where is he?" Dantonio asked.

"Down the hill, headed east," I replied tersely. "Through the jungle." I paused as I wheeled the horse around and pointed to a clear spot farther east. Damn! I could even see the ship from here! "They'll be heading for the clearing on that ridge," I said. "I've got to catch them before they get there."

"Take the road," he advised. "You'll make better time than they will going through the jungle. There's another road that goes in that direction at the base of the hill. You might even get there ahead of them. The jungle is very thick on this mountain, and will slow them down considerably. Plus, they have your Cat to deal with. They may be carrying him and not be able to move very fast."

"I hope so," I said fervently. "Thanks for your help, and thank you again for finding Ranata. She seems very happy here. If I don't return, you be sure and take good care of her. She loves you, I think." I waved to Ranata as I galloped past and headed down the road to the town.

Now, galloping downhill has never been one of my favorite pastimes, and fortunately the road curved around the mountain so it wasn't too terribly steep. I thanked God for my surefooted horse and rode like I'd never ridden before, but even so, it seemed like forever before I reached the foot of the small mountain that my sister called home.

I hadn't lost much time in getting ready to leave, and I had been moving pretty fast since then, but I knew exactly how far it was to the ship and also how far the Nedwuts had traveled in the time it had taken me to get to that point. The trouble was, they were still a good two hours ahead of me, and I knew that my horse couldn't run the whole way. To get there at all, I would have to let him walk at intervals. So, after a good long gallop on a reasonably flat stretch of road, I reluctantly reined him in and tried to keep my growing impatience from upsetting him. I took a sniff of him, noting that he didn't smell exhausted, but he would if I kept him going at that pace for long. Actually, I thought he smelled rather pleased at the thought of a rest, but he had also enjoyed the run.

"That's a good boy!" I said approvingly, patting him on the neck. "You're one helluva guy, you know that? When we catch up with Cat and have him safe, you're gonna get the best dinner and rubdown you've ever had in your life! I'll even give you a massage with some of that Marludian oil I've got in my pack. It'll make you feel so good, you could go full out for another fifty miles." I kept talking to him, just to make myself relax and let him walk. I gave him perhaps fifteen minutes and then went on again at an easy canter.

The scent trail was surprisingly easy to follow; in fact, it was *so* easy, I wondered how in the world I hadn't been able to do it before. I was certain that I could find Cat, and probably catch up to them before they got to their ship, but what I would do when I did find them, I wasn't sure. I knew that stealth was a high priority, but having an army behind me would have been a nice touch, too. It occurred to me that I probably should have gotten a bunch of unchained, mean Statzeelian males to go with me. The Nedwuts would have been running scared then, and would undoubtedly end up feeling sorry that they were ever born. Of course, I planned on making them feel that way myself, just as soon as I caught up with them. I would jerk a big, honking knot in their hairy little tails for stealing my Cat! I'd had time to think about it by then, and I was even more pissed off than I was before, but at the same time, I was calm and I could think. I was doing something rather than floundering about aimlessly searching for him and I knew that I would not fail.

I was gaining on them. They were moving much more slowly than I was, for they weren't mounted, as yet. Horses don't travel very well through jungles, so I figured that they must have left their own somewhere near the road. I could smell horses, but I wasn't sure they weren't merely others out on the road being ridden by someone else. Cat, however, I could smell with crystal clarity: it was as though he was emitting a homing signal that I could follow with my eyes closed. I knew he was with the four Nedwuts, though their scent was more vague, being less familiar. Cat was with them, and was hurt, that much I knew, but no more—except that I would make them so fuckin' sorry....

I walked the horse again, and spent the next fifteen minutes trying to divert my mind by coming up with a name for him, finally deciding on Buckaroo Banzai after ruling out Tonto. It probably didn't fit him all that well, but it had a nice ring to it. I'd run across the name in my perusal of ancient texts once and had thought it sounded intriguing. Then I spent the next mile or so at a trot, chanting some nasty little ditties I'd learned on Farstal Six about the sexual potency of their males—which was obviously written by an irate female who wasn't getting any since it basically referred to all of the men as dick-less shitheads. I'd print it here, but it only rhymes when you sing it in Farstalese and it would probably lose something in the translation, especially since I'm not much of a poet.

Essentially, what I was trying to do was to allay some of my anger since I knew it would cloud my judgment. I'd always thought sex messed up my brain, but concern for Cat's welfare was just as bad, if not worse. He would be okay, I told myself. He'll be fine. They had just roughed him up a little bit when they captured him and he would be fine and dandy when I caught up with him. The Nedwuts would hand him over at gunpoint and I would send them on their way to their ship, perhaps even warning them that the local authorities had been alerted to their illegal presence on a planet from which they'd been banned. I would be civil, but firm in my dealings with them. I would keep my head clear and I would not let my temper get the better of me.

Yeah, *right*! Who did I think I was trying to kid? The sonsabitches would be lucky if I didn't skin them alive! I was mad as hell and I was gonna stay that way for a good long while. It was an interesting exercise in mental discipline to presume that I would be able to control my anger when I found them, but that's all it was. I actually pitied the poor, dumb bastards.

I let Buckaroo walk for a while and tried to think of another song to sing, but I couldn't come up with one. I was getting closer, and it was getting harder and harder to put it out of my mind. I could smell Cat more clearly the farther I went, and he was not only hurt, he was bleeding. I could smell it, and as far as I was concerned, those Nedwuts were already dead meat. They should be saying their prayers, asking God for anything they could think of to slow me down, though I'd have been willing to bet they had no idea that I was after them. They should have known it, though. Should have guessed. They knew about Zetithians and must have known why they were destroyed, but obviously didn't take into account that I would go through hell or high water to get him back—or perhaps they *did* know it, and were even counting on it. Maybe it was a trap for me, since they were well aware that Earth women were valuable on this world. I would have to be very, very careful.

Alanna had said that she would report their presence, but I wondered who she had told and what form the enforcement of the law would take. I hadn't seen any

kind of lawmen—or women—anywhere since we'd
landed. I mean, there were all of these fuckin' rules, but
I sure as hell hadn't noticed anyone out there enforcing
them! Maybe I'd just missed it. I mean, I hadn't actually
seen anyone being hauled off to jail, and besides, what
would be the point since most people were already in
chains, anyway?

I was almost to the point where their trail would cross
the road—had *already* crossed the road. *Dammit!* They
were staying in the jungle! The horses I'd smelled must
not have been theirs after all. It occurred to me then that
they were being awfully sneaky about this and the whole
scenario smacked of premeditation. The notion that it was
a trap for me grew and took shape in my mind. Cat was
still with them, but was probably alert, for I could smell
his anger overshadowing the pain; he was conscious, and
he was *pissed.* Unfortunately, I knew I was going to have
to leave Buckaroo behind for the time being and go the
rest of the way on foot. Dismounting, I rummaged
through the saddle bags and found a pair of hobbles which
I put on Buckaroo's forelegs, then removed his bridle and
tied it to the saddle. With any luck, he would still be there
grazing alongside the road when I came back.

I stuck a few supplies in the pockets of my overalls,
slung one pulse rifle over my back and, carrying the
other one at the ready and set for the highest stun level,
crept through the jungle right on their trail. I couldn't see
them as yet—even perfect vision won't help you a whole
lot in a jungle, because you can't see through trees—but
they were close and didn't seem to be moving anymore,
which I thought was rather odd.

I discovered that the best thing about being able to smell my way was that it freed me from the necessity of trying to decide which way to go, or to even look where I was going. All I had to do was follow my nose and concentrate on moving quickly and quietly. As a result, I was upon them almost before I knew it.

Peering through the dense foliage, I could see that there were indeed four of them, but I couldn't see Cat from where I stood. I toyed with the idea of using a wide-beam stun, but with all the trees, a lot of the energy would ricochet off to who knows where, and I needed a more precise means of picking them off. Nedwuts were born hunters, and their sense of smell was pretty good, too, though as far as I could tell, they hadn't realized I was there yet. I circled around to approach them from downwind, noting as I moved that they were in a small clearing, and also that Cat was tied to a tree.

Apparently, they'd decided to stop for lunch and a little sport. I heard pulse blasts and figured they must be cooking something, because they'd gotten a small fire going. They were laughing and talking among themselves and appeared to be roasting their catch on the end of long sticks. Then one of them took his stick, red hot on the end, and went over to Cat. Poor Cat! Once again I'd waited a moment too long. I heard him roar out in pain and I started firing.

I took out the one closest to Cat first, and then took a wide circle around to get a clear shot at the rest of them, for after the first shot, they knew I was there and took cover. They might not have realized that there was only one of me, but I knew a few tricks, and

Nedwuts aren't the smartest thugs in the galaxy by any stretch of the imagination. What I didn't count on was that they had Cat and had every intention of using him against me.

"The Zetithian is as good as dead," one of them shouted. "Surrender yourself, or he dies."

"In your dreams, slimeball!" I yelled back. I hoped Cat appreciated my use of the term. It was one of his favorite Earth expressions, after all. "If you touch so much as another hair on his head, believe me, you'll wish you hadn't!"

"Empty threats!" the Nedwut sneered. "We have taken Earth females before. They pose no danger."

"Yeah, well, you've never dealt with me before, asshole!" I argued. "I'm just a little bit different, and I want my Cat back!" One of them was moving. I could smell them, and hear them. They were trying to circle around and come in behind me. What they didn't realize was that I knew exactly where each of them was. I swore to myself right then and there that if I ever saw Delamar again, I was going to give him a big, fat kiss right smack dab on top of his weird little alien head!

"We knew you would follow him, which is why we took him," the Nedwut snarled. "*You* are the prize here, not him. There is a bounty on Zetithians, and we will collect it whether he is alive or dead, but you, my lovely Terran, you are worth far more alive and well. Killing him means no loss to us. We could kill him right now."

"If you did that, I'd just leave," I replied. "There would be no reason for me to stay." There would be no reason for me to do much of anything if Cat died; but I'd probably turn the pulse rifle on myself. No way would I let these bastards take me alive. "Well, guys," I said nonchalantly, hoping that Cat wouldn't hear me and lose hope. On the other hand, he wasn't saying anything either. I had only heard him scream, which didn't bode well for his condition when I finally got to him. "If he's as good as dead, I might as well give up and go home right now. No point in hanging around here anymore. See ya!"

One of the Nedwuts was still moving around to position himself to get the drop on me, but I knew precisely where he was, even though he wasn't making a sound. I took a deep breath, spun on my heels and fired a fairly wide stun shot in his direction and took him out. I heard his body crash heavily into the underbrush.

"That's two for me and none for you," I yelled. "You guys better get lost or I'm gonna pick off the rest of you: one by hairy fuckin' one! Let's be sensible about this!" The trouble was, if I didn't take them out a little quicker, the ones I'd already shot would begin coming around and then we'd be starting all over again. "So far, I haven't killed any of you, but that could change if you keep this up. You're trying my patience here."

I scented something else, then. Cat was still bleeding, and quite a bit from the smell of it. I had to hurry. "Like I said," I shouted, "my patience is wearing pretty damned thin! You guys better get lost or I'll kill all four of you!"

"You are weak, female!" the Nedwut spat out. "You should have killed us all while you had the chance. Now you are paying for it."

Actually, Cat was the one paying for it. I had to do something quick because Cat was bleeding and might even be dying. I looked at the clearing, peering up into the trees, and there, thanks to my improved vision, I was able to see the answer. One of the little wild primates was up there, perched high in the branches of the canopy, staring down at us all with a marked degree of curiosity. Moving as quietly as possible, I shifted to a new location, going for a position where I had a clear shot at the network of branches above the clearing. "Sorry, buddy," I muttered, taking a bead on the limb next to him and pulling the trigger.

The poor little bugger screamed and scrambled to a new perch as the one he was on gave way beneath him. As diversions go, it was fairly effective, for one of the Nedwuts raised up and fired off a pulse, missing the animal completely, but at the same time exposing himself to me. He might have missed his shot, but I didn't, for he dropped to the ground in a nerveless heap. I took a moment to make a mental note that these Nedwut pulse rifles were far more effective against Nedwuts than mine were—which made sense because they tended to bicker among themselves just as much as they did with everyone else, and undoubtedly took pot shots at each other from time to time. I was terribly glad I'd brought them with me.

"Okay, buddy," I yelled. "There's only one of you left. Now, I've got a really nice pulse rifle here—you know, the one that I took from your dead leader?-It shoots pretty well, doesn't it? And maybe you'd like to get it back, but right now, there's another question that you should be asking yourself, and that is, do I feel lucky?"

"Luck has nothing to do with it!" the Nedwut snarled. "We will prevail! You are weak and a female! We will not fail. You will be our prisoner and we will sell you into slavery and the Zetithian will die. We will take his hide for the bounty and you will spend the rest of your life in harsh servitude while we go on to enjoy the wealth that we have acquired as a result of our meeting."

"Yeah, well, there's something you should know about this planet, you stupid jerk! Just in case you haven't noticed, there are females walking around this planet without chains on, but there are no males that are free. It's the *males* who are enslaved here, you idiot, it just doesn't look that way." I knew I was in deep do-do for giving away such a major secret, but I doubted that he would believe me anyway.

"You lie!" he hissed. *See, what did I tell ya?* "It is the *women* who bring the high price! You know nothing of this world."

"You might be surprised," I said with a chuckle. "I know more than you might think. I also know that the authorities have been alerted to your presence here and even if you leave right now, you'll still get caught. I spotted your ship on that ridge, and you may find that there's a little greeting party waiting for you when you get there."

"There is no law on this planet!" the Nedwut growled. "The people are all sheep, and need no governing. It is a pity that other worlds will not pay for them, for we could take as many as we wished, and no one would stop us."

I hated to admit it, but I sort of believed that, as well. The men didn't get into trouble because they all had responsible females looking after them. It would be very difficult for the males to get together a gang of cutthroats and go out on a killing spree. The form of control and law enforcement was of a sexual nature and I seriously doubted that they had much call for police or prisons or even much of a judicial system. The female neighborhood grapevine seemed to be a much more effective means of controlling the native males; it was the offworlders who needed policing, which was the problem I was currently experiencing. We were all offworlders, and if we got caught, they would probably throw every last one of us in the slammer.

"Yeah, well, you might be right," I conceded, "but I gotta tell ya, I'm getting sick and tired of all this shit I've had to take from you. I think I've had enough and I also think it just might be a good day to die." I knew that while we were arguing, Cat was probably dying and I was tired of crouching behind my friendly log, anyway, so I decided to go for broke. I fired a couple of shots to distract him and took off for the clearing, firing as I went. I got close enough to deliver a wide-range stun that would stop him—for a while, at least—and I fired again.

This time I heard him fall, and I went straight for Cat. When I saw what they'd done to him, I didn't hesitate for one second. I reset the rifle and went around to each of the Nedwuts and I killed every single, solitary one of them, for Cat was either dead or dying, bleeding profusely from a gaping wound at the base of his neck, and there wasn't a damned thing I could do for him.

But, of course, I tried anyway. I cut him down from the tree to which he'd been bound and tried to staunch the bleeding with my bare hands, but I was in despair of ever saving him, for he was extremely pale and was barely breathing. I had nothing in my overall pockets but an Orknal first-aid kit and the Derivian ointment, which, as you know, was pretty good stuff, but it wasn't *that* good. I was too late. I should have just gone in shooting and taken my chances. I'd been too slow and, as a result, I was going to lose my darling Cat forever.

I pulled what medicines I had with me out of my pockets and applied them to his wounds anyway. I knew it wasn't much—and wasn't nearly enough either—but at least I was doing *something* for him. I pulled him into my arms and held him, sobbing into his mane as he died. I'd already died once that day because I'd lost him. Now it appeared that I was simply going to have to die all over again.

I had been sitting there with him for several minutes, leaning against the tree, holding him in my arms, when, suddenly, I realized that I wasn't alone anymore. The little primate had come down from the canopy and was crouching there beside me, holding out a tentative hand. It reached out and touched Cat's hair, and then looked up at me with big, round, gleaming eyes that seemed to reflect my despair.

"He's dying," I whispered sadly, "I can't save him." I doubted that it understood a word I was saying, but in a situation such as that, I probably would have been talking to the trees if I'd thought they might be listening; this furry little creature with its monkey-like body and big, lemur eyes could at least hear me. It raised a hand to touch the tears on my face with its tiny little fingers, tasting them briefly before scampering off once more into the brush.

I'd never felt so alone in my life. I could hear sounds of birds and insects and other animals all around me, but the smell of death was so strong, it overpowered any others that I might have noted. I wondered if I would die when Cat did—if the bond we had was that strong. Delamar had told us only that I would be able to track him, not that I could save him or outlive him, and to tell you the truth, I didn't really care. I was losing the only man I'd ever loved in my entire life, and it made my own life seem utterly worthless.

Somewhere, through the scent of blood and death, I became aware of my furry little friend as it returned once more. It appeared to have been eating something, for its cheeks were bulging, and it was still chewing as it approached. Life goes on, I thought. Cat and I would die here and become part of the cycle of life in the jungle, for our deaths meant nothing in the overall fate of the stars. Cat was the last of his kind, the memory of which would pass into legend, then myth, and then be forgotten in the mists of time. What a waste, I thought as I watched him die. What a goddamned, useless waste….

The little monkey sat at Cat's feet, regarding us both with its big, dark eyes for a long moment before it came closer, climbing up onto Cat. With a quiet chirping sound, it pulled my hand away from Cat's neck with its nimble little fingers, removed a wad of chewed leaves from its mouth, and then applied it to the wound. Placing my hand over Cat's wound again, it gazed up at me with those deep, brown eyes, pressed its hand on top of mine, and began to sing.

At least, that's what it sounded like to me. It was a rhythmic, whirring sound that rose and fell with each breath, but it also had a melody that was repeated at least five times before it stopped. Giving me a nod and touching my tear-stained cheek once more, the tiny creature moved away and disappeared into the jungle.

I watched it until it was lost to my sight, only to be replaced in my line of vision by a well-armed squadron of the biggest, toughest-looking Amazons I'd ever beheld in my long and varied experience. If these were members of the local army, then they were definitely of a different breed from anyone else I'd seen thus far—and they were all female. Dressed in swerg skins and armed to the teeth, with long, dark hair and glowing blue eyes, they looked like a jungle-dwelling SWAT team.

They might have appeared to be unrelated to any Statzeelian I'd seen so far, but they did speak an understandable dialect of Stantongue with only a mild accent. "He is dead?" the leader asked.

I shook my head. "Not quite, but nearly there," I replied wearily. "I was too late. The Nedwuts have killed him." I gestured at the bodies lying in and around the clearing. "And I killed them." Which had been pointless because Cat was going to die anyway; it had merely been my revenge. I might have told myself that I'd killed them just so they could cause us no further harm, but the truth was, it had been purely out of vengeance; I wanted them dead for what they had done to my Cat.

"You have saved us the trouble then," the leader said gravely. "Their lives were forfeit once they set foot on our soil and they knew this to be true. Killing a Nedwut is not a crime on this world, but killing someone else is, and we take great pains to prevent it. We have a healer with us, would you let her see him?"

"Sure," I replied. "Whatever." I was fairly certain that they couldn't possibly do him any harm, but I cherished little hope that there was anything that could be done to save him. Not now, not after he'd been abused for so many years in the past and had lost so much blood in such a short period of time. I could console myself with the fact that he'd at least had a few days with me that hadn't been torture for him. Poor Cat. I'd wanted to keep him forever, but forever hadn't turned out to be very long, had it?

Their ranks parted and a small, pale creature came forward, which, to my surprise, looked very much like Delamar, except that this one had blue, as opposed to red, eyes. She noted my surprise and seemed equally surprised to see me—and especially my own red eyes.

"You have been treated by one of our males and bonded with this man, have you not?" Her voice was the same breathy whisper as Delamar's had been, but was much more musical, and lighter in tone.

I nodded in response to her query. So, I had been bonded to him. I'd thought as much.

"It is a process that is only effective if you already love the one with whom you are to be bonded," she said. "To be bonded as you have been, you must love him very much indeed."

"I love him more than anything," I murmured. "My sweet Cat."

"You will not live if he dies," she said softly. "There-fore, we must save him in order to save you." She directed her glowing blue gaze into my red one. "You would not wish to live if he dies, would you?"

I shook my head. "No," I replied. "I would not." In fact, I would welcome death, and I was beginning to fade already, losing my will, and not caring that it was slipping away from me, just as Cat was.

The blue-eyed female came closer, taking Cat's face in her hands. "A Zetithian male," she murmured. "So rare and so beautiful—so much so that they were destroyed because of it. It would be a great pity to lose this one, for he is very precious, is he not?"

"Oh, yeah," I sighed. "He's precious to me, all right. More than anything else in the universe."

She nodded. "I am called Tudrock," she said. "And I will do my best to save you both, but you must let me have him for few moments. I assure you that he will come to no harm."

It sounded like what the male had said to me before filling me up with his aquamarine slime. I wondered briefly what strange thing she would have to do to Cat to help him, but relinquished him to her anyway, realizing that I really didn't care anymore.

A collective gasp could be heard from all of the women, including Tudrock, as my hand slipped away from Cat's wound, revealing the mass of chewed leaves that had been applied to it. The leaves had apparently stopped the bleeding—either that or Cat was simply out of blood altogether.

"What is this?" Tudrock exclaimed as she examined the poultice that the monkey had pressed into the wound. "The Guardians have helped you?"

I looked up at her, realizing that my vision was beginning to fade and I had less than perfect control of the muscles in my neck. "Guardians?"

"The creatures of the jungle," she replied. "They did this for you?"

I nodded weakly. "A little monkey with big eyes put it there and then left, just before you came. I've seen several of them while we were traveling on the road through the jungle. Are you telling me that there is something…special about them?"

The tall woman who had spoken before replied. "The Guardians live in the canopy of the jungle, but they are timid creatures and rarely seen. To see one is considered good luck, for they have powers that heal the body, the mind, and the spirit. You are very fortunate, indeed."

Yeah, right! I thought. So fortunate that Cat is lying here dying in my arms! No, scratch that, because he was dying in Tudrock's arms now, for she had taken his inert body into her grasp, holding him closely as she opened his eyes with her long, tapered fingers.

"My work will be made easier because of the Guardian's help," Tudrock said. "I will bring his body back from death, but it is the Guardians who will return his spirit."

"Whatever," I mumbled, with a wave that never truly materialized into a full gesture. With Cat out of my arms, I felt myself growing weaker by the second. "Please save my Cat, if you can," I sighed. "I'm dying anyway."

Tudrock nodded, directing her blue gaze into Cat's glittering eyes. I could see that the golden glow was fading from his cat-like pupils, but the black irises still gleamed like obsidian. I watched, not caring, merely observing, as her eyes changed colors similar to the way Delamar's had done, fading first from blue to purple before turning red. Gradually the red became more yellow, and when her eyes reached a deep shade of orange, her tongue protruded just as the male's had, and then slid past Cat's parted lips. I could see his throat expanding as it passed down and he seemed to swallow it in the only movement I'd seen him make since I'd found him. Then, just as before with Delamar, a ball formed in her mouth and passed through her tongue, down Cat's throat and into his stomach.

The bolus having been delivered, Tudrock's tongue whipped back into her mouth and she laid Cat back down so that his head rested on my chest. I was leaning back against the trunk of the tree he'd been tied to and I had no strength left to move, not even to raise my arms to hold him.

And I *did* want to hold him! I knew that Tudrock had done her best, but I still felt so weak, so helpless. I wanted so much to hold my sweet Cat, but I hadn't the strength. Then my vision faded to black and I felt no more.

Chapter Fifteen

I GUESS ALANNA MUST HAVE ALERTED THE RIGHT people, for they seemed to know precisely where Cat and I belonged. I have a vague recollection of being hauled up the mountain road behind Buckaroo on a makeshift travois of sorts, nestled closely to Cat as I regained some of my senses. My smeller still seemed to work fairly well, for, as before, I could identify and place the people around us from their scent alone. The Amazonian SWAT team and Tudrock escorted us to Ranata and Dantonio's house, and I felt some of my strength returning—though slowly—as we traveled.

Cat, however, never stirred throughout the entire journey, and I'll admit to being somewhat doubtful that he would ever make a full recovery. Of course, the fact that I, myself, was improving was a good sign—that is, if these people were to be believed. He did feel warm and seemed to be breathing normally, so I told myself not to worry. Between the Guardian and Tudrock he *had* to get better—he had to!—if for no other reason than to spread the word that the Nedwuts had been responsible for the destruction of Zetith.

Something had to be done about those snarling little shits, and I would see to it that they got what was coming to me the rest of my natural life to do it. Of course, the prosecution of the Nedwuts would undoubtedly involve whoever had paid them to destroy Zetith, since I still felt that it was a given that they couldn't do something like that on their own. The network of drug smugglers and other perpetrators of organized crime would be gunning for us, which made me sort of want to keep my mouth shut, but the word was undoubtedly already spreading, for the old man we'd met had said that he would see to it. Word of mouth moved pretty quickly despite the distances between planets, for—the theories of star movement and the expansion of the universe notwithstanding—our galaxy, at least, seemed to be getting smaller with each passing year. Soon, I hoped, the Nedwuts and others of their ilk would be banned from every planet in the galaxy but their own. It might even get a sort of peacekeeping force going, though things like that had a way of getting out of control, as well. No, just the knowledge that they were capable of such a heinous crime would be enough to get them shunned by the people of probably every planet I'd ever been on—and I'd been on quite a few. We were growing up as a galaxy, and we hoped things would become more peaceful and prosperous as time went on.

I, of course, could go on with my life, trading in legal commodities and traveling the galaxy with my Cat, perhaps, or maybe we'd just go home—though first I had to get him well. The trouble was, I wasn't worth a whole lot at the time, myself, and for once in my life, I had to depend on my little sister to take care of me!

I'll have to admit that for a recuperative period, it certainly had its advantages. Cat and I were cleaned up and tucked into that lovely soft, cozy bed in our room at Ranata's house, and fed well and often. I could have stayed there forever, except that for the first day and a half, Cat was still unconscious. I told Tudrock I wanted a second opinion if he didn't wake up soon, but she just laughed in that odd, wheezy little chuckle that her kind all seemed to possess, and told me to be a patient patient.

"Ha, ha, ha!" I said grimly. "Very funny!"

"He will recover," she assured me, "but it will not happen overnight. Stay close to him and eat well to regain your own health; he will regain his strength from contact with you, as well as your presence nearby."

Which, of course, I had no problem doing whatsoever. If only doctor's orders were always so easy to follow! I'd once had a doctor on Resulus tell me that standing on my head three times a day would help my stiff neck after I'd gotten into a fight with a drunken little shithead who thought I'd overcharged him for some engine parts. I told him he could sit on it and spin—well, actually, I told both of them the same thing since I thought it sounded a little nicer than telling them they ought to go fuck themselves. I found it odd that they didn't view my consideration for them in quite the same light; one of them punched me and the other just gave me a shot of pain-killer and booted me out of his office. Fuckin' assholes! I didn't stay too long on Resulus anyway. The air was unhealthy and the people were all a bunch of whiny little shits.

I remember lying in that soft, warm bed one morning with Cat and, though I'd been dozing, I was wide awake the moment he started purring. I had massaged him with Marludian oil for perhaps an hour

or so and had finally grown too tired to continue. He
smelled nice after I'd finished, though, and my mind
began to drift from the scent of it. I wondered if his
scars would fade if I used enough of it on him—which
reminded me of a line I'd heard once: *"Pain heals,
chicks dig scars, but glory lasts forever."*

I couldn't remember the name of the old movie that
one was from, but I know it was about football players.
The game is still played nowadays, of course, but the
football isn't just a ball anymore. It's a droid and has a
mind of its own—a nasty, tricky little mind, too! I played
football when I was in school, and one time the damned
ball tackled me! I got out of sports after that, preferring
more lucrative pastimes.

Yes, I'll admit it: I'm the one who sold the extra
cookies I asked Mom to put in my lunch, rather than
giving them away to my friends—but I charged the
going rate, so you really couldn't call me a swindler. It
wasn't my fault that the going rate for my mother's
chocolate chip-macadamia nut-marshmallow cookies
was slightly inflated; I mean, she made some truly
awesome cookies! I was *very* popular!

But I'd never been loved—at least not in the way that
my Cat loved me. I knew from the moment I heard him
purr that he would be okay and that he didn't hold it
against me for not getting to him before the Nedwuts
nearly killed him. I thought I might have been a little
pissed, if I'd been in his place, but I wouldn't have cared
if he'd awakened and been mad at me for the rest of my
life—well, maybe I would have cared a *little* bit! On the
other hand, I *was* bonded to him, and he'd simply have

to learn to put up with me. I sighed deeply and snuggled up a little closer to him.

"Mm-m, Kittycat," I murmured. "I'm feeling very laetralant this morning. How about you?"

I didn't really expect an answer, but I got one, anyway. "Yes, Jacinth," Cat replied. "Very laetralant! I could lie here and let you do that to me all day."

"Do what?"

"Mm-m," he purred. "Your hands on my body. It was very…intoxicating."

Obviously he'd been playing possum for quite a while. The purring gave him away, though. "That massage oil is pretty good stuff, isn't it? I've sold cases and cases of it anywhere I've gone. I haven't met a species yet that didn't think it was wonderful—even the hairier ones like it."

"I am not speaking of the oil," Cat said. "I am referring to your hands. They are what intoxicate me, not the oil."

"What a nice thing to say!" I exclaimed. "But I'll bet it's really because of the oil. You weren't purring before I started using that!"

"I can see that you are still very stubborn," he said. "And very odd."

"But you like odd, don't you?" I asked anxiously. "I mean, you *did* say that once."

"Yes, I like odd," he agreed. "*Your* kind of odd." He rolled over to face me and stretched, yawning hugely and displaying all of those sharp fangs of his. "I feel very well now. I believe I could get out of bed."

I sighed again. "Yes, but do you *want* to get out of bed? Really?" I was pretty comfortable myself. All I had to do was get up to go to the potty now and then—everything else was done for me. I'd never been so pampered in all my life!

"No," he replied truthfully. "I do not. I wish to lie here and mate with you all day and all night, my lovely one."

"I'm not sure you're quite up to that yet," I said firmly. "I mean, you almost died and have been unconscious for a couple of days, Cat! I really think you should rest now."

"But I *have* rested," he growled. "Now I wish to mate."

I just love it when he says things like that! "You big, sweet-talking Kittycat! C'mere and kiss your master! She's been very lonely without you, and should probably tie you up to make sure you never run off like that again."

"If you wish," Cat purred, "I will remain chained to you forever."

"I wish," I replied, looking up into his eyes. What I saw there made me gasp. "Cat!" I exclaimed. "Your eyes have turned blue! Well, the pupils have, anyway. They have a blue glow now instead of gold."

"And your eyes are red," he said as he studied my own eyes. "We have both changed, have we not?"

I nodded. "I guess our kittens will end up having purple eyes then," I said thoughtfully. "You know: if you mix red and blue, you get purple?"

"Kittens?"

"Oh, you know!" I said impatiently. "Baby cats! On Earth, we call them kittens."

"Jacinth!" he demanded sharply. "Are you telling me that you are having kittens?"

I giggled helplessly. "No, but Tudrock tells me that we will be able to—someday. She says it's my responsibility to have as many kittens as possible so that your bloodline is not lost."

"And who is Tudrock?" he inquired.

"Your doctor," I replied. "She's the reason your eyes are blue, and also the reason you're still alive. Boy, have I got a lot to tell you! A lot of strange things have happened since you wandered off and got lost."

"I did not wander off and get lost!" Cat protested in something of a huff. "I was stunned and taken prisoner by Nedwuts."

"Yeah, well, it was your own damn fault *that* happened!" I informed him. "Did you know that killing Nedwuts isn't a crime here? They're dead meat once they set foot on the planet! If you'd just killed all of them when we first saw them, we wouldn't have gotten into such a fix, and then I wouldn't have had to go and bump off the rest of them!"

"You did that?" he asked gently. "I would not have believed you capable of such a thing."

"What?" I squeaked. "Because I'm a girl? Listen, I've had to kill before, Cat! This wasn't the first time, but I hope it's the last." I paused for a moment. "I killed them because of what they did to you, Cat. I thought you were dead—or at least dying."

"But I *am* dying, my lovely master," he whispered softly, reaching out to stroke my arm. "I am dying for your touch and your kiss. I have been denied for far too long."

"Too long?" I exclaimed. "Gee whiz, Cat! It's only been, what, two or three days? And before that it was how many years?"

"But I am yours now," he reminded me. "I must have you often."

"And just how often is often?" I asked cautiously.

His up-swept brows lifted and his pupils dilated with a blue glow. "Now and as many times as I can before the sun rises again."

I tried real hard to look serious, but I'm not sure I was very successful. "Cat, we're gonna have to lay some ground rules here; we can't be mating all the time! I mean, we'll never get anywhere or get anything done, and besides that, who will take care of the kittens?"

"We will get a—what do you call someone who cares for children?"

"A nanny?" I suggested. "Or a babysitter, or—how about a cat-sitter?"

"Yes, a nanny," he said, eyeing me in a rather irritated fashion. I don't think he appreciated the "cat-sitter" remark. "If we are to have many children, then we must mate often."

"Oh, so that's how you'll justify it! Gee," I said morosely. "I can hardly *wait* to be pregnant all the time! You know, I'm not so sure I would like that. Maybe we could, um, loan some semen to some other women who'd like to have kittens, too. I know some ladies who apparently trade semen around the way most neighbors trade recipes."

"Oh, and where is that?" Cat inquired.

"I promised not to tell, but if you'll just give me some, I'll be sure it gets to the right people."

Of course, I wasn't entirely sure that the locals would want to introduce Cat's genes into the pool—though he only *looked* fierce; he was really just a big pussycat after all. It might also be difficult to explain to a flat-nosed, round-eared, and flat-toothed man why his children all came out looking feline. Then again, these Statzeelian males apparently weren't all that bright: after all, the women had convinced them that they needed to inter-breed with Terrans. I wasn't sure just how they would convince the guys to let their women bear Cat's children, but they were a pretty resourceful bunch, and I was pretty sure they'd think of something. On the other hand, if it were to get out that Cat's coronal fluid could cause repeated orgasms, the women would possibly decide that it was worth the risk, whether the males approved or not. We'd have to be sure to include a good-sized dose of that along with the semen, I decided—though snard packed a pretty healthy wallop all by itself! I would have to consult Tudrock about the possibilities. Maybe they could cross Cat with those Amazon SWAT team members—now *they* would have some seriously nice kittens! Cat, however, had a one-track mind when it came to mating.

"Oh, I will give you some snard," he promised. "I will give you as much as I can. Beginning right now."

I guess it was my own damn fault for teasing him for so long, but I thought it best not to spoil him too much—after all, I couldn't have him getting as ornery as the Statzeelians! Anyway, when he pulled me up against him I bumped into a very hard, very wet, very aroused Cat cock. "You weren't kidding, were you?"

"No, I never kid about such things," he purred. "When I say I want to mate with you all day and all night, that is exactly what I mean."

"Are you sure you wouldn't like to eat something first?" I suggested helpfully. "I know I'm supposed to have provided strength for you while you were sleeping, but I'm sure that eating a good hearty breakfast would be much better for you."

"I do not want to eat," Cat reminded me. "If I had wanted to eat, I would have asked for food."

"Always say what you mean, don't you?"

"Yes," he replied. "Do you not wish to mate with me?"

"Well, I don't know," I muttered. "I just haven't felt like it lately." I was lying through my teeth, of course, but for some reason I felt like teasing him a little—just to see what he'd do.

"Then you must lick me and taste me to increase your desire," he said, pushing my head down to his cock. "Lick me, my lovely master, and I will bring you joy unlike any you have ever known."

"Now where have I heard *that* before?" I wondered aloud.

"Sh-h," he whispered. "We have talked enough. Lick me."

His cockhead was thick and hard and oozing buckets of coronal fluid. How could I possibly resist it? Well, I couldn't because I'd been thinking about it the whole time I'd been giving him that massage, just hoping that he'd wake up in an amorous mood. I didn't stall any longer, but lapped up his sweet syrup and waited for it to take effect. I wondered if it would be any different considering all that had happened to us since the last time, but it still worked—possibly even better, for the orgasm was slower to build, before blossoming into full-blown ecstasy.

"Good?" he purred.

I couldn't answer him for a moment—being in a total body spasm sort of limits your ability to speak. "Yes," I gasped. "Very good. I think I'm ready for you now. In fact, I've been ready for hours."

"You have been toying with me," he accused, directing a glowering look in my general direction. "You will pay for that."

"Whatcha gonna do, Cat?" I taunted him. "Fuck me to death?"

"No," he replied. "I will only do it until you are helpless and speechless and fall asleep in my arms."

"Ooo, sounds nice!" I said with heartfelt approval. "Go for it, Cat! Knock me out."

And he did. He rolled me over and slid that big, ruffled cock inside me and began stroking my slick tunnel with his intoxicating penis. I must say that for someone so recently near death, he showed surprising stamina; he didn't stop for a very long time, getting into a steady rhythm that sent my mind and body into orbit. When he finally came with a deep, throaty growl, I was truly helpless and speechless, and I did fall asleep—just about the time Alanna came in with lunch. I told Cat to eat for both of us while I drifted off. Damn! I sure do love my big, purring, beautiful, lovable—and *extremely* fuckable Cat!

Chapter Sixteen

WE STAYED WITH RANATA FOR A FEW WEEKS, AND during that time I discovered that perhaps I could get used to the quiet, domestic life after all. I did grumble a bit about all the trouble I'd gone to finding Ranata when I could have been doing something much more constructive—especially seeing as how I'd spent the past six years chasing her across the galaxy only to find her happy as a clam with a bun in the oven. I had to explain that statement to Cat, of course—he got quite a kick out of the bun in the oven thing, but he never did get the part about why a clam would be so happy, although the more I thought about it, the more I became convinced that people only thought they were happy because their shells were sort of curved like a smile. But all in all, I had to admit that the past six years hadn't been a total waste. I mean, I certainly wouldn't have found Cat if I'd stayed closer to home, so I didn't fuss too much about it.

Following Tudrock's instructions, I was able to collect a lot of Cat's semen to give to her to disperse as she saw fit. I was threatened with all sorts of dire consequences if I passed along the secret manner in which it was "collected." Tudrock seemed to think that my suggestion of crossing Cat with the SWAT team women was a good one. I thought I'd like to go back someday and see how they turned out, but so far I haven't made it back there.

The question of what to do with my life posed the biggest problem now. Cat didn't care what we did, being of the opinion that almost anything would be an improvement over what he'd done in his life up to that point, so he left it up to me. I was a little tired of the constant travel and Statzeel was a beautiful place; living there would have had its advantages, but I decided that the see-through clothes and the collar and leash thing would probably grate on me after a while. It made me wish that there was a wilder part of the planet where we could disappear to, but unfortunately such a place didn't exist—well, I guess we could have carved out a place to live in the deep jungle, but between the swergs and the bugs, we probably would have been pretty miserable.

Besides, it was an agrarian society on the whole, and I didn't think I'd make a very good farmer. Cat could probably do almost anything since he'd had to do all sorts of things as a slave; but, in all honesty, we really didn't have to do anything at all, for I had enough credits to enable the two of us to live quite comfortably for the rest of our lives if we were frugal—which, generally speaking, I usually was. I wasn't in the habit of decking myself out with rare jewels, for example, and Cat had nothing at all. I wondered if he'd stay naked all the time unless he left the house, the way he had when he was on my ship. While I did like the idea, I really didn't think it was necessary since I was pretty sure he'd take his clothes off anytime I asked.

I did like the horses we'd gotten from the Nedwuts, but taking them with me on the ship would have been difficult. And since they'd undoubtedly been stolen from someone else, we'd eventually have to give them back once the owners were found if we stayed there on Statzeel. I was in limbo, and I felt lost, almost as though I'd suddenly been blinded. My life had no purpose anymore, other than to be with Cat, and I knew I could do that anywhere.

I felt that our parents should know that Ranata was safe and sound, though she had no intention of ever returning to Earth. So, in the end, I decided to take the simplest course and head for home, doing a little trading along the way and helping to spread the word about the Nedwuts and the drug dealers. I just hoped we didn't run into any of them while we were at it since knowing that there was a bounty on Zetithians made avoiding them an absolute must.

So, one bright, sunny morning, Cat and I saddled up and headed back to the spaceport, retracing our journey through the jungle. Cat and I rode unhurriedly on that trip, except in the section where we'd run into the swergs and all the bugs, where we made some serious tracks! Our trek was made bittersweet by the knowledge that I would be leaving my sister behind, as well as Buckaroo, of whom I'd become increasingly fond. We didn't see any of the Guardians on that trip: I guess we'd gotten all the luck we would need for the rest of our lives with our previous encounters. I had hoped that one of them would at least wave goodbye to us, but if they did, I never saw them.

Passing through the villages again, we sold a good bit of what we'd brought along with us and made about a bajillion pairs of new shoes for the locals with my

Shoemaker in a Box for a fraction of the cost of new ones. I doubt that the local cobblers were terribly pleased with me, but everyone else sure was! Once again I considered selling samples of Cat's coronal fluid to the women, knowing full well that I could make a fortune from it, but decided not to since it would have undoubtedly caused a riot. We'd made enough credits to pay for any fines we might have incurred for leaving my ship in the port for so long, so we probably didn't need the extra money anyway. I did think about bottling his fluid and selling it on other worlds along our route back to Earth—just not telling anyone what it was or where it came from. I decided I'd have to experiment with it some and see if it lost its potency over time—although I couldn't imagine anyone *ever* leaving it on the shelf long enough for it to go bad!

We spent our nights in a tent along the road, making love in a delightfully carnal fashion each evening, not even caring that hordes of insects were bombarding the tent all night long—though I did make liberal use of some repellent Ranata gave me. I had no desire to get knocked out by a mosquito ever again!

Cat and I both found that we had difficulty functioning if we were ever so much as out of each other's sight, so it seemed that whatever we did for the rest of our lives, we were definitely going to have to do it together. But I, for one, didn't mind, because I loved looking at Cat as much as I loved doing anything else with him.

I didn't get to see Delamar again before we left, and I'd wished I could have since I felt I owed him a great deal for his help. I left a message at the restaurant for him, though, and I hope he got it. I had a feeling that Tudrock had a few choice words for him, herself, for not explaining all of the implications of his "treatment" to us. I got the distinct impression that he'd done it before, and also that it was ever so slightly against the rules.

We didn't stay long in port once we got back to the *Jolly Roger*, and, oddly enough, it felt good to get back into space. Cat stripped off his clothes as soon as we had everything aboard, including a hundred bolts of the local see-through fabric. If I didn't make a small fortune selling that stuff, then I couldn't very well call myself a trader!

I taught Cat how to fly the ship, and we spent a fair amount of time improving his knowledge of Earth's history and lore. Oddly enough, he'd actually heard the "Do I feel lucky?" remark I'd made to the Nedwuts and asked me about its origin—which, of course, meant that he had to watch every *Dirty Harry* movie I had in the computer database. It took a little time, but time was now something that we both had in abundance.

When we got back to Earth, I wasn't sure what made my parents more pleased: the fact that Ranata was alive and well, or the fact that I'd finally hooked up with a man. Mom thought Cat was really cool, although my father remained a bit tepid about the relationship until I actually married him and we had our first litter. I say litter, because there were three of them: all males and all just like their father, except that they had gold pupils rather than purple. It seemed that the changes the healers had made in us weren't hereditary, which was a pity, for I would have liked to have seen at least one with purple eyes.

The story of the destruction of Zetith grew with the telling, and I'm happy to say that the Nedwuts have been singing small for quite a number of years now. Most of them don't dare set foot on another world, for even if they aren't shot on sight, they are harassed to the point that they don't stick around very long.

We stayed on Earth for a while, but soon space began calling to me again, so we loaded up the kittens and went back to trading. Cat and I have visited many worlds and discovered that Cat was *not* the last of his kind. There were other survivors, but I leave it to them to tell their own stories.

We never made it back to Statzeel, but received word in a roundabout way that the breeding program was proceeding well and had exceeded all expectations. It wasn't made clear whether it was Cat's offspring or Ranata's that were responsible, but I'd like to think that they both were.

I am quite old now. Cat and I have had many children, and though our litters have all grown and have had litters of their own, even my great-grandchildren still look like Zetithians. I have no idea how many generations must pass before the bloodline is too dilute to produce the same characteristics, but I doubt that I will see it in my lifetime.

Cat and I have been together for sixty-five years, and though we are both showing our age, my love for him has only grown stronger with each passing year, and I still feel the fire in my soul each time I look upon him, just as I did when I first saw him there in chains on Orpheseus Prime so many years ago.

I remember remarking to Cat on our fiftieth anniversary that he had now been in slavery with me for at least twice as long as he had been before I found him. He laughed, kissing me fondly and thanking me yet again for rescuing him, but I knew that no thanks were necessary, for, in truth, I hadn't been the one to rescue him at all. Oh, no, my friend! *He* was the one who rescued *me*.

About the Author

Cheryl Brooks is a critical care nurse by night and a romance writer by day. She is a member of the Romance Writers of America and lives in Bloomfield, Indiana. *Slave* is her first novel.